Reviews for Harlan Coben

Gone for Good

'An absorbing tale, with an unexpected ending.'
Daily Telegraph

'Ingenious and gripping, this is another thriller to stir the heart.'
Guardian

'Coben creates a host of striking characters ... this is top-notch
thriller writing.' *Observer*

'The plot has many satisfying twists and turns but most pleasing are
the host of striking characters Coben creates ... Great stuff.'
Waterstones' Books Quarterly, Issue 4

'Coben delivers far more than an absorbing mystery here ...
breathtaking.' *Booklist*

'I forced myself to read slowly. I wanted to savor every clue, every
detail, and I never wanted it to end. There are numerous aspects to
the clincher ending, with surprises in store for the reader until the
very last page.' *USA Today*

'A compelling and original suspense thriller ... intriguing ...
clever and unique.' *Los Angeles Times*

'A thriller of runaway tension ... Masterful suspense and explosive
twists of fate.' Iris Johansen

'A terrific thriller.' Larry King

Tell No One

'This is suspense at its finest – gut wrenching thrills and honest, heart-tugging emotion. A big book in every sense of the word.'
Jeffery Deaver

'*Tell No One* rocks the house . . . An exhilarating, bang-up, Porsche turbo of a novel that you will absolutely not put down.'
Dennis Lehane

'*Tell No One* is in another league, a pulsing, pacy, devour-at-one-sitting thriller . . . Coben grabs you with the opening paragraph and never lets you go. A class act.' *Observer*

'An increasingly frightening conspiracy with an unguessable ending . . . hard to put down.' *Sunday Telegraph*

'It is always satisfying to discover a new crime writer – and this is the business . . . this book will keep you up until 2am.' *Play*

'*Tell No One* is such a terrific thriller, you'll want to tell everyone . . . Harlan Coben delivers the near-impossible . . . a can't-put-it-down page-turner with a slam-bang surprise ending.' Lisa Scottoline

'This thriller moves from heartbreaking to heartstopping without missing a beat.' *Booklist*

The Myron Bolitar novels

Also by Harlan Coben

DARKEST FEAR

HARLAN COBEN

BCA

This edition published 2002
by BCA
by arrangement with Orion Books
an imprint of The Orion Publishing Group

CN 111923

Third reprint 2005

Typeset by Deltatype Ltd, Birkenhead, Merseyside

Printed in Great Britain by
Clays Ltd, St Ives plc

When a father gives to his son, they both laugh.
When a son gives to his father, they both cry.

Yiddish proverb

This one is for your father. And mine.

'What is your darkest fear?' the voice whispered. 'Close your eyes now and picture it. Can you see it? Do you have it yet? The very worst agony you can imagine?'

After a long pause, I say, 'Yes.'

'Good. Now imagine something worse, something far, far worse . . .'

'The Mind of Terror' by Stan Gibbs,
column in the New York Herald, January 16

1

An hour before his world exploded like a ripe tomato under a stiletto heel, Myron bit into a fresh pastry that tasted suspiciously like a urinal cake.

'Well?' Mom prompted.

Myron battled his throat, won a costly victory, swallowed. 'Not bad.'

Mom shook her head, disappointed.

'What?'

'I'm a lawyer,' Mom said. 'You'd think I'd have raised a better liar.'

'You did the best you could,' Myron said.

She shrugged and waved a hand at the, uh, pastry. 'It's my first time baking, *bubbe*. It's okay to tell me the truth.'

'It's like biting into a urinal cake,' Myron said.

'A what?'

'In men's public bathrooms. In the urinals. They put them there for the smell or something.'

'And you eat them?'

'No—'

'Is that why your father takes so long in there? He's having a little Tastykake? And here I thought his prostate was acting up.'

'I'm joking, Mom.'

She smiled through blue eyes tinged with a red that Visine could never hope to get out, the red you can only get through slow, steady tears. Normally Mom was heavily into histrionics. Slow, steady tears were not her style. 'So am I, Mr Smarty Pants. You think you're the only one in this family with a sense of humor?'

Myron said nothing. He looked down at the, uh, pastry, fearing or perhaps hoping it might crawl away. In the thirty-plus years his mother had lived in this house, she had never baked – not from a recipe, not from scratch, not even from one of those Pillsbury morning croissant thingies that came in small mailing tubes. She could barely boil water without strict instructions and pretty much never cooked, though she could whip up a mean Celeste frozen pizza in the microwave, her agile fingers dancing across the numerical keypad in the vein of Nureyev at Lincoln Center. No, in the Bolitar household, the kitchen was more a gathering place – a Family Room Lite, if you will – than anything related to even the basest of the culinary arts. The round table held magazines and catalogs and congealing white boxes of Chinese takeout. The stovetop saw less action than a Merchant-Ivory production. The oven was a prop, strictly for show, like a politician's Bible.

Something was definitely amiss.

They were sitting in the living room with the dated pseudo-leather white modular couch and aqua-tinged rug whose shagginess reminded Myron of a toilet-seat cover. Grown-up Greg Brady. Myron kept stealing glances out the picture window at the For Sale sign in the front yard as though it were a spaceship that had just landed and something sinister was about to step out.

'Where's Dad?'

Mom gave a weary wave toward the door. 'He's in the basement.'

'In my room?'

'Your *old* room, yes. You moved out, remember?'

He did – at the tender age of thirty-four no less. Childcare experts would salivate and tsk-tsk over that one – the prodigal son choosing to remain in his split-level cocoon long after the deemed appropriate deadline for the butterfly to break free. But Myron might argue the opposite. He might bring up the fact that for generations and in most cultures, offspring lived in the familial home until a ripe old age, that adopting such a philosophy could indeed be a societal boom, helping people stay rooted to something tangible in this era of the disintegrating nuclear family. Or, if that rationale didn't float your boat, Myron could try another. He had a million.

But the truth of the matter was far simpler: He liked hanging out in the 'burbs with Mom and Dad – even if confessing such a sentiment was about as hip as an Air Supply eight track.

'So what's going on?' he asked.

'Your father doesn't know you're here yet,' she said. 'He thinks you're not coming for another hour.'

Myron nodded, puzzled. 'What's he doing in the basement?'

'He bought a computer. Your father plays with it down there.'

'Dad?'

'My point exactly. The man can't change a lightbulb without a manual – all of a sudden he's Bill Gates. Always on the nest.'

'The Net,' Myron corrected.

'The what?'

'It's called the Net, Mom.'

'I thought it was nest. The bird's nest or something.'

'No, it's Net.'

'Are you sure? I know there's a bird in there somewhere.'

'The Web maybe,' Myron tried. 'Like with a spider.'

She snapped her fingers. 'That's it. Anyway your father is on there all the time, weaving the Web or whatever. He chats with people, Myron. That's what he tells me. He chats with complete strangers. Like he used to do with the CB radio, remember?'

Myron remembered. Circa 1976. Jewish Dads in the suburbs checking for 'smokeys' on the way to the delicatessen. Mighty convoy of Cadillac Sevilles. Ten-four, good buddy.

'And that's not all,' she went on. 'He's typing his memoirs. A man who can't scribble down a grocery list without consulting Strunk and White suddenly thinks he's an ex-president.'

They were selling the house. Myron still could not believe it. His eyes wandered about the overly familiar surroundings, his gaze getting snagged on the photographs running up the stairwell. He saw his family mature via fashion – the skirts and sideburns lengthening and shortening, the quasi-hippie fringes and suede and tie-dyes, the leisure suits and bell-bottoms, the frilly tuxedos that would be too tacky for a Vegas casino – the years flying by frame by frame like one of those depressing life insurance commercials. He spotted the poses from his basketball days – a sixth-grade suburban-league foul shot, an eighth-grade drive to the hoop, a high school slam dunk – the row ending with *Sports Illustrated* cover shots, two from his days at Duke and one with his leg in a cast and a large-fonted IS HE FINISHED? emblazoned across his knee-cast image (the answer in the mind's eye being an equally large-fonted YES!).

'So what's wrong?' he asked.

'I didn't say anything was wrong.'

Myron shook his head, disappointed. 'And you a lawyer.'

'Setting a bad example?'

'It's no wonder I never ran for higher office.'

She folded her hands on her lap. 'We need to chat.'

Myron didn't like the tone.

'But not here,' she added. 'Let's take a walk around the block.'

Myron nodded and they rose. Before they reached the door, his cell phone rang. Myron snatched it up with a speed that would have made Wyatt Earp step back. He put the phone to his ear and cleared his throat.

'MB SportsReps,' he said, silky-smooth, professional-like. 'This is Myron Bolitar speaking.'

'Nice phone voice,' Esperanza said. 'You sound like Billy Dee ordering two Colt 45s.'

Esperanza Diaz was his longtime assistant and now sports-agent partner at MB SportsReps (M for Myron, the B for Bolitar – for those keeping score).

'I was hoping you were Lamar,' he said.

'He hasn't called yet?'

'Nope.'

He could almost see Esperanza frown. 'We're in deep doo-doo here,' she said.

'We're not in deep doo-doo. We're just sucking a little wind, that's all.'

'Sucking a little wind,' Esperanza repeated. 'Like Pavarotti running the Boston Marathon.'

'Good one,' Myron said.

'Thanks.'

Lamar Richardson was a power-hitting Golden Glove shortstop who'd just become a free agent – 'free agent' being a phrase agents whisper in the same way a mufti might whisper 'Praise Allah.' Lamar was shopping for new representation and had whittled his final list down to three agencies: two supersized conglomerates with enough office space to house a Price Club and the aforementioned pimple-on-the-buttocks but oh-so-personal MB SportsReps. Go, pimple-butt!

Myron watched his mother standing by the door. He switched ears and said, 'Anything else?'

'You'll never guess who called,' Esperanza said.

'Elle and Claudia demanding another ménage à trois?'

'Oooo, close.'

She would never just tell him. With his friends, everything was a TV game show. 'How about a hint?' he said.

'One of your ex-lovers.'

He felt a jolt. 'Jessica.'

Esperanza made a buzzing noise. 'Sorry, wrong bitch.'

Myron was puzzled. He'd only had two long-term relationships in his life: Jessica on and off for the past thirteen years (now very off). And before that, well, you'd have to go back to . . .

'Emily Downing?'

Esperanza made a *ding-ding* noise.

A sudden image pierced his heart like a straight-blade. He saw Emily sitting on that threadbare couch in the frat basement, smiling that smile at him, her legs bent and tucked under her, wearing his high school varsity jacket that was several sizes too big, her gesturing hands slipping down and disappearing into the sleeves.

His mouth went dry. 'What did she want?'

'Don't know. But she said that she simply *had* to talk to you. She's very breathy, you know. Like everything she says is a double entendre.'

With Emily, everything was.

'She good in the sack?' Esperanza asked.

Being an overly attractive bisexual, Esperanza viewed everyone as a potential sex partner. Myron wondered what that must be like, to have and thus weigh so many options, and then he decided to leave that road untraveled. Wise man.

'What did Emily say exactly?' Myron said.

'Nothing specific. She just spewed out a colorful assortment of breathy teasers: urgent, life-and-death, grave matters, et cetera, et cetera.'

'I don't want to talk to her.'

5

'I didn't think so. If she calls back, you want me to give her the runaround?'

'Please.'

'*Más tarde* then.'

He hung up as a second image whacked him like a surprise wave at the beach. Senior year at Duke. Emily so composed as she dumped the varsity jacket onto his bed and walked out. Not long after that, she married the man who'd ruin Myron's life.

Deep breaths, he told himself. In and out. That's it.

'Everything okay?' Mom asked.

'Fine.'

Mom shook her head again, disappointed.

'I'm not lying,' he said.

'Fine, right, sure, you always breathe like an obscene phone call. Listen, if you don't want to tell your mother—'

'I don't want to tell my mother.'

'Who raised you and . . .'

Myron tuned her out, as was his custom. She was digressing again, taking on a past life or something. It was something she did a lot. One minute she was thoroughly modern, an early feminist who marched alongside Gloria Steinem and became proof that – to quote her old T-shirt – A Woman's Place Is in the House . . . and Senate. But at the sight of her son, her progressive attire slid to the floor and revealed the babushka-clad yenta beneath the burned bra. It made for an interesting childhood.

They headed out the front door. Myron kept his eyes on the For Sale sign as though it might suddenly brandish a gun. His mind flashed onto something he had never actually seen – the sunny day when Mom and Dad had arrived here for the first time, hand in hand, Mom's belly swelling with child, both of them scared and exhilarated realizing that this cookie-cut three-bedroom split-level would be their life vessel, their SS *American Dream*. Now, like it or not, that journey was coming to an end. Forget that 'close one door, open another' crap. That For Sale sign marked the end – the end of youth, of middle age, of a family, the universe of two people who'd started here and fought here and raised kids here and worked and carpooled and lived their lives here.

They walked up the street. Leaves were piled along the curb, the surest sign of suburban autumn, while leaf blowers shattered the still air like helicopters over Saigon. Myron took the inside track so his path would skim the piles' edges. The dead leaves crackled under his sneakers and he liked that. He wasn't sure why.

'Your father spoke to you,' Mom said, half-question. 'About what happened to him.'

Myron felt his stomach tense up. He veered deeper into the leaves, lifting his legs high and crunching louder. 'Yes.'

'What did he say exactly?' Mom asked.

'That he'd had chest pains while I was in the Caribbean.'

The Kaufman house had always been yellow, but the new family had painted it white. It looked wrong with the new color, out of place. Some homes had gone the aluminum-siding route, while others had built on additions, bumping out the kitchens and master bedrooms. The young family who'd moved into the Miller home had gotten rid of the Millers' trademark overflowing flower boxes. The new owners of the Davis place had ripped out those wonderful shrubs Bob Davis had worked on every weekend. It all reminded Myron of an invading army ripping down the flags of the conquered.

'He didn't want to tell you,' Mom said. 'You know your father. He still feels he has to protect you.'

Myron nodded, stayed in the leaves.

Then she said, 'It was more than chest pains.'

Myron stopped.

'It was a full-blown coronary,' she went on, not meeting his eyes. 'He was in intensive care for three days.' She started blinking. 'The artery was almost entirely blocked.'

Myron felt his throat close.

'It's changed him. I know how much you love him, but you have to accept that.'

'Accept what?'

Her voice was gentle and firm. 'That your father is getting older. That I'm getting older.'

He thought about it. 'I'm trying,' he said.

'But?'

'But I see that For Sale sign—'

'Wood and bricks and nails, Myron.'

'What?'

She waded through the leaves and took hold of his elbow.

'Listen to me. You mope around here like we're sitting shiva, but that house is not your childhood. It isn't a part of your family. It doesn't breathe or think or care. It's just wood and bricks and nails.'

'You've lived there for almost thirty-five years.'

'So?'

He turned away, kept walking.

'Your father wants to be honest with you,' she said, 'but you're not making it any easier.'

'Why? What did I do?'

She shook her head, looked up into the sky as though willing divine inspiration, continued walking. Myron stayed by her side. She snaked her arm under his elbow and leaned against him.

'You were always a terrific athlete,' she said. 'Not like your father. Truth be told, your father was a spaz.'

'I know this,' Myron said.

'Right. You know this because your father never pretended to be something he wasn't. He let you see him as human – vulnerable even. And it had a strange effect on you. You worshipped him all the more. You turned him into something almost mythical.'

Myron thought about it, didn't argue. He shrugged and said, 'I love him.'

'I know, sweetheart. But he's just a man. A good man. But now he's getting old and he's scared. Your father always wanted you to see him as human. But he doesn't want you to see him scared.'

Myron kept his head down. There are certain things you cannot picture your parents doing – having sex being the classic example. Most people cannot – probably should not even try to – picture their parents in flagrante delicto. But right now Myron was trying to conjure up another taboo image, one of his father sitting alone in the dark, hand on his chest, scared, and the sight, while achievable, was aching, unbearable. When he spoke again, his voice was thick. 'So what should I do?'

'Accept the changes. Your father is retiring. He's worked his whole life and like most moronically macho men of his era, his self-worth is wrapped up in his job. So he's having a tough time. He's not the same. You're not the same. Your relationship is shifting and neither one of you likes change.'

Myron stayed silent, waiting for more.

'Reach out to him a little,' Mom said. 'He's carried you your whole life. He won't ask, but now it's his turn.'

When they turned the final corner, Myron saw the Mercedes parked in front of the For Sale sign. He wondered for a moment if it was a Realtor showing the house. His father stood in the front yard chatting with a woman. Dad was gesturing wildly and smiling. Looking at his father's face – the rough skin that always seemed in need of a shave, the prominent nose Dad used to 'nose punch' him during their giggling fun-fights, the heavy-lidded eyes à la Victor Mature and Dean Martin, the wispy hairs of gray that held on stubbornly after the thick black had fled – Myron felt a hand reach in and tweak his heart.

Dad caught his eye and waved. 'Look who stopped by!' he shouted.

Emily Downing turned around and gave him a tight smile. Myron looked back at her and said nothing. Fifty minutes had passed. Ten more until the heel crushed the tomato.

2

Too much history.

His parents made themselves scarce. For all their almost legendary butting in, they both had the uncanny ability to trample full tilt through the Isle of Nosiness without tripping any gone-too-far mines. They quietly disappeared into the house.

Emily tried a smile, but it just wasn't happening. 'Well, well, well,' she said when they were alone. 'If it isn't the good one I let get away.'

'You used that line last time I saw you.'

'Did I?'

They had met in the library freshman year at Duke. Emily had been bigger then, a bit fleshier, though not in a bad way, and the years had definitely slimmed her down and toned her up, though again not in a bad way. But the visual whammy was still there. Emily wasn't so much pretty as, to quote *SuperFly*, foxy. Hot. Sizzlingly so. As a young coed, she'd had long, kinky hair that always had that just-did-the-nasty muss to it, a crooked smile that could knock a movie up a rating, and a subconsciously undulating body that continuously flickered out the word *sex* like an old movie projector. It didn't matter that she wasn't beautiful; beauty had little to do with it, in fact. This was an innate thing; Emily couldn't turn it off if she donned a muumuu and put roadkill on her head.

The weird thing was, they were both virgins when they met, somehow missing the perhaps overblown sexual revolution of the seventies and early eighties. Myron always believed that the revolution was mostly hype or, at the very least, that it didn't seep past the brick façades of suburban high schools. But then again, he was pretty good at self-rationalization. More likely, it was his fault

– if you could consider not being promiscuous a fault. He'd always been attracted to the 'nice' girls, even in high school. Casual affairs never interested him. Every girl he met was gauged as a potential life partner, a soul mate, an undying love, as though every relationship should be a Carpenters song.

But with Emily it had been complete sexual exploration and discovery. They learned from each other in stuttering, though achingly blissful, steps. Even now, as much as he detested her very being, he could still feel the tightening, could still recall the way his nerve endings would sing and surge when they were in bed. Or the back of a car. Or a movie theater or a library or once even during a poly sci lecture on Hobbes's *Leviathan*. While he may have yearned to be a Carpenters man, his first long-term relationship had ended up more like something off Meat Loaf's *Bat Out of Hell* album – hot, heavy, sweaty, fast, the whole 'Paradise by the Dashboard Light.'

Still, there had to have been more to it. He and Emily had lasted three years. He had loved her, and she'd been the first to break his heart.

'There a coffee bar near here?' she asked.

'A Starbucks,' Myron said.

'I'll drive.'

'I don't want to go with you, Emily.'

She gave him the smile. 'Lost my charms, have I?'

'They lost their effect on me a long time ago.' Half lie.

She shifted her hips. Myron watched, thinking about what Esperanza had said. It wasn't just her voice or her words – even her movements ended up a double entendre. 'It's important, Myron.'

'Not to me.'

'You don't even know—'

'It doesn't matter, Emily. You're the past. So is your husband—'

'My *ex*-husband. I divorced him, remember? And I never knew what he did to you.'

'Right,' Myron said. 'You were just the cause.'

She looked at him. 'It's not that simple. You know that.'

He nodded. She was right, of course. 'I always knew why I did it,' Myron said. 'I was being a competitive dumbass who wanted to get one up on Greg. But why you?'

Emily shook her head. The old hair would have flown side to side, ending up half covering her face. Her new coif was shorter and more stylized, but his mind's eye still saw the kinky flow. 'It doesn't matter anymore,' she said.

'Guess not,' he said, 'but I've always been curious.'

'We both had too much to drink.'

'Simple as that?'

'Yes.'

Myron made a face. 'Lame,' he said.

'Maybe it was just about sex,' she said.

'A purely physical act?'

'Maybe.'

'The night before you married someone else?'

She looked at him. 'It was dumb, okay?'

'You say so.'

'And maybe I was scared,' she said.

'Of getting married?'

'Of marrying the wrong man.'

Myron shook his head. 'Jesus, you're shameless.'

Emily was about to say more, but she stopped as though her last reserves had suddenly been zapped away. He wanted her gone, but with ex-loves there is also a pulling sadness. There before you stands the true road untraveled, the lifetime what-if, the embodiment of a totally alternate life if things had gone a little different. He had absolutely no interest in her anymore, yet her words still drew out his old self, wounds and all.

'It was fourteen years ago,' she said softly. 'Don't you think it's time we moved on?'

He thought about what that 'purely physical' night had cost him. Everything, maybe. His lifelong dream, for sure. 'You're right,' he said, turning away. 'Please leave.'

'I need your help.'

He shook his head. 'As you said, time to move on.'

'Just have coffee with me. With an old friend.'

He wanted to say no, but the past had too strong a pull. He nodded, afraid to speak. They drove in silence to Starbucks and ordered their complicated coffees from an artist-wannabe *barista* with more attitude than the guy who works at the local record store. They added whatever condiments at the little stand, playing a game of Twister by reaching across one another for the nonfat milk or Equal. They sat down in metal chairs with too-low backs. The sound system was playing reggae music, a CD entitled *Jamaican Me Crazy*.

Emily crossed her legs and took a sip. 'Have you ever heard of Fanconi anemia?'

Interesting opening gambit. 'No.'

'It's an inherited anemia that leads to bone marrow failure. It weakens your chromosomes.'

Myron waited.

'Are you familiar with bone marrow transplants?'

Strange line of questioning, but he decided to play it straight. 'A little. A friend of mine had leukemia and needed a transplant. They had a marrow drive at the temple. We all went down and got tested.'

'When you say "we all"—'

'Mom, Dad, my whole family. I think Win went too.'

She tilted her head. 'How is Win?'

'The same.'

'Sorry to hear that,' she said. 'When we were at Duke, he used to listen to us making love, didn't he?'

'Only when we pulled down the shade so he couldn't watch.'

She laughed. 'He never liked me.'

'You were his favorite.'

'Really?'

'That's not saying much,' Myron said.

'He hates women, doesn't he?'

Myron thought about it. 'As sex objects, they're fine. But in terms of relationships . . .'

'An odd duck.'

She should only know.

Emily took a sip. 'I'm stalling,' she said.

'I sorta figured that.'

'What happened to your friend with leukemia?'

'He died.'

Her face went white. 'I'm sorry. How old was he?'

'Thirty-four.'

Emily took another sip, cradling the mug with both hands. 'So you're listed with the bone marrow national registry?'

'I guess. I gave blood and they gave me a donor card.'

She closed her eyes.

'What?' he asked.

'Fanconi anemia is fatal. You can treat it for a while with blood transfusions and hormones, but the only cure is a bone marrow transplant.'

'I don't understand, Emily. Do you have this disease?'

'It doesn't hit adults.' She put down her coffee and looked up. He was not big on reading eyes, but the pain was neon-obvious. 'It hits children.'

As though on cue, the Starbucks soundtrack changed to something instrumental and somber. Myron waited. It didn't take her long.

'My son has it,' she said.

Myron remembered visiting the house in Franklin Lakes when Greg disappeared, the boy playing in the backyard with his sister. Must have been, what, two, three years ago. The boy was about ten, his sister maybe eight. Greg and Emily were in the midst of a bloody take-no-prisoners custody battle, the two children pinned down in the crossfire, the kind no one walks away from without a serious hit.

'I'm sorry,' he said.

'We need to find a bone marrow match.'

'I thought siblings were an almost automatic match.'

Her eyes flicked around the room. 'One-in-four chance,' she said, stopping abruptly.

'Oh.'

'The national registry found only three potential donors. By potential I mean that the initial HLA tests showed them as possibilities. The A and B match, but then they have to do a full blood and tissue workup to see—' She stopped again. 'I'm getting technical. I don't mean to. But when your kid is sick like this, it's like you live in a snow globe of medical jargon.'

'I understand.'

'Anyway, getting past the initial screening is like winning a second-tier lottery ticket. The chance of a match is still slim. The blood center calls in the potential donors and runs a battery of tests, but the odds they'll be a close enough match to go through with the transplant are pretty low, especially with only three potential donors.'

Myron nodded, still having no idea why she was telling him any of this.

'We got lucky,' she said. 'One of the three was a match with Jeremy.'

'Great.'

'There's a problem,' she said. Again the crooked smile. 'The donor is missing.'

'What do you mean, missing?'

'I don't have the details. The registry is confidential. No one will tell me what's going on. We seemed to be on the right track, and then all of a sudden, the donor just pulled out. My doctor can't say anything – like I said, it's protected.'

'Maybe the donor just changed his mind.'

'Then we better change it back,' she said, 'or Jeremy dies.'

The statement was plain enough.

'So what do you think happened?' Myron asked. 'You think he's missing or something?'

'He or she,' Emily said. 'Yes.'

'He or she?'

'I don't know anything about the donor – age, sex, where they live, nothing. But Jeremy isn't getting any better and the odds of finding another donor in time are, well, almost nonexistent.' She kept the face tight, but Myron could see the foundation starting to crack a bit. 'We have to find this donor.'

'And that's why you've come to me? To find him?'

'You and Win found Greg when no one else could. When he disappeared, Clip went to you first. Why?'

'That's a long story.'

'Not so long, Myron. You and Win are trained in this sort of thing. You're good at it.'

'Not in a case like this,' Myron said. 'Greg is a high-profile athlete. He can take to the airwaves, offer rewards. He can buy private detectives.'

'We're already doing that. Greg has a press conference set up for tomorrow.'

'So?'

'So it won't work. I told Jeremy's doctor we would pay anything to the donor, even though it's illegal. But something else is wrong here. I'm afraid all the publicity might even backfire – that it may send the donor deeper into hiding or something, I don't know.'

'What does Greg say to that?'

'We don't talk much, Myron. And when we do, it's usually not very pretty.'

'Does Greg know you're talking to me now?'

She looked at him. 'He hates you as much as you hate him. Maybe more so.'

Myron decided to take that as a no. Emily kept her eyes on him, searching his face as though there were an answer there.

'I can't help you, Emily.'

She looked like she'd just been slapped.

'I sympathize,' he went on, 'but I'm just getting over some major problems of my own.'

'Are you saying you don't have time?'

'It's not that. A private detective would have a better chance—'

'Greg's hired four already. They can't even find out the donor's name.'

'I doubt I can do any better.'

'This is my son's life, Myron.'

'I understand, Emily.'

'Can't you put aside your animosity for me and Greg?'

He wasn't sure that he could. 'That's not the issue. I'm a sports agent, not a detective.'

'That didn't stop you before.'

'And look how things ended up. Every time I meddle, it leads to disaster.'

'My son is thirteen years old, Myron.'

'I'm sorry—'

'I don't want your sympathy, dammit.' Her eyes were smaller now, black. She leaned toward him until her face was scant inches from his. 'I want you to do the math.'

He looked puzzled. 'What?'

'You're an agent. You know all about numbers, right? So do the math.'

Myron tilted back, giving himself a little distance. 'What the hell are you talking about?'

'Jeremy's birthday is July eighteenth,' she said. 'Do the math.'

'What math?'

'One more time: He's thirteen years old. He was born July the eighteenth. I was married October tenth.'

Nothing. For several seconds, he heard the mothers chatting over one another, one baby cry, one *barista* call out an order to another, and then it happened. A cold gust blew across Myron's heart. Steel bands wrapped around his chest, making it almost impossible to breathe. He opened his mouth but nothing came out. It was like someone had whacked his solar plexus with a baseball bat. Emily watched him and nodded.

'That's right,' she said. 'He's your son.'

3

'You can't know that for sure,' Myron said.

Emily's whole persona screamed exhaustion. 'I do.'

'You were sleeping with Greg too, right?'

'Yes.'

'And we only had that one night during that time. You probably had a whole bunch with Greg.'

'True.'

'So how can you possibly know—?'

'Denial,' she interjected with a sigh. 'The first step.'

He pointed a finger at her. 'Don't hand me that psychology-major crap, Emily.'

'Moving quickly to anger,' she continued.

'You can't know—'

'I've always known,' she interrupted.

Myron sat back. He stayed composed but underneath he could almost feel the fissure widening, his foundation starting to shift.

'When I first got pregnant, I figured like you: I'd slept with Greg more, so it was probably his baby. At least, that's what I told myself.' She closed her eyes. Myron stayed very still, the knot in his stomach tightening. 'And when Jeremy was born, he favored me, so who was to say? But – and this is going to sound so goddamn stupid – a mother knows. I can't tell you how. But I knew. I tried to deny it too. I told myself I was just feeling guilty over what we'd done, and that this was God's way of punishing me.'

'How Old Testament of you,' Myron said.

'Sarcasm,' she said with almost a smile. 'Your favorite defense.'

'Your maternal intuition hardly counts as evidence, Emily.'

'You asked before about Sara.'

'Sara?'

'Jeremy's sister. You wondered about her matching as a donor. She didn't.'

'Right, but you said there was only a one-in-four chance with siblings.'

'For *full* siblings, yes. But the match wasn't even close. Because she's only Jeremy's half sister.'

'The doctor told you this?'

'Yes.'

Myron felt the stone footing beneath his feet give way. 'So . . . Greg knows?'

Emily shook her head. 'The doctor pulled me aside. Because of the divorce, I'm Jeremy's primary custodian. Greg has custody too, but the children live with me. I'm in charge of the medical decisions.'

'So Greg still believes . . . ?'

'That Jeremy is his, yes.'

Myron was floundering in deep water with no land in sight. 'But you said you've always known.'

'Yes.'

'Why didn't you tell me?'

'Are you kidding? I was married to Greg. I loved him. We were starting our life together.'

'You still should have told me.'

'When, Myron? When should I have told you?'

'As soon as the baby was born.'

'Aren't you listening? I just told you I wasn't sure.'

'A mother knows, you said.'

'Come on, Myron. I was in love with Greg, not you. You with your corny sense of morality – you would have insisted I divorce Greg and marry you and live some suburban fairy tale.'

'So instead you chose to live a lie?'

'It was the right decision based on what I knew then. With hindsight' – she stopped, took a deep sip – 'I probably would have done a lot of things differently.'

He tried to let some of it sink in, but it was a no-go. Another group of stroller-laced soccer moms entered the coffee shop. They took a corner table and started jabbering about little Brittany and Kyle and Morgan.

'How long have you and Greg been separated?' Myron's voice sounded sharper than he intended. Or maybe not.

'Four years now.'

'And you were no longer in love with him, right? Four years ago?'

'Right.'

'Earlier even,' he went on. 'I mean, you probably fell out of love with him a long time ago, right?'

She looked confused. 'Right.'

'So you could have told me then. At least four years ago. Why didn't you?'

'Stop cross-examining me.'

'You're the one who dropped this bombshell,' he said. 'How do you expect me to react?'

'Like a man.'

'What the hell does that mean?'

'I need your help. Jeremy needs your help. That's what we should be concentrating on.'

'I want some answers first. I'm entitled to that much.'

She hesitated, looked like she might argue, then nodded wearily. 'If it'll help you get past this—'

'Get past this? Like it's a kidney stone or something?'

'I'm too tired to fight with you,' she said. 'Just go on. Ask your questions.'

'Why didn't you tell me before now.'

Her eyes drifted over his shoulder. 'I almost did,' she said. 'Once.'

'When?'

'Do you remember when you came to the house? When Greg first vanished?'

He nodded. He had just been thinking about that day.

'You were looking out the window at him. He was in the yard with his sister.'

'I remember,' Myron said.

'Greg and I were going through that nasty custody battle.'

'You accused him of abusing the children.'

'It wasn't true. You realized that right away. It was just a legal ploy.'

20

'Some ploy,' Myron said. 'Next time accuse him of war atrocities.'

'Who are you to judge me?'

'Actually,' Myron said, 'I think I'm just the person.'

Emily pinned him with her eyes. 'Custody battles are war without the Geneva Accords,' she said. 'Greg got nasty. I got nasty back. You do whatever you have to in order to win.'

'And that includes revealing that Greg wasn't Jeremy's father?'

'No.'

'Why not?'

'Because I won custody anyway.'

'That's not an answer. You hated Greg.'

'Yes.'

'Still do?' he asked.

'Yes.' No hesitation.

'So why didn't you tell him?'

'Because as much as I loathe Greg,' she said, 'I love Jeremy more. I could hurt Greg. I'd probably enjoy it. But I couldn't do that to my son – take away his father like that.'

'I thought you'd do anything to win.'

'I'd do anything to Greg,' she said, 'not Jeremy.'

It made sense, he guessed, but he suspected she was holding something back. 'So you kept this secret for thirteen years.'

'Yes.'

'Do your parents know?'

'No.'

'You never told anyone?'

'Never.'

'So why are you telling me now?'

Emily shook her head. 'Are you being purposely dense, Myron?'

He put his hands on the table. They weren't shaking. Somehow he understood that these questions came from more than mere curiosity; they were part of the defense mechanism, the internal barbed wire and moat he'd lavishly built to keep Emily's revelation from reaching him. He knew that what she was telling him was life altering in a way nothing he'd ever heard before was. The words *my son* kept floating through his subconscious. But they were just words right now. They'd get through eventually, he guessed, but for now the barbed wire and moat were holding.

'You think I wanted to tell you? I practically begged you to help, but you wouldn't listen. I'm desperate here.'

'Desperate enough to lie?'

'Yes,' she said, again with no hesitation. 'But I'm not, Myron. You have to believe that.'

He shrugged. 'Maybe someone else is Jeremy's father.'

'Excuse me?'

'A third party,' he said. 'You slept with me the night before your wedding. I doubt I was the only one. Could be one of a dozen guys.'

She looked at him. 'You want your pound of flesh, Myron? Go ahead, I can take it. But this isn't like you.'

'You know me that well, huh?'

'Even when you got angry – even when you had every right to hate me – you've never been cruel. It's not your way.'

'We're in uncharted waters here, Emily.'

'Doesn't matter,' she said.

He felt something well up, making it hard to breathe. He grabbed his mug, looked into it as though it might have an answer on the bottom, put it back down. He couldn't look at her. 'How could you do this to me?'

Emily reached across the table and put her hand on his forearm. 'I'm sorry,' she said.

He pulled away.

'I don't know what else to say. You asked before why I never told you. My main concern was always Jeremy's welfare, but you were a consideration too.'

'Bull.'

'I know how you are, Myron. I know you can't just shrug this off. But for now you have to. You have to find the donor and save Jeremy's life. We can worry about the rest after that.'

'How long has' – he almost said *my son* – 'Jeremy been ill?'

'We learned about it six months ago. When he was playing basketball. He started getting bruised too easily. Then he was short of breath for no reason. He started falling down . . .' Her voice tailed off.

'Is he in the hospital?'

'No. He lives at home and goes to school and he looks fine, just a little pale. But he can't play competitive sports or anything like that. He seems to be doing well, but . . . it's just a matter of time. He's so anemic and his marrow cells are so weak that something will get him. Either he'll contract a life-threatening infection or if he manages to get past that, malignancies will eventually develop. We treat him with hormones. That helps, but it's a temporary treatment, not a cure.'

'And a bone marrow transplant would be a cure?'

'Yes.' Her face brightened with an almost religious fervor. 'If the transplant takes, he can be completely cured. I've seen it happen with other kids.'

Myron nodded, sat back, crossed his legs, uncrossed them. 'Can I meet him?'

She looked down. The sound of the blender, probably making a frappuccino, exploded while the espresso maker shrieked its familiar mating call to the various lattes. Emily waited for the noise to die down. 'I can't stop you. But I'm hoping you'll do the right thing here.'

'That being?'

'It's hard enough being thirteen years old and almost terminally ill. Do you really want to take away his father too?'

Myron said nothing.

'I know you're in shock right now. And I know you have a million more questions. But you have to forget that for now. You have to work through your confusion, your anger, everything. The life of a thirteen-year-old boy – our son – is at stake. Concentrate on that, Myron. Find the donor, okay?'

He looked back toward the soccer moms, still cooing about their children. Listening to them, he felt an overwhelming pang.

'Where can I find Jeremy's doctor?' he asked.

4

When the elevator doors opened into the reception area of MB SportsReps, Big Cyndi reached out to Myron with two arms the approximate circumference of the marble columns at the Acropolis. Myron almost leaped out of the way – involuntary survival reflex and all – but he stayed still and closed his eyes. Big Cyndi embraced him, which was like being wrapped in wet attic insulation, and lifted him into the air.

'Oh, Mr Bolitar!' she cried.

He grimaced and rode it out. Eventually she put him back down as though he were a porcelain doll she was returning to a shelf. Big Cyndi is six-six and on the planetoid side of three hundred pounds, the former intercontinental tag-team wrestling champion with Esperanza, aka Big Chief Mama to Esperanza's Little Pocahontas. Her head was cube shaped and topped with hair spiked to look like the Statue of Liberty on a bad acid trip. She wore more makeup than the cast of *Cats*, her clothing form-fitted like sausage casing, her scowl the stuff of sumos.

'Uh, everything okay?' Myron ventured.

'Oh, Mr Bolitar!'

Big Cyndi looked like she was about to hug him again, but something stopped her, perhaps the stark terror in Myron's eyes. She picked up luggage that in her manhole-paw resembled a Close'N Play phonograph from the early seventies. She was that kind of big, the kind of big where the world around her always looked like a bad B-monster movie set and she was walking through a miniature Tokyo, knocking over power lines and swatting at buzzing fighter planes.

Esperanza appeared in her office doorway. She folded her arms and rested against the frame. Even after her recent ordeal,

Esperanza still looked immensely beautiful, the shiny black ringlets still falling over her forehead just so, the dark olive skin still radiant – the whole image a sort of gypsy, peasant-blouse fantasy. But he could see some new lines around the eyes and a slight slouch in the perfect posture. He'd wanted her to take time off after her release, but he knew she wouldn't. Esperanza loved MB Sports-Reps. She wanted to save it.

'What's going on?' Myron asked.

'It's all in the letter, Mr Bolitar,' Big Cyndi said.

'What letter?'

'Oh, Mr Bolitar!' she cried again.

'What?'

But she didn't respond, hiding her face in her hands and ducking into the elevator as though entering a tepee. The elevator doors slid closed, and she was gone.

Myron waited a beat and then turned to Esperanza. 'Explanation?'

'She's taking a leave of absence,' Esperanza said.

'Why?'

'Big Cyndi isn't stupid, Myron.'

'I didn't say she was.'

'She sees what's going on here.'

'It's only temporary,' Myron said. 'We'll snap back.'

'And when we do, Big Cyndi will come back. In the meantime she got a good job offer.'

'With Leather-N-Lust?' Big Cyndi worked nights as a bouncer at an S&M bar called Leather-N-Lust. Motto: Hurt the ones you love. Sometimes – or so he had heard – Big Cyndi was part of the stage show. What part she played Myron had no idea nor had he worked up the courage to ask – another taboo abyss his mind did its best to circumvent.

'No,' Esperanza said. 'She's returning to FLOW.'

For the wrestling uninitiated, FLOW is the acronym for the Fabulous Ladies of Wrestling.

'Big Cyndi is going to wrestle again?'

Esperanza nodded. 'On the senior circuit.'

'Excuse me?'

'FLOW wanted to expand its product. They did some research,

25

saw how well the PGA is doing with the senior golf tour and . . .' She shrugged.

'A senior ladies' wrestling tour?'

'More like retired,' Esperanza said. 'I mean, Big Cyndi is only thirty-eight. They're bringing back a lot of the old favorites: Queen Qaddafi, Cold War Connie, Brezhnev Babe, Cellblock Celia, Black Widow—'

'I don't remember the Black Widow.'

'Before our time. Hell, before our parents' time. She must be in her seventies.'

Myron tried not to make a face. 'And people are going to pay money to see a seventy-year-old woman wrestle?'

'You shouldn't discriminate on the basis of age.'

'Right, sorry.' Myron rubbed his eyes.

'And professional women's wrestling is struggling right now, what with the competition from Jerry Springer and Ricki Lake. They need to do something.'

'And grappling old ladies is the answer?'

'I think they're aiming more for nostalgia.'

'A chance to cheer on the wrestler of your youth?'

'Didn't you go see Steely Dan in concert a couple of years ago?'

'That's different, don't you think?'

She shrugged. 'Both past their prime. Both mining more on what you remember than what you see or hear.'

It made sense. Scary sense maybe. But sense. 'How about you?' Myron asked.

'What about me?'

'Didn't they want Little Pocahontas to return?'

'Yep.'

'Were you tempted?'

'To what? Return to the ring?'

'Yes.'

'Oh, sure,' Esperanza said. 'I busted my shapely ass working full-time while getting my law degree, so I could once again don a suede bikini and grope aging nymphs in front of drooling trailer trash.' She paused. 'Still, it is a step above being a sports agent.'

'Ha-ha.' Myron walked over to Big Cyndi's desk. There was an envelope with his name scrawled across the top in glow-in-the-dark orange.

'She wrote it in crayon?' Myron said.

'Eye shadow.'

'I see.'

'So are you going to tell me what's wrong?' she asked.

'Nothing,' Myron said.

'Bullshit,' she said. 'You look like you just heard Wham split up.'

'Don't bring that up,' Myron said. 'Sometimes, late at night, I still suffer flashbacks.'

Esperanza studied his face a few more seconds. 'This have something to do with your college sweetheart?'

'Sort of.'

'Oh Christ.'

'What?'

'How do I say this nicely, Myron? You are beyond moronic in the ways of women. Exhibits A and B are Jessica and Emily.'

'You don't even know Emily.'

'I know enough,' she said. 'I thought you didn't want to talk to her.'

'I didn't. She found me at my parents' place.'

'She just showed up there?'

'Yep.'

'What did she want?'

He shook his head. He still wasn't ready to talk about it yet. 'Any messages?'

'Not as many as we'd like.'

'Win upstairs?'

'I think he went home already.' She picked up her coat. 'I think I'll do likewise.'

'Good night.'

'If you hear anything from Lamar—'

'I'll call you.'

Esperanza put on her coat, flipping the glistening black flow out of the collar. Myron headed into his office and made a few phone calls, mostly of a recruiting nature. It was not going well.

Several months ago, a friend's death had sent Myron into a tailspin, causing him to – and we're using complex psychiatric jargon here – wig out. Nothing overly drastic, no nervous breakdown or institutional commitment. He had instead fled to a deserted

27

Caribbean island with Terese Collins, a beautiful TV anchorwoman he didn't know. He had told no one – not Win, not Esperanza, not even Mom and Dad – where he was going or when he'd be back.

As Win put it, when he wigged out, he wigged out in style.

By the time Myron was forced to return, their clients were scattering into the night like kitchen help during an immigration bust. Now Myron and Esperanza were back, attempting to revive the comatose and perhaps dying MB SportsReps. This was no easy task. The competition in this business was a dozen starving lions, and Myron was one heavily limping Christian.

The MB SportsReps office was nicely situated on Park Avenue and Forty-sixth Street in the Lock-Horne Building, owned by the family of Myron's college-and-current roommate, Win. The building was in primo midtown location and offered up some semi-dazzling views of the Manhattan skyline. Myron soaked it in for a moment and then looked down at the suits speeding below. The sight of the working ants always depressed him, a chorus of 'Is That All There Is?' playing in his head.

He turned now toward his Client Wall, the one with action shots of all the athletes represented by MB SportsReps, which now looked as spotty and sparse as a bad hair transplant. He wanted to care, but unfair as it was to Esperanza, his heart wasn't really in it. He wanted to go back, to love MB and have that old hunger, but no matter how much he tried to stoke the old fire, it wouldn't flame up.

Emily called about an hour later.

'Dr Singh doesn't have office hours tomorrow,' Emily said. 'But you can hook up during rounds tomorrow morning.'

'Where?'

'Babies and Children's Hospital. It's part of Columbia Presbyterian on 167th Street. Tenth floor, south.'

'What time?'

'Rounds start at eight,' Emily said.

'Okay.'

Brief silence.

'You okay, Myron?'

'I want to see him.'

28

It took her a few seconds. 'Like I said before, I can't stop you. But sleep on it, okay?'

'I just want to see him,' Myron said. 'I won't say anything. Not yet, at least.'

'Can we talk about this tomorrow?' Emily asked.

'Yeah, sure.'

She hesitated again. 'Do you have Web access, Myron?'

'Yes.'

'We have a private URL.'

'What?'

'A private Web address. I take photos with the digital camera and post them there. For my parents. They moved to Miami last year. They check it out every week. Get to see new pictures of the grandkids. So if you want to see what Jeremy looks like . . .'

'What's the address?'

She gave it to him and Myron typed it in. He hung up before hitting the return button. The images came up slowly. He drummed his fingers on the desk. On top of the screen was a banner saying HI, NANA AND POP-POP. Myron thought about his parents and shook it off.

There were four photographs of Jeremy and Sara. Myron swallowed. He placed the arrow on Jeremy's image and clicked the mouse, zooming in closer, enlarging the boy's face. He tried to keep his breathing steady. He stared at the boy's face for a long time without really registering anything. Eventually his vision blurred, his own face reflecting on the monitor over the boy's, blending the images together, creating a visual echo of he knew not what.

5

Myron heard the cries of ecstasy through the door.

Win – real name: Windsor Horne Lockwood III – was letting Myron temporarily crash at his apartment in the Dakota on Seventy-second Street and Central Park West. The Dakota was an old New York landmark whose rich and lush history had been totally eclipsed by the murder of John Lennon twenty-some-odd years ago. Entering meant crossing over the spot where Lennon had bled to death, the feeling not unlike trampling over a grave. Myron was finally getting used to it.

From the outside, the Dakota was beautiful and dark and resembled a haunted house on steroids. Most apartments, including Win's, had more square footage than a European principality. Last year, after a lifetime of living in Mom and Dad's suburban sprawl, Myron had finally moved out of the basement and into a SoHo loft with his ladylove, Jessica. It was a huge step, the first sign that after more than a decade, Jessica was ready to – gasp! – commit. So the two lovers clasped hands and took the live-together plunge. And like so many plunges in life, it ended in an ugly splat.

More cries of ecstasy.

Myron pressed his ear against the door. Cries, yes, and a soundtrack. Not live action, he decided. He used his key and pushed open the door. The cries were coming from the TV room. Win never used that room for, uh, filming. Myron sighed and stepped through the portal.

Win wore his casual WASP uniform: khakis, shirt with a color so loud you couldn't look at it straight on except through a pinhole, loafers, no socks. His blond locks had been parted with the precision of old ladies dividing up a lunch check; his skin was the color of white china with dabs of golf-ruddy red on both cheeks. He sat yoga-lotus-style, his legs pretzeled to a point man was never supposed to achieve. His index fingers and thumbs formed two circles, the hands resting against the knees. Yuppie Zen. Old World European clashing heads with Ancient Oriental. The sweet smell of Main Line mixed with the heavy Asian incense.

Win breathed in for a twenty count, held it, breathed out for a twenty count. He was meditating, of course, but with a Win-like twist. He did not, for example, listen to soothing nature sounds or chimes; no, he preferred meditating to the sound tracks of, uh, skin flicks from the seventies, which basically sounded like a bad Jimi Hendrix impersonator making wah-wah-wah noises on an electric kazoo. Just listening to it was enough to make you rush out for a shot of antibiotics.

Win did not close his eyes either. He did not visualize a deer sipping water by a lapping stream or a gentle waterfall against green foliage or any of that. His gaze remained fixed on the television screen; more specifically, on homemade videotapes of himself and a pot-pourri of females in the throes of passion.

Myron stepped fully into the room. Win turned one of his finger-Os into a flat-palm stop sign, then lifted the index finger up to indicate he wanted another moment. Myron risked a glance at the screen, saw the writhing flesh, turned away.

A few seconds later, Win said, 'Hello.'

'I'd like my disgust noted for the record,' Myron said.

'So noted.'

Win moved fluidly from the lotus position to a full stand. He popped out the tape and put it in a box. The box was labeled *Anon 11*. *Anon*, Myron knew, stood for *Anonymous*. It meant Win had either forgotten her name or never learned it.

'I can't believe you still do this,' Myron said.

'Are we moralizing again?' Win asked with a smile. 'How nice for us.'

'Let me ask you something.'

'Oh, please do.'

'Something I always wanted to know.'

'My ears are all atwitter.'

'Putting aside my repugnancy for a moment—'

'Not on my account,' Win said. 'I so enjoy when you're superior.'

'You claim this' – Myron motioned vaguely at the videotape and then the TV screen – 'relaxes you.'

'Yes.'

'But doesn't it also . . . I mean, sick as it is . . . doesn't it also arouse you?'

'Not at all,' Win replied.

'That's the part I don't understand.'

'Viewing the act does not arouse me,' Win explained. 'Thinking about the act does not arouse me. Videos, dirty magazines, *Penthouse Forum*, cyber-porn – none of them arouse me. For me, there is no substitute for the real thing. A partner must be present. The rest has the same effect as tickling myself. It's why I never masturbate.'

Myron said nothing.

'Problem?' Win asked.

'I'm just wondering what possessed me to ask,' Myron said.

Win opened a Ming dynasty cabinet that had been converted into a small fridge and tossed Myron a Yoo-Hoo. He poured himself a snifter of cognac. The room was lush antiques and rich tapestries and Oriental carpets and busts of men with long, curly hair. If not for the state-of-the-art home entertainment system, the room could have been something you'd stumble across on a tour of a Medici palace.

They grabbed their usual seats.

Win said, 'You look troubled.'

'I have a case for us.'

'Ah.'

'I know I said we weren't going to do this anymore. But this is sort of a special circumstance.'

'I see,' Win said.

'Do you remember Emily?'

Win did that swirl thing with his snifter. 'College girlfriend. Used to make monkey noises during sex. Dumped you in the beginning of our senior year. Married your arch-enemy Greg Downing. Dumped him too. Probably still makes monkey noises.'

'She has a son,' Myron said. 'He's sick.' He quickly explained the situation, leaving out the part about possibly being the kid's father. If he couldn't talk about it with Esperanza, there was no way he could raise the subject with Win.

When he finished, Win said, 'It shouldn't be too difficult. You're going to talk to the doctor tomorrow?'

'Yes.'

'Find out what you can about who handles the records.'

Win picked up the remote and flicked on the television. He flipped the channels because there were a lot of commercials on and because he was male. He stopped at CNN. Terese Collins was anchoring the news.

'Is the lovely Ms Collins visiting us tomorrow?' Win asked.

Myron nodded. 'Her flight comes in at ten.'

'She's been visiting quite a bit.'

'Yep.'

'Are you two' – Win crinkled his face as if someone had just flashed him a particularly nasty case of jock rot – 'getting serious?'

Myron looked at Terese on the screen. 'Still too new,' he said.

There was an *All in the Family* marathon on cable, so Win flipped to it. They ordered in some Chinese food and watched two episodes. Myron tried to get lost in the bliss of Archie and Edith, but it wasn't happening. His thoughts naturally kept returning to Jeremy. He managed to deflect the paternity issue, concentrating, as Emily had asked, on the disease and task at hand. Fanconi anemia. That was what she said the boy had. Myron wondered if they had anything about it on the Web.

'I'll be back in a little while,' Myron said.

Win looked at him. 'The Stretch Cunningham funeral episode is up next.'

'I want to check something on the Web.'

'The episode where Archie gives the eulogy.'

'I know.'

'Where he comments that he never thought Stretch Cunningham was Jewish because of the "ham" in his last name.'

'I know the episode, Win.'

'And you're willing to miss it for the sake of the Web?'

'You have it on tape.'

'That's not the point.'

The two men looked at each other, comfortable in the silence. After some time passed, Win said, 'Tell me.'

He barely hesitated. 'Emily said I'm the boy's father.'

Win nodded and said, 'Ah.'

'You don't sound surprised.'

Win used the chopsticks to grab another shrimp. 'You believe her?'

'Yes.'

'Why?'

'For one thing, it's a hell of a thing to lie about it.'

'But Emily is good at lying, Myron. She's always lied to you. She lied to you in college. She lied to you when Greg disappeared. She lied in court about Greg's behavior with the children. She betrayed Greg the night before their wedding by sleeping with you. And, if you will, if she is telling the truth now, she lied to you for the better part of thirteen years.'

Myron thought about it. 'I think she's telling the truth about this.'

'You *think*, Myron.'

'I'm going to take a blood test.'

Win shrugged. 'If you must.'

'What does that mean?'

'I'll let the statement speak for itself.'

Myron made a face. 'Didn't you just say I should find out for sure?'

'Not at all,' Win said. 'I was merely pointing out the obvious. I didn't say it made a difference.'

Myron thought about it. 'You're confusing me.'

'Simply put,' Win said, 'so what if you are the boy's biological father? What difference does it make?'

'Come on, Win. Not even you can be that cold.'

'Quite the opposite. As strange as this might sound, I am using my heart on this one.'

'How do you figure?'

Win swirled the liquid again, studied the amber, took a sip. It colored his cheeks a bit. 'Again I'll put it simply: No matter what a blood test might indicate, you are not Jeremy Downing's father. Greg is. You may be a sperm donor. You may be an accident of lust and biology. You may have provided a simple microscopic cell structure that combined with one slightly more complex. But you are not this boy's father.'

'It's not that simple, Win.'

'It is that simple, my friend. The fact that you insipidly choose to confuse the issue does not change the fact. I'll demonstrate, if you'd like.'

'I'm listening.'

'You love your father, correct?'

'You know the answer to that.'

'I do,' Win said. 'But what makes him your father? The fact that he once grunted on top of Mommy after a few drinks – or the way he has cared for you and loved you for the past thirty-five years?'

Myron looked down at the can of Yoo-Hoo.

'You owe this boy nothing,' Win continued, 'and equally important, he owes you nothing. We will try to save his life, if that is what you wish, but that should be where it ends.'

Myron thought about it. The only thing scarier than Win irrational was when Win made sense. 'Maybe you're right.'

'But you still don't think it's that simple.'

'I don't know.'

On the television, Archie approached the pulpit, a yarmulke on his head. 'It's a start,' Win said.

6

Myron mixed childlike Froot Loops and very adult All-Bran into a bowl and poured on skim milk. For those not reading the Cliffs Notes, this act denotes that there is still a great deal of boy in the man. Heavy symbolism. How poignant.

The Number 1 train took Myron to a platform on 168th Street so far below ground that commuters had to take a urine-encapsulated elevator to reach the surface. The elevator was big and dark and shaky and brought on images of a PBS documentary on coal mining.

Located in Washington Heights, a quick stone's toss from Harlem and directly across Broadway from the Audubon Ballroom where Malcolm X was gunned down, Columbia Presbyterian Medical Center's famed pediatric building was called Babies and Children's Hospital. It used to be called just Babies Hospital, but a committee of learned medical experts was formed and after hours of intense study, they decided to change the name from Babies Hospital to Babies and Children's Hospital. Moral of the story: Committees are really, really important.

But the name, while not exactly Madison Avenue, does adequately reflect the reality of the situation – the hospital is strictly pediatric and deliveries, a well-worn twelve-floor edifice with eleven of them devoted to sick children. There was something very wrong with that, but probably nothing beyond the theologically obvious.

Myron stopped before the entranceway and looked up at the pollution-brown brick. Lots of misery in the city and much of it ended up here. He ducked inside and checked in at the security desk. He gave his name to a guard. The guard tossed him a pass, almost glancing up from his *TV Guide* in the process. Myron waited a long time for the elevator, reading the Patient's Bill of Rights, which was printed in both English and Spanish. There was a sign for the Sol Goldman Heart Center right next to a sign for the hospital's Burger King. Mixed messages or assuring future business – Myron wasn't sure which.

The elevator opened on the tenth floor. Directly in front of him, there was a rainbow-hued 'Save the Rain Forest' mural, painted, according to the sign, by the 'pediatric patients' of the hospital. Save the Rain Forest. Oh, like these kids didn't have enough on their plate, right?

Myron asked a nurse where he might find Dr Singh. The nurse pointed to a woman leading a dozen interns through the corridor. Myron was a little surprised to see that Dr Singh was of the female persuasion, mostly because he had somehow imagined her being a man. Terribly sexist, but there you go.

Dr Singh was, as her name strongly implied, Indian, from-India Indian as opposed to Native American Indian. Mid-thirties, he figured, her hair a lighter brown than what he was used to seeing on India Indians. She wore a white doctor coat, of course. So did all the interns, most of them appearing to be about fourteen years of age, their white coats more like smocks, like they were about to finger-paint or maybe dissect a frog in a junior high biology class. Some wore grave expressions that were almost laughable on their cherubic faces, but most emanated that medical-intern exhaustion from too many nights on call.

Only two of the interns were men – boys really – both sporting blue jeans, colorful ties, and white sneakers like waiters at Bennigan's. The women – to call them girls would use up Myron's anti-PC quota for the week – favored hospital scrubs. So young. Babies taking care of babies.

Myron followed the group at a semi-discreet distance. Every once in a while he glanced in a room and immediately regretted it. The corridor walls were festive and brightly painted, jammed with Disney/Nick Junior/PBS kiddie images and collages and mobiles, but Myron only saw black. A floor filled with dying children. Bald little boys and girls in pain, their veins blackened by toxins and poisons. Most of the children looked so calm and unafraid and unnaturally brave. If you wanted to see the stark terror, you had to look in the eyes of the parents, as though Mom and Dad were sucking the horror toward them, taking it on so that their child wouldn't have to.

'Mr Bolitar?'

Dr Singh met his eye and held out her hand. 'I'm Karen Singh.'

Myron almost asked her how she did this, how she stayed on this floor day in and day out, watching children die. But he didn't. They exchanged the usual pleasantries. Myron had expected an Indian accent, but the only thing he picked up was a little Bronx.

'We can talk in here,' she said.

She pushed open one of the superheavy, superwide doors endemic to hospitals and nursing homes, and they stepped into an empty room with stripped beds. The barrenness ignited Myron's imagination. He could almost see a loved one rushing into the hospital, repeatedly pushing the elevator call button, diving inside, pushing more buttons, sprinting down the corridor into this silent room, the bed being stripped by a nurse, then the sudden cry of anguish . . .

Myron shook his head. He watched too much TV.

Karen Singh sat on the corner of the mattress, and Myron studied her face for a moment. She had long sharp features. Everything pointed down – her nose, her chin, her eyebrows. Sort of harsh.

'You're staring,' she said.

'I don't mean to.'

She pointed to her forehead. 'You were maybe expecting a dot?'

'Er, no.'

'Very good, then let's get to it, shall we?'

'Okay.'

'Mrs Downing wants me to tell you whatever you want to know.'

'I appreciate your taking the time.'

'Are you a private investigator?' she asked.

'More like a family friend.'

'Did you play basketball with Greg Downing?'

Myron was always surprised by the memory of the public. After all these years, people could still recall his big games, his big shots, sometimes with more clarity than Myron could. 'You're a fan?'

'Nope,' she said. 'Can't stand sports actually.'

'So how did you—'

'Just a deduction. You're tall and about the right age and you said you were a family friend. So . . .' She shrugged.

'Nice deduction.'

'It's what we do here when you think about it. Deduce. Some diagnoses are easy. Others must be deduced from the evidence. You ever read Sherlock Holmes?'

'Sure.'

'Sherlock said that you should never theorize before you have facts – because then you twist facts to suit theories rather than twisting theories to suit facts. If you see a misdiagnosis, nine times out of ten they ignored Sherlock's axiom.'

'Did that happen with Jeremy Downing?'

'As a matter of fact,' she said, 'it did.'

Somewhere down the hall, a machine started beeping. The sound hit the nerves like a police taser.

'So his first doctor screwed up?'

'I won't get into that. But Fanconi anemia isn't common. And because it looks like other things, it's often misdiagnosed.'

'So tell me about Jeremy.'

'What's to tell? He has it. Fanconi anemia, that is. In simple terms, his bone marrow is corrupted.'

'Corrupted?'

'In layman's term, it's shit. It makes him susceptible to a host of infections and even cancers. It commonly turns into AML.' She saw the puzzled look on his face and added, 'That's acute myelogenous leukemia.'

'But you can cure him?'

' "Cure" is an optimistic word,' she said. 'But with a bone marrow transplant and treatments with a new fludarabine compound, yes, I believe his prognosis is excellent.'

'Fluda-what?'

'Not important. We need a bone marrow donor that matches Jeremy. That's what counts here.'

'And you don't have one.'

Dr Singh shifted on the mattress. 'That's correct.'

Myron felt the resistance. He decided to back off, test another flank. 'Could you take me through the transplant process?'

'Step by step?'

'If it's not too much trouble.'

She shrugged. 'First step: find a donor.'

'How do you go about that?'

'You try family members, of course. Siblings have the best chance of matching. Then parents. Then people of similar background.'

'When you say people of similar background—'

'Blacks with blacks, Jews with Jews, Latino descent with Latino descent. You'll see that quite often in marrow drives. If the patient is, for example, a Hasidic Jew, the donation drives will take place within their shuls. Mixed blood is usually the hardest to match.'

'And Jeremy's blood or whatever you need to match – it's fairly rare?'

'Yes.'

Emily and Greg were both of Irish descent. Myron's family came from the usual pot-pourri of old Russia and Poland and even a little Palestine thrown in. Mixed blood. He thought about the paternity implications.

'So after you exhausted the family, how do you search for the match?'

'You go to the national registry.'

'Where are they located?'

'In Washington. You listed?'

Myron nodded.

'They keep computer records there. We search for a preliminary match in their banks.'

'Okay, now assuming you find a match in the computer—'

'A *preliminary* match,' she corrected. 'The local center calls the potential donor and asks them to come in. They run a battery of tests. But the odds of matching are still fairly slim.'

Myron could see that Karen Singh was relaxing, comfortable with the familiar subject matter, which was exactly what he wanted. Interrogations are a funny thing. Sometimes you go for the full frontal attack, and sometimes you sidle up, friendly-like, and sneak in the back. Win put it simpler: Sometimes you get more ants with honey, but you should always pack a can of Raid.

'Let's suppose you find a full-fledged donor,' Myron said. 'What then?'

'The center acquires the donor's permission.'

'When you say "center," do you mean the national registry in Washington?'

'No, I mean the local center. Do you have your donor card in your wallet?'

'Yes.'

'Let me see it.'

Myron took out his wallet, flipped through about a dozen supermarket discount cards, three video club memberships, a couple of those buy-a-hundred-coffees-get-ten-cents-off-the-hundredth coupon, that sort of thing. He found the donor card and handed it to her.

'See here,' she said, pointing to the back. 'Your local center is in East Orange, New Jersey.'

'So if I was a preliminary match, the East Orange center would call me?'

'Yes.'

'And if I ended up being a full match?'

'You'd sign some papers and donate marrow.'

'Is that like donating blood?'

Karen Singh handed the card back to him and shifted again. 'Harvesting bone marrow is a more invasive procedure.'

Invasive. Every profession has its own buzzwords. 'How so?'

'For one thing, you have to be put under.'

'Anesthesia?'

'Yes.'

'And then what do they do?'

'A doctor sticks a needle through the bone and sucks the marrow out with a syringe.'

Myron said, 'Eeuw.'

'As I just explained, you're not awake during the procedure.'

'Still,' Myron said, 'it sounds much more complicated than giving blood.'

'It is,' she said. 'But the procedure is safe and relatively painless.'

'But people must balk. I mean, most probably signed up the same way I did: They had a friend who was sick and ran a drive. For someone you know and care about, sure, you're willing to make a sacrifice. But for a stranger?'

Karen Singh's eyes found his and settled in hard. 'You are saving a life, Mr Bolitar. Think about that. How many opportunities do you get to save a fellow human being's life?'

He had hit a nerve. Good. 'Are you saying people don't balk?'

'I'm not saying it never happens,' she said, 'but most people do the right thing.'

'Does the donor get to meet the person he or she is saving?'

'No. It's totally anonymous. Confidentiality is very important here. Everything is held in the utmost secrecy.'

They were getting to it now, and Myron could sense that her defenses were starting to slide back up like a car window. He decided to pull back again, let her resettle on comfy ground. 'What's the patient going through during all this?' he asked.

'At what point?'

'While the marrow is being harvested. How do you prep the patient?' Prep. Myron had said 'prep.' Like a real doctor. Who said watching *St Elsewhere* was a waste of time?

'It depends on what you're treating,' Dr Singh said. 'But for most diseases, the recipient goes through about a week's worth of chemotherapy.'

Chemotherapy. One of those words that hush a room like a nun's scowl. 'They get chemo before the transplant?'

'Yes.'

'I would think that would weaken them,' Myron said.

'To some degree, yes.'

'Why would you do it, then?'

'You have to. You're giving the recipient new bone marrow. Before you do that, you have to kill the old marrow. With leukemia, for example, the amount of chemo is high because you have to kill off all the living marrow. In the case of Fanconi anemia, you can be less aggressive because the marrow is already very weak.'

'So you kill off all the bone marrow?'

'Yes.'

'Isn't that dangerous?'

Dr Singh gave him the steady eyes again. 'This is a dangerous procedure, Mr Bolitar. You are in effect replacing a person's bone marrow.'

'And then?'

'And then the patient is infused with new marrow through an IV. He or she is kept isolated in a sterile environment for the first two weeks.'

'Quarantined?'

'In effect. Do you remember the old TV movie *The Boy in the Plastic Bubble*?'

'Who doesn't?'

Dr Singh smiled.

'Is that what the patient lives in?' Myron asked.

'A bubble chamber of sorts, yes.'

'I had no idea,' Myron said. 'And this works?'

'Rejection is always a possibility, of course. But our success rate is quite high. In the case of Jeremy Downing, he can live a normal, active life with the transplant.'

'And without it?'

'We can keep treating him with male hormones and growth factors, but his premature death is inevitable.'

Silence. Except for that steady mechanical beep coming from down the hall.

Myron cleared his throat. 'When you said that everything involving the donor is confidential—'

'I meant totally.'

Enough wading. 'How does that sit with you, Dr Singh?'

'What do you mean?'

'The national registry located a donor who matched Jeremy, didn't they?'

'I believe so, yes.'

'So what happened?'

She tapped her chin with her index finger. 'May I speak candidly?'

'Please.'

'I believe in the need for secrecy and confidentiality. Most people don't understand how easy, painless, and important it is to put their name in the registry. All they have to do is give a little blood. Just a little tube of the stuff, less than you would for any blood donation. Do that simple act – and you can save a life. Do you understand the significance of that?'

'I think so.'

'We in the medical community must do all we can to encourage people to join the bone marrow registry. Education, of course, is important. So, too, is confidentiality. It has to be honored. The donors have to trust us.'

She stopped, crossed her legs, leaned back on her hands. 'But in this case, something of a quandary has developed. The importance of confidentiality is bumping up against the welfare of my patient. For me, the quandary is easy to resolve. The Hippocratic oath trumps all. I'm not a lawyer or a priest. My priority must be to save the life, not protect confidences. My guess is that I'm not the only doctor that feels that way. Perhaps that's why we have no contact with the donors. The blood center – in your case, the one in East Orange – does everything. They harvest the marrow and ship it to us.'

'Are you saying that you don't know who the donor is?'

'That's right.'

'Or if it's a he or she or where they live or anything?'

Karen Singh nodded. 'I can only tell you that the national registry found a match. They called and told me so. I later received a call telling me that the donor was no longer available.'

'What does that mean?'

'My question exactly.'

'Did they give you an answer?'

'No,' she said. 'And while I see things on the micro level, the national registry has to remain macro. I respect that.'

'You just gave up?'

She stiffened at his words. Her eyes went small and black. 'No, Mr Bolitar, I did not give up. I raged against the machine. But the people at the national registry are not ogres. They understand that this is a life-or-death situation. If a donor backs out, they try their best to bring them back into the fold. They do everything I would do to convince the donor to go through with it.'

'But nothing worked here?'

'That seems to be the case.'

'The donor would be told that he's sentencing a thirteen-year-old boy to death?'

She didn't hesitate. 'Yes.'

Myron threw up his hands. 'So what do we conclude here, Doctor? That the donor is a selfish monster?'

Karen Singh chewed on that one for a moment. 'Perhaps,' she said. 'Or perhaps the answer is simpler.'

'For example?'

'For example,' she said, 'maybe the center can't find the donor.'

Hello. Myron sat up a bit. 'What do you mean, "can't find"?'

'I don't know what happened here. The center won't tell me, and that's probably how it should be. I'm the patient's advocate. It's their job to deal with the donors. But I believe they were' – she stopped, searching for the right word – 'perplexed.'

'What makes you say that?'

'Nothing concrete. Just a feeling that this might be more than a donor with cold feet.'

'How do we find out?'

'I don't know.'

'How do we find the donor's name?'

'We can't.'

'There has to be a way,' Myron said. 'Play pretend with me. How could I do it?'

She shrugged. 'Break into the computer system. That's the only way I know.'

'The computer in Washington?'

'They network with the local centers. But you'd have to know codes and passwords. Maybe a good hacker could get through, I don't know.'

Hackers, Myron knew, worked better in the movies than in real life. A few years ago, maybe – but most computer systems nowadays were secure against such invasions.

'How long do we have here, Doctor?'

'There's no way of telling. Jeremy is reacting well to the hormones and growth factors. But it's only a question of time.'

'So we have to find a donor.'

'Yes.' Karen Singh stopped, looked at Myron, looked away.

'Is there something else?' Myron asked.

She did not face him. 'There is one other remote possibility,' she said.

'What?' Myron asked.

'Keep in mind what I said before. I'm the patient's advocate. It's my job to explore every possible avenue to save him.'

Her voice was funny now.

'I'm listening,' Myron said.

Karen Singh rubbed her palms on her pant legs. 'If Jeremy's biological parents were to conceive again, there is a twenty-five percent chance that the offspring would be a match.'

She looked at Myron.

'I don't think that's a possibility,' he said.

'Even if it's the only way to save Jeremy's life?'

Myron had no reply. An orderly walked by, looked in the room, mumbled an apology, left. Myron stood and thanked her.

'I'll show you to the elevator,' Dr Singh said.

'Thank you.'

'There's a lab on the first floor in the Harkness Pavilion.' She handed him a slip of paper. Myron looked at it. It was an order form. 'I understand you might want to take a certain confidential blood test.'

Neither of them said anything else as they walked toward the elevators. There were several children being wheeled through the corridor. Dr Singh smiled at them, the pointed features softening into something almost celestial. Again the children looked unafraid. Myron wondered if the calmness spawned from ignorance or acceptance. He wondered if the children did not understand the gravity of what was happening to them or if they possessed a quiet clarity their parents would never know. Such philosophical queries, Myron knew, were best left to those more learned. But maybe the answer was simpler than he imagined: The children's suffering would be relatively short; their parents' would be eternal.

When they reached the elevator, Myron said, 'How do you do it?'

She knew what he meant. 'I could say something fancy about finding solace in helping, but the truth is, I block and I compartmentalize. It's the only way.'

The elevator door opened, but before Myron could move he heard a familiar voice say, 'What the hell are you doing here?'

Greg Downing stepped toward him.

7

Too much history. Again.

The last time the two men had been in the same room, Myron was straddled over Greg's chest, trying to kill him, punching him repeatedly in the face until Win – Win of all people – pulled him off. Three years ago. Myron hadn't seen him since, except on highlight films during the evening news.

Greg Downing glared at Myron, then at Karen Singh, then back at Myron as though he expected him to have evaporated by then.

'What the hell are you doing here?' he asked again.

Greg was clad in a flannel shirt over some waffle knit you'd buy at Baby Gap, faded jeans, and preternaturally scuffed work boots. The Suburban Lumberjack.

Something sparked hot in Myron's chest, ignited, took flight.

From the day they first battled for a rebound in the sixth grade, Greg and Myron were the pure definition of cross-town rivals. In high school, where their competitive cup truly runneth over, Greg and Myron met up eight times, splitting the games evenly. Rumor had it that there was bad blood between the budding superstars, but that was just standard sports hyperbole. The truth was, Myron barely knew Greg off the court. They were killer competitors, sure, willing to do just about anything to win, but once the final buzzer sounded, the two boys shook hands and the rivalry hibernated until the next opening tap.

Or so Myron had always thought.

When he accepted a scholarship at Duke and Greg chose the University of North Carolina, basketball fans rejoiced. Their seemingly innocent rivalry was ready for ACC prime time. Myron and Greg did not disappoint. The Duke-UNC matchups drew fantastic television ratings, no game decided by more than three points. Both had spectacular college careers. Both were named first-team All-Americans. Both were on covers of *Sports Illustrated*, once even sharing it. But the rivalry stayed on the court. They would do battle until bloody, but the competition never overlapped into their personal arenas.

Until Emily.

Before the start of senior year, Myron broached the subject of marriage with Emily. The next day she came to him, held his hands, looked into his eyes, and said, 'I'm not sure I love you.' Bam, like that. He still wondered what happened. Too much too soon, he guessed. A need to spread the proverbial wings a bit, play the proverbial field, what have you. Time passed. Three months, by Myron's count. Then Emily took up with Greg. Myron publicly shrugged it off – even when Greg and Emily got engaged just before graduation. The NBA draft took place right about then too. Both went in the first round, though Greg was surprisingly picked before Myron.

That was when it all unraveled.

The end result?

Almost a decade and a half later, Greg Downing was winding down an All-Star pro basketball career. People cheered him. He made millions and was famous. He played the game he loved. For Myron, his lifelong dream had ended before it had begun. During his first preseason game with the Celtics, Big Burt Wesson had slammed into him, sandwiching Myron's knee between himself and another player. There was a snap, crackle, pop – and then a hot, ripping pain, as though metal talons were shredding his kneecap into thin strips.

His knee never recovered.

A freak accident. Or so everyone thought. Including Myron. For more than ten years, he'd believed that the injury was merely a fluke, the fickle work of the Fates. But now he knew better. Now he knew the man who stood in front of him had been the cause. Now he knew that their seemingly innocent childhood rivalry had grown monstrous, had feasted upon his dream, had slaughtered Greg and Emily's marriage, and had in all probability led to the birth of Jeremy Downing.

He felt his hands tighten into fists. 'I was just leaving.'

Greg put a hand on Myron's chest. 'I asked you a question.'

Myron stared at the hand. 'One good thing,' he said.

'What?'

'No transportation time,' Myron said. 'We're already at the hospital.'

Greg sneered. 'You sucker-punched me last time.'

'You want to go again?'

'Pardon me,' Karen Singh said. 'But are you guys for real?'

Greg kept glaring at Myron.

'Stop it,' Myron said, 'or I'll wet myself.'

'You're a son of a bitch.'

'And you're not on my Christmas card list either, Greggy-poo.'

Greggy-poo. Very mature.

Greg leaned closer. 'You know what I'd like to do to you, Bolitar?'

'Kiss me on the lips? Buy me flowers?'

'Flowers for your grave maybe.'

Myron nodded. 'Good one, Greg. I mean, ouch, I'm wounded.'

Karen Singh said, 'Just because this is a children's floor doesn't mean you two have to act like one.'

Greg took a step back, his eyes never leaving Myron. 'Emily,' he spat suddenly. 'She called you, right?'

'I have nothing to say to you, Greg.'

'She asked you to find the donor. Like you found me.'

'You always were a bright boy.'

'I'm calling a press conference today. I'm going to make a direct appeal to the donor. Offer a reward.'

'Good.'

'So we don't need you, Bolitar.'

Myron looked at Greg, and for a moment they were back on the court, faces drenched with sweat, the crowd cheering, the clock ticking down, the ball bouncing. Nirvana. Gone for ever. Snatched away by Greg. And by Emily. And maybe most of all, when he looked at it honestly, by Myron's own stupidity.

'I've got to go,' Myron said.

Greg took a step back. Myron moved past him and pressed the elevator button.

'Hey, Bolitar.'

He faced Greg.

'I came here to talk to the doc about my son,' Greg said, 'not rehash our past.'

Myron said nothing. He turned back to the elevator.

'You think you can help save my boy?' Greg asked.

Myron's mouth went dry. 'I don't know.'

The elevator dinged and opened. There were no good-byes, no nods, no further communication of any sort. Myron stepped inside and let the doors close. When he reached the first level, he went to the lab. He rolled up his sleeve. A woman drew his blood, untied the tourniquet, and said, 'Your doctor will be in touch with you about the results.'

8

Win was bored, so he drove Myron to the airport to pick up Terese. His foot pushed down on the gas pedal as though it had offended him. The Jag flew. As was his custom when driving with Win, Myron kept his eyes averted.

'It would appear,' Win began, 'that our best option would be to locate a satellite marrow clinic in a somewhat remote area. Upstate maybe or in western Jersey. We would then break in at night with a computer expert.'

'Won't work,' Myron said.

'*Por qua?*'

'The Washington center shuts down the computer network at six o'clock. Even if we were to break in, we couldn't bring up the mainframe.'

Win said, 'Hmm.'

'Don't fret,' Myron said. 'I have a plan.'

'When you talk like that,' Win said, 'my nipples harden.'

'I thought only the real thing aroused you.'

'This isn't the real thing?'

They parked in JFK Airport's short-term parking and reached the Continental Airlines gate ten minutes before the flight touched down. When the passengers began to appear, Win said, 'I'll stand over in the corner.'

'Why?'

'I wouldn't want to cast a shadow on your greeting,' he said. 'And standing over there affords me a better view of Ms Collins's derriere.'

Ah, Win.

Two minutes later, Terese Collins – to use a purely transportational term – disembarked. She was casually decked out in a white

51

blouse and green slacks. Her brown hair was up in a ponytail. People lightly elbowed one another, whispering and subtly gesturing, giving her that surreptitious glance, the one that says 'I recognize you but don't want to appear fawning.'

Terese approached Myron and offered up her breaking-to-commercial smile. It was small and tight, trying to be friendly but reminding viewers that she was telling them about war and pestilence and tragedy and that maybe a big happy smile would be somewhat obscene. They hugged a little too tightly, and Myron felt the familiar sadness overwhelm him. It happened to him every time they hugged – a sense that something inside of him was crumbling anew. He sensed that the same thing happened to her.

Win came over.

'Hello, Win,' she said.

'Hello, Terese.'

'Checking out my ass again?'

'I prefer the term "derriere." And yes.'

'Still choice?'

'Grade A.'

'Ahem,' Myron said. 'Please wait for the meat inspector.'

Win and Terese looked at each other and rolled their eyes.

Myron had been wrong before. Emily was not Win's favorite. Terese was – though it was strictly because she lived far away. 'You are the pitiful, needy type who feels incomplete without a steady girlfriend,' Win had told him. 'Who better than a career woman who lives a thousand miles away?'

Win headed for his Jag while they waited for her luggage. Terese watched Win walk away.

Myron said, 'Is his ass better than mine?'

'No ass is better than yours,' she said.

'I know that. I was just testing you.'

Terese kept looking. 'Win is an interesting fellow,' she said.

'Oh yeah,' Myron agreed.

'On the outside, he's all cold and detached,' she said. 'But underneath that – way down deep inside – he's all cold and detached.'

'You read people well, Terese.'

Win dropped them off at the Dakota and returned to the office. When Myron and Terese got inside the apartment, she kissed him hard. Always an urgency with Terese. A desperation in their love-making. Pleasant, sure. Awesome even. But there was still the aura of sadness. The sadness didn't go away when they made love, but for a little while it lifted like cloud cover, hovering above instead of weighing them down.

They had hooked up at a charity function a few months back, both dragged there by well-meaning friends. It was their mutual misery that drew them, as though it were one of those psychic crowns only they could spot on each other. They met and ran away that very night to the Caribbean on a let's-just-flee dare. For the usually predictable Myron, the spontaneous act felt surpris-ingly right. They spent a numbingly blissful three weeks alone on a private island, trying to stave off the flow of pain. When Myron was finally forced to return home, they'd both assumed it was over. They'd assumed wrong. At least, it appeared that way.

Myron recognized that his own healing was finally under way. He wasn't back to full strength or normal or any of that. He doubted he ever would be. Or even wanted to be. Giant hands had twisted him and then let go, and while his world was slowly untwisting, he knew that it would never fully return to its original position.

Again with the poignant.

But whatever had happened to Terese – whatever had brought on the sadness and twisted her world, if you will – still held firm, refusing to let go.

Terese's head lay on his chest, her arms wrapped around him. He could not see her face. She never showed him her face when they finished.

'You want to talk about it?' he asked.

She still hadn't told him, and Myron rarely asked. Doing so, he knew, was breaking an unspoken though cardinal rule.

'No.'

'I'm not pushing,' he said. 'I just wanted you to know that if you're ever ready, I'm here.'

'I know,' she said.

He wanted to say something more, but she was still at a place where words were either superfluous or they stung. He stayed quiet and stroked her hair.

'This relationship,' Terese said. 'It's bizarre.'

'I guess.'

'Someone told me you're dating Jessica Culver, the writer.'

'We broke up,' he said.

'Oh.' She did not move, still holding him a little too tightly. 'Can I ask when?'

'A month before we met.'

'And how long were you two together?'

'Thirteen years, on and off.'

'I see,' she said. 'Am I the recovery?'

'Am I yours?'

'Maybe,' she said.

'Same answer.'

She thought about that a little. 'But Jessica Culver is not the reason you ran away with me.'

He remembered the cemetery overlooking the school yard. 'No,' he said, 'she's not the reason.'

Terese finally turned to him. 'We have no chance. You know that, right?'

Myron said nothing.

'That's not unusual,' she went on. 'Plenty of relationships have no chance. But people stay in them because it's fun. This isn't fun either.'

'Speak for yourself.'

'Don't get me wrong, Myron. You're a hell of a lay.'

'Could you put that in a sworn affidavit?'

She smiled but there was still no joy. 'So what do we have here?'

'Truth?'

'Preferably.'

'I always overanalyze,' Myron said. 'It's my nature. I meet a woman, and I immediately picture the house in the 'burbs and the white picket fence and the two-point-five kids. But for once I'm not doing that. I'm just letting it happen. So, to answer your question, I don't know. And I'm not sure I care.'

She lowered her head. 'You realize that I'm pretty damaged.'

'I guess.'

'I have more baggage than most.'

'We all have baggage,' Myron said. 'The question is, does your baggage go with mine?'

'Who said that?'

'I'm paraphrasing from a Broadway musical.'

'Which one?'

'*Rent.*'

She frowned. 'I don't like musicals.'

'Sorry to hear that,' Myron said.

'You do?'

'Oh yeah.'

'You're in your mid-thirties, single, sensitive, and you like show tunes,' she said. 'If you were a better dresser, I'd say you were gay.'

She pressed a hard, quick kiss to his lips, and then they held each other a little more. Once again he wanted to ask her what had happened to her, but he wouldn't. She would tell him one day. Or she wouldn't. He decided to change subjects.

'I need your help with something,' Myron said.

She looked at him.

'I need to break into a bone marrow center's computer system,' he said. 'And I think you can help.'

'Me?'

'Yup.'

'You got the wrong technophobe,' she said.

'I don't need a technophobe. I need a famous anchorwoman.'

'I see. And you're asking for this favor postcoital?'

'Part of my plan,' Myron said. 'I've weakened your will. You cannot refuse me.'

'Diabolical.'

'Indeed.'

'And if I refuse?'

Myron wiggled his eyebrows. 'I'll once again use my brawny body and patented lovemaking technique to make you succumb.'

' "Succumb," ' she repeated, pulling him closer. 'Is that one word or two?'

9

It took a shockingly short time to set up.

Myron told Terese his plan. She listened without interruption. When he finished, she started placing calls. She never asked why he was looking for the donor or how he and the donor were connected. The unspoken rule again, he guessed.

Within the hour a news van complete with a hand-held television camera was delivered to the Dakota. The director of the Bergen County Blood Center – a nearby New Jersey bone marrow center – had agreed to drop everything for an immediate interview with Terese Collins, anchorwoman extraordinaire. The power of the idiot box.

They took the Harlem River Drive up to the George Washington Bridge, crossing the Hudson and exiting onto Jones Road in Englewood, New Jersey. After they parked, Myron hoisted up the camera. Heavier than he thought. Terese showed him how to hold it, how to lean it against his shoulder and aim. There was something bazooka-like about the whole thing.

'Do you think I should wear a disguise?' Myron asked.

'Why?'

'People still recognize me from my playing days.'

She made a face.

'I'm rather famous in certain circles.'

'Get real, Myron. You're an ex-jock. If someone by some miracle recognizes you, they'll think you got lucky and didn't end up in a gutter like most ex-jocks.'

He thought about it. 'Fair enough.'

'One other thing,' she said. 'And this will be nearly impossible for you.'

'What?'

'You have to keep your big mouth shut,' Terese said.

'Egads.'

'You're just the cameraman here.'

'We prefer to be called "photographic artists."'

'Just play your part. Trust me to handle him.'

'Can I at least use a pseudonym?' He put the camera to his eye. 'You can call me Lens. Or Scoop.'

'How about Bozo? No, wait, that would be a synonym.'

Everyone's a wise guy.

When they entered the clinic's lobby, people turned toward Terese and did that surreptitious stare again. Myron realized that today was the first time he had been with her in public. He had never quite thought about how famous she was.

'You get these stares wherever you go?' he whispered.

'Pretty much.'

'Does it bother you?'

She shook her head. 'That's horseshit.'

'What is?'

'Celebrities who complain about people staring at them. Want to really piss off a celebrity? Let him go someplace and not be recognized.'

Myron smiled. 'You're so self-realized.'

'That a new way of saying cynical?'

The receptionist said, 'Mr Englehardt will see you now.'

She led them down a corridor with thin plaster walls and a bad paint job. Englehardt sat behind a plastic-wood desk. He was probably late twenties with a slight build and a chin weaker than machine-dispensed coffee.

Myron quickly noted the computer setup. Two of them. One on his desk. One on the credenza. Hmm.

Englehardt jumped up as though he'd just been passed a note that his chair had cooties. His eyes were wide and fixed on Terese. Myron was ignored and felt like, well, the cameraman. Terese smiled brightly at Englehardt, and he was lost.

'I'm Terese Collins,' she said, extending her hand. Englehardt did everything but take a knee and kiss it. 'This is my cameraman, Malachy Throne.'

Myron sort of smiled. After the Broadway-musical debacle, he had worried. But Malachy Throne? Genius. Pure genius.

They all exchanged quick pleasantries. Englehardt kept touching his hair, trying very hard to look subtle about it and not like he
was prepping for the camera. Not happening, bub. Finally Terese
signaled that they were ready to begin.

'Where would you like me to sit?' Englehardt asked.

'Behind the desk would be nice,' she said. 'Don't you agree,
Malachy?'

'Behind the desk,' Myron said. 'Yeah, that's the ticket.'

The interview began. Terese kept her gaze on her subject;
Englehardt, trapped in the beam, could look nowhere else. Myron
put his eye to the camera. The consummate professional. Very
Richard Avedon.

Terese asked Englehardt how he'd gotten started in this
business, his background, general crap, relaxing him, putting him
on that comfy ground, not all that different from the technique
Myron had used with Dr Singh. She was in on-air mode now.
Her voice was different, her eyes steadier.

'So the national registry in Washington keeps track of all
donors?' Terese asked.

'That's correct.'

'But you can access the records?'

Englehardt tapped the computer on his desk. The screen faced
him, the back of the monitor toward them. Okay, Myron thought,
so it was the one on his desk. That would make it more difficult,
but not impossible.

Terese looked at Myron. 'Why don't you get a back shot,
Malachy?' Then turning to Englehardt, 'If that's okay with you.'

'No problem at all,' Englehardt said.

Myron started moving into position. The monitor was off. No
surprise.

Terese continued to hold Englehardt's gaze. 'Does everyone in
the office have access to the national registry's computer?'

Englehardt shook his head firmly. 'I'm the only one.'

'Why's that?'

'The information is confidential. We don't breach the secrecy
under any circumstance.'

'I see,' she said. Myron was in place now. 'But what's to stop
someone from coming in here when you're not around?'

'I always lock my office door,' Englehardt said, up on his

haunches and eager to please. 'And you can only access the network with a password.'

'You're the only one who knows the password?'

Englehardt tried not to preen, but he didn't try too hard. 'That's correct.'

Ever see those hidden-camera stories on *Dateline* or *20/20*? They always shoot from some strange angle and in black-and-white. Truth is, it's easy for any layperson to buy one and it's even easy to get one that films in color. There are stores that sell them right in Manhattan, or you can go online and search under 'spy stores.' You'll see hidden cameras in clocks, pens, briefcases and, most common of all, smoke detectors – available to anyone with the proper buckage. Myron had one that looked like a film case. He dropped it now on the window ledge with the lens pointing toward the computer monitor.

When it was in place, Myron tapped his nose with his finger, à la Redford in *The Sting*. Their signal. *Bolitar. Myron Bolitar. A Yoo-Hoo. Shaken not stirred.* Terese picked up her cue. The smile dropped off her face like an anvil.

Englehardt looked startled. 'Ms Collins? Are you okay?'

For a moment she could not bear to face him. Then: 'Mr Englehardt,' Terese said, her voice Gulf War-grave, 'I must confess something.'

'I'm sorry?'

'I am here under somewhat false pretenses.'

Englehardt looked confused. Terese was so good, Myron almost looked confused.

'I sincerely believe you are doing important work here,' she continued. 'But others are not so sure.'

Englehardt's eyes were widening. 'I don't understand.'

'I need your help, Mr Englehardt.'

'Billy,' he corrected.

Myron made a face. Billy?

Terese didn't miss a beat. 'Someone is trying to disrupt your work, Billy.'

'My work?'

'The national registry's work.'

'I'm still not sure what you—'

'Are you familiar with the case of Jeremy Downing?'

59

Englehardt shook his head. 'I never know the names of patients.'

'He's the son of Greg Downing, the basketball star.'

'Oh, wait, yes, I heard about this. His son has Fanconi anemia.' Terese nodded. 'That's correct.'

'Isn't Mr Downing supposed to hold a press conference today? To track down a donor?'

'Exactly, Billy. And that's the problem.'

'What is?'

'Mr Downing has found the donor.'

Still confused. 'That's a problem?'

'No, of course not. If the person is the donor. And if the person is telling the truth.'

Englehardt looked at Myron. Myron shrugged and moved back to the front of the desk. He left the film case on the windowsill.

'I'm not following you, Ms Collins.'

'Terese,' she said. 'A man has come forward. He claims that he is the matching donor.'

'And you think he's lying?'

'Let me finish. He not only claims he's the donor, but he says that the reason he refused to donate his marrow was because of the terrible treatment he received from this center.'

Englehardt nearly tipped back. 'What?'

'He claims he was treated shabbily, that your staff was rude, and that he's even debating leveling a lawsuit.'

'That's ridiculous.'

'Probably.'

'He's lying.'

'Probably,' she said again.

'And he'll be found out,' Englehardt continued. 'They'll test his blood and see he's a phony.'

'But when, Billy?'

'What?'

'When will they do that? A day from now? A week from now? A month? But by then the damage is done. He's going to appear at the press conference today with Greg Downing. The media will be there in force. Even if it ends up being false, no one remembers the retraction. They just remember the allegation.'

Englehardt sat back. 'Jesus.'

'Let me be frank, Billy. A number of my colleagues believe him. I don't. I smell a publicity hound. I'm having some of my best investigators dig into this man's past. So far they've come up with nothing, and time is running short.'

'So what can I do?'

'I need to *know* it's not true. I can't stop it merely because I *believe* it's not true. I have to know for certain.'

'How?'

Terese chewed on her lower lip. Deep thought. 'Your computer network.'

Englehardt shook his head. 'The information in here is confidential. I explained that before. I can't tell you—'

'I don't need to know the name of the donor.' She leaned forward. Myron moved as far away from the action as possible, trying to be no threat whatsoever. 'I need to know what's *not* the name.'

Englehardt looked hesitant.

'I'm sitting over here,' she said. 'I can't see the monitor. Malachy is by the door.' She turned to Myron. 'Your camera is off, Malachy?'

'Yes, Terese,' Myron said. He put it down for emphasis.

'So here is what I suggest,' Terese said. 'You look up Jeremy Downing in your computer. It will list a donor. I give you a name. You tell me if the name matches. Simple?'

Englehardt still looked hesitant.

'You wouldn't be violating anyone's confidentiality,' she said. 'We can't see your screen. We can even leave the room while you look it up, if you'd like.'

Englehardt said nothing. Terese said nothing either. Waiting him out. The perfect interviewer. She finally turned to Myron. 'Grab your stuff,' she said to him.

'Wait.' Englehardt's eyes slid left, then right, up then down. 'Jeremy Downing, you say?'

'Yes.'

He did another quick series of eye-slides. When he saw that the coast was clear, he hunched over the keyboard and typed quickly. A few seconds later, he asked, 'What's the name of this supposed donor?'

'Victor Johnson.'

Englehardt looked at the monitor and smiled. 'That's not him.'

'You're sure?'

'Absolutely.'

Terese matched the smile. 'That's all we needed to know.'

'You'll stop him?'

'He won't even get to the press conference.'

Myron grabbed the film case and camera, and they hurried down the corridor. Once outside he turned to her and said, 'Malachy Throne?'

'You know who he is?'

'He played False Face on *Batman*.'

Terese smiled and nodded. 'Very good.'

'Can I tell you something?'

'What?'

'It turns me on when you talk *Batman*,' he said.

'And even when I don't.'

'Are you trying to make a point?'

Five minutes later they were watching the tape in the van.

10

Mr Davis Taylor
221 North End Ave
Waterbury, Connecticut

The social security and phone numbers were there too. Myron took out his cell phone and dialed. After two rings, a machine picked up and a robotic voice, the default greeting, asked him to leave a message at the tone. He left his name and mobile number and asked Mr Taylor to return his call.

'So what are you going to do?' Terese asked.

'I guess I'll drive up and try to talk to Mr Davis Taylor.'

'Hasn't the clinic already tried that?'

'Probably.'

'But you're more persuasive?'

'Questionable.'

'I have to cover the Waldorf tonight,' she said.

'I know. I'll go alone. Or maybe I'll bring Win.'

She still would not face him. 'This boy who needs the transplant,' she said. 'He's not a stranger, is he?'

Myron was not sure how to answer that. 'I guess not.'

Terese nodded in a way that told him not to say any more. He didn't. He picked up the phone and called Emily. She answered halfway through the first ring.

'Hello?'

'When is Greg doing the news conference?' he asked.

'In two hours,' Emily said.

'I need to reach him.'

He heard a hopeful gasp. 'Did you find the donor for Jeremy?'

'Not yet.'

'But you have something.'

'We'll see.'

'Don't patronize me, Myron.'

'I'm not patronizing you.'

'This is my son's life we're talking about here.'

And mine? 'I have a lead, Emily. That's all.'

She gave him the number. 'Myron, please call me if—'

'The moment I know something.'

He hung up and called Greg.

'I need you to put off the press conference,' Myron said.

'Why?' Greg asked.

'Just give me till tomorrow.'

'You have something?'

'Maybe,' Myron said.

'Maybe nothing,' Greg said. 'Do you have something or not?'

'I have a name and address. It might be our man. I want to check it out before you make a public plea.'

'Where does he live?' Greg asked.

'Connecticut.'

'You driving up?'

'Yes.'

'Right now?'

'Pretty much.'

'I want to go with you,' Greg said.

'That's not a good idea.'

'He's my kid, dammit.'

Myron closed his eyes. 'I understand that.'

'So then you'll understand this: I'm not asking your permission. I'm going. So stop dicking around and tell me where you want me to pick you up.'

Greg drove. He had one of those fancy SUV four-by-fours that are all the rage with New Jersey suburbanites whose idea of 'off-road' is a speed bump at the mall. Très truck chic. For a long while neither man spoke. The tension in the air was more than the cut-with-a-knife variety; it pressed against the car windows, weighed Myron down, made him tired and gloomy.

'How did you get this name?' Greg asked.

'It's not important.'

Greg left it alone. They drove some more. On the radio, Jewel earnestly insisted that her hands were small, she knew, but they were hers and not someone else's. Myron frowned. Not exactly 'Blowing in the Wind,' was it?

'You broke my nose, you know,' Greg said.

Myron kept quiet.

'And my vision hasn't been the same. I'm having trouble focusing on the basket.'

Myron could not believe what he was hearing. 'You blaming me for your crappy season, Greg?'

'I'm just saying—'

'You're getting old, Greg. You've played fourteen seasons, and sitting out the strike didn't help you.'

Greg waved a hand. 'You wouldn't understand.'

'You're right.' Myron's knob turned from Simmer to Boil. 'I never got to play pro ball.'

'Right, and I never fucked my friend's wife.'

'She wasn't your wife,' Myron said. 'And we weren't friends.'

They both stopped then. Greg kept his eyes on the road. Myron turned away and stared out the passenger window.

Waterbury is one of those cities you bypass to reach another city. Myron had probably taken this stretch of 84 a hundred times, always remarking that at a distance Waterbury was a butt-ugly city. But now that he had the opportunity to see the city up close, he realized that he had underestimated the city's offensiveness to the eyes, that indeed the city had a butt-ugly quality to it that you just couldn't appreciate from afar. He shook his head. And people make fun of New Jersey?

Myron had gotten directions from the MapQuest Web site. He read them off to Greg in a voice he barely recognized as his own. Greg followed them in silence. Five minutes later, they pulled up to a dilapidated clapboard house in the middle of a street of dilapidated clapboards. The houses were uneven and crammed so close together, they looked like a set of teeth needing extensive orthodontic work.

They got out of the car. Myron wanted to tell Greg to stay back, but that would be pointless. He knocked on the door and almost immediately a gruff voice said, 'Daniel? That you, Daniel?'

Myron said, 'I'm looking for Davis Taylor.'

'Daniel?'

'No,' Myron said, yelling through the door. 'Davis Taylor. But maybe he calls himself Daniel.'

'What are you talking about?' An old man opened the door, already in full-suspicious squint. He wore glasses too small for his face, so that the metal earpieces were embedded into the folds of skin beneath both temples, and a bad yellow wig, like something Carol Channing wore once too often, adorned his crown. He had on one slipper and one shoe, and his bathrobe looked as if it'd been trampled over during the Boer War.

'I thought you was Daniel,' the old man said. He tried to readjust the glasses, but they wouldn't move. He squinted again. 'You look like Daniel.'

'Must be the clouds in your eyes,' Myron said.

'What?'

'Never mind. Are you Davis Taylor?'

'What do you want?'

'We're looking for Davis Taylor.'

'Don't know no Davis Taylor.'

'This is 221 North End Drive?'

'That's right.'

'And there's no Davis Taylor living here?'

'Just me and my boy Daniel. But he's been away. Overseas.'

'Spain?' Myron asked. He pronounced it Spahhheeeeen. Elton would have been proud.

'What?'

'Never mind.' The old man turned to Greg, tried again to readjust the glasses, gave another squint. 'I know you. You play basketball, right?'

Greg gave the old man a gentle if not superior smile – Moses gazing down at a skeptic after the Red Sea parted. 'That's right.'

'You're Dolph Schayes.'

'No.'

'You look like Dolph. Helluva shooter. Saw him play in St Louis last year. What a touch.'

Myron and Greg exchanged a glance. Dolph Schayes had retired in 1964.

'I'm sorry,' Myron said. 'We didn't catch your name.'

'You're not wearing uniforms,' the old man said.

'No, sir, he only wears it on the court.'

'Not that kind of uniform.'

'Oh,' Myron said, though he had no idea why.

'So you can't be here about Daniel. That's what I mean. I was afraid you were with the army and . . .' His voice drifted off then.

Myron saw where this was going. 'Your son is stationed overseas?'

The old man nodded. 'Nam.'

Myron nodded, feeling bad now about the Elton John teasing. 'We still didn't catch your name.'

'Nathan. Nathan Mostoni.'

'Mr Mostoni, we're looking for someone named Davis Taylor. It's very important we find him.'

'Don't know no Davis Taylor. He a friend of Daniel's?'

'Might be.'

The old man thought about it. 'Nope, don't know him.'

'Who else lives here?'

'Just me and my boy.'

'And it's just the two of you?'

'Yep. But my boy is overseas.'

'So right now you live here alone?'

'How many different ways you gonna ask that question, boy?'

'It's just that it's a pretty big house,' Myron said.

'So?'

'Ever take in any boarders?'

'Sure. Had a college girl just moved out of here.'

'What was her name?'

'Stacy something. I don't remember.'

'How long did she live here?'

'About six months.'

'And before that?'

That one took some thought. Nathan Mostoni scratched his face like a dog going after his own belly. 'A guy named Ken.'

'Did you ever have a tenant named Davis Taylor?' Myron asked. 'Or something like that?'

'Nope. Never.'

'Did this Stacy have a boyfriend?'

'I don't think so.'

'Do you know her last name?'

67

'My memory ain't so good. But she's at the college.'

'Which college?'

'Waterbury State.'

Myron turned to Greg and another thought hit him. 'Mr Mostoni, have you heard the name Davis Taylor before today?'

Another squint. 'What do you mean?'

'Has anybody else visited you or called you and asked about Davis Taylor?'

'No, sir. Never heard the name before.'

Myron looked at Greg again, then turned back to the old man. 'So no one from the bone marrow center has been in touch with you?'

The old man cocked his head and put a hand to his ear. 'The bone what?'

Myron asked a few more questions, but Nathan Mostoni started time-traveling again. There was nothing more to get here. Myron and Greg thanked him and headed back down the cracked pathway.

When they were back in the car, Greg asked, 'Why didn't the bone marrow center contact this guy?'

'Maybe they did,' Myron said. 'Maybe he just forgot.'

Greg didn't like it. Neither did Myron. 'So what's next?' Greg asked.

'We run a background check on Davis Taylor. Find out everything we can about him.'

'How?'

'It's easy nowadays. Just a few keystrokes and my partner will know it all.'

'Your partner? You mean that violent wacko you used to room with in college?'

'A, it is unhealthy to refer to Win as a violent wacko, even when he appears not to be in the vicinity. B, no, I mean my partner at MB SportsReps, Esperanza Diaz.'

Greg looked back at the house. 'What do I do?'

'Go home,' Myron said.

'And?'

'And be with your son.'

Greg shook his head. 'I don't get to see him until the weekend.'

'I'm sure Emily wouldn't mind.'

'Yeah, right.' Greg smirked, shook his head. 'You don't know her too well anymore, do you, Myron?'

'I guess not, no.'

'If she had her way, I'd never get to see Jeremy again.'

'That's a bit harsh, Greg.'

'No, Myron. If anything, it's being generous.'

'Emily told me that you're a good father.'

'Did she also tell you what she charged in our custody battle?'

Myron nodded. 'That you abused the kids.'

'Not just abused them, Myron. *Sexually* abused them.'

'She wanted to win.'

'And that's an excuse?'

'No,' Myron said. 'It's deplorable.'

'More than that,' Greg said. 'It's sick. You have no idea what Emily's capable of doing to get her way.'

'For example?'

But Greg just shook his head and started up the car. 'I'll ask you again: What can I do to help?'

'Nothing, Greg.'

'No good. I'm not sitting around while my kid is dying, you understand?'

'I do.'

'You have anything besides this name and address?'

'Nope.'

'Fine,' Greg said. 'I'll drop you off at the train station. I'm staying up here and watching the house.'

'You think the old man is lying?'

Greg shrugged. 'Maybe he's just confused and forgot. Or maybe I'm wasting my time. But I got to do something.'

Myron said nothing. Greg continued to drive.

'You'll call me if you hear something?' Greg asked.

'Sure.'

During the train ride back to Manhattan, Myron thought about what Greg had said. About Emily. And about what she'd done – and what she'd do – to save her son.

11

Myron and Terese started out the next morning showering together. Myron controlled the temperature and kept the water hot. Prevents, er, shrinkage.

When they stepped out of the steamy stall, he helped Terese towel off.

'Thorough,' she said.

'We're a full-service operation, ma'am.' He toweled her off some more.

'One thing I notice when I shower with a man,' Terese said.

'What's that?'

'My breasts always end up squeaky clean.'

Win had left several hours ago. Lately he liked to get to the office by six. Overseas markets or something. Terese toasted a bagel while Myron fixed himself a bowl of cereal. Quisp cereal. They didn't have it in New York anymore, but Win had it shipped in from a place called Woodsman's in Wisconsin. Myron downed an industrial-size spoonful; the sugar rush came at him so fast he nearly ducked.

Terese said, 'I have to go back tomorrow morning.'

'I know.'

He took another spoonful, feeling her eyes on him.

'Run away with me again,' Terese said.

He glanced up at her. She looked smaller, farther away.

'I can get us the same house on the island. We can just hop on a plane and—'

'I can't,' he interrupted.

'Oh,' she said. Then: 'You need to find this Davis Taylor?'

'Yes.'

'I see. And after that . . . ?'

70

Myron shook his head. They ate some more in silence.

'I'm sorry,' Myron said.

She nodded.

'Running away isn't always the answer, Terese.'

'Myron?'

'What?'

'Do I look in the mood for platitudes?'

'I'm sorry.'

'Yeah, you said that already.'

'I'm just trying to help.'

'Sometimes you can't help,' she said. 'Sometimes all that's left is running away.'

'Not for me,' he said.

'No,' she agreed. 'Not for you.'

She wasn't angry or upset, just flat and resigned, and that scared him all the more.

An hour later Esperanza came into Myron's office without knocking.

'Okay,' she began, grabbing a seat, 'here's what we've got on Davis Taylor.'

Myron leaned back and put his hands behind his head.

'One, he's never filed a tax return with the IRS.'

'Never?'

'Glad you're paying attention,' Esperanza said.

'Are you saying he's never shown any income?'

'Will you let me finish?'

'Sorry.'

'Two, he has virtually no paperwork. No driver's license. One credit card, a Visa recently issued by his bank. It has very little activity. Only one bank account, with a current balance of under two hundred dollars.'

'Suspicious,' Myron said.

'Yes.'

'When did he open the account?'

'Three months ago.'

'And before that?'

'Nada. At least nada that I've been able to come up with so far.'

71

Myron stroked his chin. 'No one flies that far below the radar screen,' he said. 'It has to be an alias.'

'I thought the same thing,' Esperanza said.

'And?'

'The answer is yes and no.' Myron waited for the explanation. Esperanza tucked some loose tresses behind both ears. 'It appears to be a name change.'

Myron frowned. 'But we got his social security number, right?'

'Right.'

'And most records are kept by social security number, not name, right?'

'Another right.'

'So I don't get it,' Myron said. 'You can't change your social security number. A name change might make you harder to find, but it wouldn't wipe out your past. You'd still have tax returns and stuff like that.'

Esperanza turned both palms upward. 'That's what I mean by yes and no.'

'There's no paperwork under the social security number either?'

'That's correct,' Esperanza said.

Myron tried to digest this. 'So what's Davis Taylor's real name?'

'I don't have it yet.'

'I would have thought it'd be easy to locate.'

'It would,' she said, 'if he had any records at all. But he doesn't. The social security number has no hits. It's as though this person hasn't done a thing in his whole life.'

Myron thought about it. 'Only one explanation,' he said.

'That being?'

'A fake ID.'

Esperanza shook her head. 'The social security number exists.'

'I don't doubt that. But I think someone pulled the classic tombstone-fake-ID trick.'

'That being?'

'You go to a graveyard and find the tombstone of a dead child,' Myron said. 'Someone who would be about your age if he'd lived. Then you write and request his birth certificate and paperwork and *voilà*, you've set up the perfect fake ID. Oldest trick in the book.'

Esperanza gave him the look she saved for his most idiotic moments. 'No,' she said.

'No?'

'You think the police don't watch TV, Myron? That doesn't work anymore. Hasn't worked in years, except maybe on cop shows. But just to make sure, I double-checked.'

'How?'

'Death records,' she said. 'There's a Web site that has the social security numbers of all the deceased.'

'And the number isn't there.'

'Ding, ding, ding,' Esperanza said.

Myron leaned forward. 'This makes absolutely no sense,' he said. 'Our phony Davis Taylor has gone to a great deal of trouble to create this phony ID – or at least to fly below the radar, right?'

'Right.'

'He wants no records, no paperwork, nothing.'

'Right again.'

'Even changes his name.'

'You go, boy.'

Myron put his arms out. 'Then why would he sign up to be a bone marrow donor?'

'Myron?'

'Yeah.'

'I don't know what you're talking about,' Esperanza said.

True enough. He'd called last night and asked her to check out Davis Taylor. He had not yet told her why.

'I guess I owe you an explanation,' he said.

She shrugged.

'I sort of promised you I wouldn't be doing this anymore,' he said.

'Investigating,' she said.

'Right. And I meant it. I wanted this to be a straight agency from now on.'

She didn't respond. Myron glanced at the wall behind her. The sparse Client Wall again reminded him of a hair transplant that hadn't taken. Maybe he should paint on a couple of coats of Rogaine.

'You remember Emily's call?' he said.

'It was yesterday, Myron. My memory can sometimes go back a whole week.'

He explained it all. Some men – men Myron grudgingly admired – keep it all inside, bury their secrets, hide the pain, the whole cliché. Myron rarely did. He was not one to walk down the mean streets alone – he liked Win to be his backup. He didn't grab a bottle of whiskey and drown his sorrows – he discussed them with Esperanza. Not very macho, but there you have it.

Esperanza stayed silent as he spoke. When he got to the part about being Jeremy's father, she let out a small groan and closed her eyes and kept them shut for a very long time. When she finally opened them, she asked, 'So what are you going to do?'

'I'm going to find the donor.'

'That's not what I meant.'

He knew that. 'I don't know,' he said.

She thought about it, shook her head in disbelief. 'You have a son.'

'Seems so.'

'And you don't know what you're going to do about it?'

'That's right.'

'But you're leaning,' she said.

'Win made a pretty good case for not saying anything.'

She made a sound. 'Win would.'

'Actually he claims to be using his heart.'

'If only he had one.'

'You don't agree?'

'No,' she said. 'I don't agree.'

'You think I should tell Jeremy?'

'I think first and foremost you should put aside your Batman complex,' she said.

'What the hell does that mean?'

'It means you always try a little too hard to be heroic.'

'And that's bad?'

'Sometimes it clouds your thinking,' she said. 'The heroic thing is not always the right thing.'

'Jeremy already has a family. He has a mother and a father—'

'He has,' Esperanza interrupted, 'a lie.'

They sat there and stared at each other. The phone, usually so

74

active, was silent, as it had been for too long now. Myron wondered how he could explain it so that she would understand. She stayed still, waiting.

'We were both lucky when it came to parents,' Myron said.

'Mine are dead, Myron.'

'That's not what I mean,' he said. He took a deep breath. 'How many days pass that you don't still miss them?'

'None,' she said without hesitation.

He nodded. 'We were both loved unconditionally and we both loved our parents the same way.'

Esperanza's eyes started misting. 'So?'

'So – and this was what Win said – isn't that what makes a mother or father? Isn't it about who raised us and loved us and not simply an accident of biology?'

Esperanza leaned back. 'Win said that?'

Myron smiled. 'He has his moments.'

'That he does,' she said.

'And think about your father – the one who raised and loved you. What happens to him?'

Her eyes were still misty. 'My love for him is strong enough to survive the truth. Isn't yours?'

He tilted back as though the words were jabs at his chin. 'Sure,' he said. 'But it would still hurt him.'

'Your father would be hurt?'

'Of course.'

'I see,' Esperanza said. 'So now you're worried about poor Greg Downing?'

'Hardly. You want to hear something awful?'

'Love to.'

'When Greg constantly refers to Jeremy as "my son," I want to yell out the truth. Right in his smug face. Just to see his reaction. Just to watch his world crumble.'

'So much for your Batman complex,' Esperanza said.

Myron held out his hands. 'I have my moments too,' he said.

Esperanza stood and headed for the door.

'Where you going?'

'I don't want to talk about this anymore,' she said.

He sat back.

'You're blocking,' she said. 'You know that?'

He nodded slowly.

'When you move past it – and you will – we'll talk about it again. Otherwise, we're wasting our time here, okay?'

'Okay.'

'Just don't be stupid.'

' "Don't be stupid," ' he repeated. 'Check.'

Her departing smile was brief.

12

Myron spent the rest of the day working the phones. He strapped on his Ultra Slim headset and paced the office. He talked up college coaches, mining for potential free agents. He touched base with his clients and listened to their problems, both real and imagined, therapist-style, which was a large part of his job. He sifted through his Rolodex of companies, trying to conjure up a few endorsement deals.

One serious lead came a-knocking on its own:

'Mr Bolitar? I'm Ronny Angle from Rack Enterprises. Are you familiar with us?'

'You run a bunch of topless bars, right?'

'We prefer they be called upscale exotic nightclubs.'

'And I prefer to be called a well-endowed stallion,' Myron said. 'What can I do for you, Mr Angle?'

'Ronny please. Can I call you Myron?'

'Myron please.'

'Great, Myron. Rack Enterprises is entering a new venture.'

'Uh-huh.'

'You've probably read about it. A chain of coffee-houses called La, La, Latte.'

'For real?'

'Pardon?'

'Well, I think I did see something about this, but I figured it was a joke.'

'It's no joke, Mr Bolitar.'

'So you guys are really going to open up topless coffee bars?'

'We prefer they be called upscale erotic coffee experiences.'

'I see. But you're, uh, *baristas* will be topless, correct?'

'Correct.'

Myron thought about it. 'Makes asking for milk something of a double entendre, don't you think?'

'That's very funny, Myron.'

'Thanks, Ronny.'

'We're going to open with a big splash.'

'That another milk joke, Ronny?'

'No, Myron, but you're a pretty funny guy.'

'Thanks, Ronny.'

'Let me cut right to it, okay? We like Suzze T.' Suzze T was Suzze Tamirino, a journeyman (or is it journeywoman?) on the pro tennis circuit. 'We saw her picture in the *Sports Illustrated* swimsuit issue, and, well, we were very impressed. We'd like her to do a cameo for our grand opening.'

Myron rubbed the bridge of his nose with his thumb and forefinger. 'When you say cameo—'

'A brief performance.'

'How brief?'

'No more than five minutes.'

'I don't mean brief in terms of time. I mean in terms of clothing.'

'We'd require full frontal nudity.'

'Well, thanks for thinking of us, Ronny, but I don't think Suzze will be interested.'

'We're offering two hundred thousand dollars.'

Myron sat up. Easy to hang up, but with this kind of dough, he had a responsibility to follow up. 'How about if she wears a small top?'

'No.'

'A bikini?'

'No.'

'An itsy-bitsy, teeny-weeny bikini?'

'Like in the song?'

'Exactly,' Myron said. 'Like in the song.'

'I'm going to state this as plainly as I can,' Ronny said. 'There must be nipple visibility.'

'Nipple visibility?'

'This point is non-negotiable.'

'So to speak.'

Myron promised to call him back later in the week. The two men hung up. Negotiating nipple visibility. What a business.

Esperanza came in without knocking. Her eyes were wide and bright.

'Lamar Richardson is on line one,' she said.

'Lamar himself?'

She nodded.

'No relative or personal manager or favorite astrologer?'

'Lamar himself,' Esperanza repeated.

They both nodded. This was a good thing.

Myron picked up the phone. 'Hello.'

'Let's meet,' Lamar said.

'Sure,' Myron said.

'When?'

'You name it.'

'When are you free?'

'You name it,' Myron said.

'I'm in Detroit right now.'

'I'll catch the next plane out.'

'Just like that?' Lamar said.

'Yup.'

'Shouldn't you pretend you're really busy?'

'We going to date, Lamar?'

Lamar chuckled. 'No, I don't think so.'

'Then I'll skip the playing-hard-to-get stage. Esperanza and I want you to sign up with MB SportsReps. We'll do a good job. We'll make you a priority. And we won't play mind games with you.'

Myron smiled at Esperanza. Was he good or what?

Lamar said he was going to be in Manhattan later in the week and would like to meet then. They set up a time. Myron hung up. He and Esperanza sat there and smiled at each other.

'We have a chance,' she said.

'Yep.'

'So what's our strategy?'

'I thought I'd impress him with my nimble mind,' he said.

'Hmm,' Esperanza said. 'Maybe I should wear something low cut.'

'I was kinda counting on that.'

'Hit him with brains and beauty.'

'Yes,' Myron said. 'But which one of us is which?'

When Myron got back to the Dakota, Win was heading out with his leather gym bag and Terese was gone.

'She left a note,' Win said, handing it to Myron.

Had to go back early. I'll call.
Terese

Myron read the note again. It didn't change. He folded it up and put it away.

'You going to Master Kwon's?' Myron asked. Master Kwon was their martial arts instructor.

Win nodded. 'He's been asking for you.'

'What did you tell him?' Myron asked.

'That you wigged out.'

'Thanks.'

Win gave a slight bow and lifted his gym bag. 'May I make a suggestion?'

'Shoot.'

'You haven't been to the *dojang* in a long while.'

'I know.'

'You have a great deal of stress in your life,' Win said. 'You need an outlet. You need some focus. Some balance. Some structure.'

'You're not going to make me snatch a pebble from your hand, are you?'

'Not today, no. But come with me.'

Myron shrugged. 'I'll grab my stuff.'

They were halfway out the door when Esperanza called. He told her they were just on their way out.

'Where?' she asked.

'Master Kwon's.'

'I'll meet you there.'

'Why? What's up?'

'I got some information on Davis Taylor.'

'And?'

'And it's more than a little strange. Is Win going with you?'

'Yes.'

80

'Ask him if he knows anything about Raymond Lex's family.'

Silence. 'Raymond Lex is dead, Esperanza.'

'Duh, Myron. I said *family*.'

'This has something to do with Davis Taylor?'

'It'll be easier to explain in person. I'll see you down there in an hour.'

She hung up.

One of the doormen had already fetched Win's Jag. It sat waiting for them on Central Park West. The rich. Myron settled into the lush leather. Win hit the accelerator pad. He was big with the accelerator pad; he had a bit more trouble when it came to the brake.

'Do you know Raymond Lex's family?'

'They used to be clients,' Win said.

'You're kidding?'

'Oh yes, I'm a regular Red Buttons.'

'Were you directly involved in this inheritance squabble?'

'Calling this a squabble would be similar to calling nuclear Armageddon a campfire.'

'Hard to divide up billions, huh?'

'Indeed. So why are we discussing the Lex clan?'

'Esperanza is going to meet us down at the *dojang*. She has some information on Davis Taylor. Somehow the Lex family is connected.'

Win arched his eyebrow. 'The plot doth thicken.'

'So tell me a little about them.'

'Most of it was in the media. Raymond Lex writes a controversial bestseller called *Midnight Confessions*. Said bestseller becomes an Oscar-winning blockbuster. Suddenly he goes from obscure junior-college instructor to millionaire. Unlike most of his artistic brethren, he understands business. He invests and amasses private holdings with a substantial yet confidential net worth.'

'The papers place it in the billions.'

'I won't argue.'

'That's a lot of money.'

'The way you word things,' Win said. 'It's like Proust.'

'He never wrote another book?'

'No.'

'Odd.'

'Not really,' Win said. 'Harper Lee and Margaret Mitchell never wrote another book. And at least Lex kept busy. It's hard to build one of the largest privately held corporations and do book signings.'

'So now that he's dead, his family is – how to say it? – nuclear Armageddoning?'

'Close enough.'

Master Kwon had moved his headquarters and main *dojang* into the second floor of a building on Twenty-third Street near Broadway. Five rooms – studios really – with hardwood floors, mirrored walls, high-tech sound system, sleek and shiny Nautilus equipment – oh, and some of those rice-paper Oriental scroll-posters. Gave the place a real Old World Asia feel.

Myron and Win slipped into their *dobok*, a white uniform, and tied their black belts. Myron had been studying tae kwon do and *hapkido* since Win had first introduced him to them in college, but he hadn't been to a *dojang* more than five times in the past three years. Win, on the other hand, remained devoutly lethal. Don't tug on Superman's cape, don't spit in the wind, don't pull the mask off the ol' Lone Ranger, and you don't mess around with Win. Bah, bah, dee, dee, dee, dee, dee.

Master Kwon was in his mid-seventies but could easily pass for two decades younger. Win had met him during his Asian travels when he was fifteen. As near as Myron could tell, Master Kwon had been a high priest or some such thing at a small Buddhist monastery straight out of a Hong Kong revenge flick. When Master Kwon emigrated to the United States, he spoke very little English. Now, some twenty years later, he spoke almost none. As soon as the wise master hit our shores, he opened up a chain of state-of-the-art tae kwon do schools – with Win's financial backing, of course. Once he saw the *Karate Kid* movies, Master Kwon started playing the old wise man to the hilt. His English disappeared. He started dressing like the Dalai Lama and began every sentence with the words 'Confucius say,' ignoring the small fact that he was Korean and Confucius was Chinese.

Win and Myron headed to Master Kwon's office. At the entrance, both men bowed deeply.

'Please in,' Master Kwon said.

The desk was fine oak, the chair rich leather and orthopedic looking. Master Kwon was standing near a corner. He held a putter in his hands and wore a splendidly tailored suit. His face brightened when he saw Myron, and the two men embraced.

When they broke apart, Master Kwon said, 'You better?'

'Better,' Myron agreed.

The old man smiled and grabbed his own lapel. 'Armani,' he said.

'I thought so,' Myron said.

'You like?'

'Very nice.'

Satisfied, Master Kwon said, 'Go.'

Win and Myron bowed deeply. Once in the *dojang*, they fell into their customary roles: Win led and Myron followed. They started with meditation. Win loved meditating, as we already graphically witnessed. He sat in the lotus position, palms tilted up, hands resting on knees, back straight, tongue folded against the upper teeth. He breathed in through his nose, forcing the air down, letting his abdomen do all the work. Myron tried to duplicate – had been trying for years – but he had never quite gotten the hang of it. His mind, even during less chaotic times, wandered. His bad knee tightened. He got fidgety.

They cut down the stretching to only ten minutes. Again Win was effortless, executing splits and toe touches and deep bends with ease, his bones and joints as flexible as a politician's voting record. Myron had never been a naturally limber guy. When he was training seriously, he could touch his toes and complete a hurdle stretch with little problem. But just then, that felt like a long time ago.

'I'm already sore,' Myron said through a grunt.

Win tilted his head. 'Odd.'

'What?'

'That's precisely what my date said last night.'

'You weren't kidding before,' Myron said. 'You really are another Red Buttons.'

They did a little sparring, and Myron immediately realized how out of shape he was. Sparring is the most tiring activity in the world. Don't believe it? Find a punching bag and pretend-box with it for one three-minute round. Just a bag that can't fight back. Try it, just one round. You'll see.

When Esperanza came in, the sparring mercifully ceased and Myron grabbed his knees, sucking wind. He bowed to Win, threw a towel over his shoulder, grabbed some Evian. Esperanza folded her arms and waited. A group of students walked past the door, saw Esperanza, did a double take.

Esperanza handed Myron a sheet of paper. 'The birth certificate of Davis Taylor né Dennis Lex.'

'Lex,' Myron repeated. 'As in . . . ?'

'Yep.'

Myron scanned the photocopy. According to the document, Dennis Lex would be thirty-seven years old. His father was listed as one Raymond Lex, his mother as Maureen Lehman Lex. Born in East Hampton, New York.

Myron handed it to Win.

'They had another child?'

'Apparently so,' Esperanza said.

Myron looked at Win. Win shrugged.

'He must have died young,' Win said.

'If he did,' Esperanza said, 'I can't find it anywhere. There's no death certificate.'

'No one in the family ever mentioned another child?' Myron asked Win.

'No one,' Win said.

He turned back to Esperanza. 'What else you got?'

'Not much. Dennis Lex changed his name to Davis Taylor eight months ago. I also found this.' She handed him a photocopy of a news clipping. A small birth announcement from the *Hampton Gazette* dated thirty-seven years ago:

Raymond and Maureen Lex of Wister Drive in East Hampton are delighted to announce the birth of their son, Dennis, six pounds eight ounces on June 18th. Dennis joins his sister Susan and his brother Bronwyn.

Myron shook his head. 'How could no one know about this?'

'It's not all that surprising,' Win said.

'How do you figure?'

'None of the Lex family holdings are public. They are fiercely protective of their privacy. Security around them is around-the-clock and the best money can buy. Everyone who works with them must sign confidentiality agreements.'

'Even you?'

'I don't do confidentiality agreements,' Win said. 'No matter how much money is involved.'

'So they never asked you to sign one?'

'They asked. I refused. We parted ways.'

'You gave them up as clients?'

'Yes.'

'Why? I mean, what would have been the big deal? You keep everything confidential anyway.'

'Exactly. Clients hire me not only because of my brilliance in the ways of finance but because I am the very model of discretion.'

'Don't overlook your startling modesty,' Myron added.

'I don't need to sign a contract saying I won't reveal anything. It should be a given. It's the equivalent of signing a document saying that I won't burn down their house.'

Myron nodded. 'Nice analogy,' he said.

'Yes, thank you, but I'm trying to illustrate how far this family will go to maintain their privacy. Until this inheritance feud erupted, the media had no idea how extensive Raymond Lex's holdings were.'

'But come on, Win. This is Raymond Lex's son. You'd know about a son.'

Win pointed to the top of the clipping. 'Notice when the child was born – *before* Raymond Lex's book came out, when Lex was just a typical small-town professor. It wouldn't make news.'

'You really buy that?'

'Do you have a better explanation?'

'So where is the kid now? How can the son of one of America's wealthiest families have no paperwork? No credit cards, no driver's license, no IRS filings, no trail at all? Why did he change his name?'

'The last one is easy,' Win said.

'Oh?'

'He's hiding.'

'From?'

'His siblings perhaps,' Win said. 'As I said before, this inheritance battle is rather nasty.'

85

'That might make sense – and I stress the word "might" – if he'd been around before. But how can there be no paperwork on him? What is he hiding from? And why on earth would he put his name in the bone marrow registry?'

'Good questions,' Win said.

'Very good,' Esperanza added.

Myron reread the article and looked at his two friends. 'Nice to have a consensus,' he said.

13

The mobile phone blew him out of his sleep like a shotgun blast. Myron's hand reached up blindly, his fingers bouncing along the night table until they located the phone.

'Hello?' he croaked.

'Is this Myron Bolitar?'

The voice was a whisper.

'Who is this?' Myron asked.

'You called me.'

Still whispering, the sound like leaves skittering across pavement.

Myron sat upright, his heartbeat picking up a little steam. 'Davis Taylor?'

'Sow the seeds. Keep sowing. And open the shades. Let the truth come in. Let the secrets finally wither in the daylight.'

Ooookay. 'I need your help, Mr Taylor.'

'Sow the seeds.'

'Yes, of course, we'll sow away.' Myron flicked on the light. 2:17 A.M. He checked the LCD display on the phone. The Caller ID was blocked. Damn. 'But we have to meet.'

'Sow the seeds. It's the only way.'

'I understand, Mr Taylor. Can we meet?'

'Someone must sow the seeds. And someone must unlock the chains.'

'I'll bring a key. Just tell me where you are.'

'Why do you wish to see me?'

What to say? 'It's a matter of life and death.'

'Whenever you sow the seeds, it's a matter of life and death.'

'You donated blood for a bone marrow drive. You're a match. A young boy will die if you don't help.'

Silence.

'Mr Taylor?'

'Technology cannot help him. I thought you were one of us.' Still whispering but sad now.

'I am. Or at least I want to be—'

'I'm hanging up now.'

'No, wait—'

'Good-bye.'

'Dennis Lex,' Myron said.

Silence, except for the sound of breathing. Myron wasn't sure if the sound was coming from him or the caller.

'Please,' Myron said. 'I'll do whatever you ask. But we have to meet.'

'Will you remember to sow the seeds?'

Small chunks of ice dropped down his back.

'Yes,' Myron said, 'I'll remember.'

'Good. Then you know what you must do.'

Myron gripped the receiver. 'No,' he said. 'What must I do?'

'The boy,' the voice whispered. 'Say one last good-bye to the boy.'

14

'Sow the seeds?' Esperanza said.

They were in Myron's office. The morning sun striped the floor with Venetian slits, two cutting across Esperanza's face. She didn't seem to mind.

'Right,' Myron said. 'And something about that phrase keeps gnawing at me.'

'It was a Tears for Fears song,' Esperanza said.

' "Sowing the Seeds of Love." I remember.'

'Wasn't that the name of the tour too? We saw them at the Meadowlands in, what, 1988?'

'Eighty-nine.'

'What happened to those guys?'

'They broke up,' Myron said.

'Why do they all do that?'

'Got me.'

'Supertramp, Steely Dan, the Doobie Brothers—'

'Not to mention Wham.'

'They break up and then they never make anything decent on their own. They flounder around and end up a segment of VH-1's *Where Are They Now?*'

'We're getting off the subject.'

Esperanza handed him a slip of paper. 'Here's the office number for Susan Lex, Dennis's older sister.'

Myron read the number like it was in code and might mean something. 'I had another thought.'

'What's that?'

'If Dennis Lex exists, then he had to have gone to school, right?'

'Maybe.'

89

'So let's see if we can find out where the Children Lex schooled – public, private, whatever.'

Esperanza frowned. 'You mean like college?'

'Start there, yes. Not that siblings go to the same school, but maybe they did. Or maybe they all went to Ivy League schools. Something like that. You might want to start with high school. It's more likely that they all went to the same one.'

'And if I don't find any record of him in high school?'

'Go back even further.'

She crossed her legs, folded her arms. 'How far?'

'As far as you can.'

'And what good will this exercise in futility do us?'

'I want to know when Dennis Lex fell off the radar screen. Did people know him in high school? In college? In grad school?'

She did not look impressed. 'And assuming I somehow manage to find, say, his elementary school, what exactly is that going to do for us?'

'Damn if I know. I'm grasping at straws here.'

'No, you're asking *me* to grasp at straws.'

'Then don't do it, Esperanza, okay? It was just a thought.'

'Nah,' she said with a wave of her hand. 'You may be right.'

Myron put his palms on his desk, arched his back, looked left, looked right, looked up, looked down.

'What?' she said.

'You said I may be right. I'm waiting for the world as we know it to end.'

'Good one,' Esperanza said, standing. 'I'll see what I can dig up.'

She left the room. Myron picked up the telephone and dialed Susan Lex's number. The receptionist transferred the call, and a woman identifying herself as Ms Lex's secretary picked it up. She had a voice like a steel-wool tire over gravel.

'Ms Lex does not see people she doesn't know.'

'It's a matter of grave importance,' Myron said.

'Perhaps you did not hear me the first time.' Classic battle-ax. 'Ms Lex does not see people she doesn't know.'

'Tell her it's about Dennis.'

'Excuse me?'

'Just tell her that.'

Battle-ax put Myron on hold without another word. Myron listened to a Muzak version of Al Stewart's 'Time Passages.' Myron had thought the original was Muzak-y enough, thank you very much.

The battle-ax came back with a snap. 'Ms Lex does not see people she doesn't know.'

'I've been thinking about that, but it doesn't really make sense.'

'Excuse me?'

'I mean, at some time she must see people she doesn't know – otherwise she'd never meet anybody new. And if we follow my logic, how did you ever get to see her for the first time? She was willing to see you before she knew you, right?'

'I'm hanging up now, Mr Bolitar.'

'Tell her I know about Dennis.'

'I just—'

'Tell her if she doesn't agree to see me, I'll go to the press.'

Silence. 'Hold.' A click and then the Muzak came back on. Time passed. So, mercifully, did 'Time Passages,' replaced by the Alan Parsons Project's 'Time.' Myron nearly slipped into a coma.

Battle-ax returned. 'Mr Bolitar?'

'Yes?'

'Ms Lex will give you five minutes of her time. I have an opening on the fifteenth of next month.'

'No good,' Myron said. 'It has to be today.'

'Ms Lex is a very busy woman.'

'Today,' Myron said.

'That simply will not be possible.'

'At eleven. If I'm not let in, I go immediately to the press.'

'You're being terribly rude, Mr Bolitar.'

'To the press,' Myron repeated. 'Do you understand?'

'Yes.'

'Will you be there?'

'What possible difference could that make?'

'All this sexual tension is driving me batty. Maybe afterward we could get together for a nice cool latte.'

He heard the phone go click and smiled. The charm, he thought. It's baaaaack.

Esperanza buzzed in. 'Topless tennis, anyone?'

'What?'

'I got Suzze T on line one.'

He hit a button. 'Hey, Suzze.'

'Hey, Myron, what's shaking?'

'I got an offer for you to refuse.'

'You mean you're going to hit on me?'

The charm suffers a setback. 'Where are you going to be this afternoon?'

'Same place as now,' she said. 'The Morning Mosh. You know it?'

'No.'

She gave him the address, and Myron agreed to meet her there in a few hours. He hung up the phone and leaned back.

' "Sow the seeds," ' he said out loud.

He stared at the wall. An hour to kill before he headed over to the Lex Building on Fifth Avenue. He could sit here and think about life and maybe contemplate his navel. No, too much of that already. He swiveled his seat to the computer, double-clicked the proper icon, connected to the Net. He tried Yahoo first and typed *sow the seeds* into the search field. Only one hit: a Web site for the San Francisco League of Urban Gardeners. They went by the acronym SLUG. Tough guys probably. A gang. Probably wore green bandannas and engaged in drive-by waterings.

He tried Alta Vista's search engine next, but they listed 2,501 Web pages. It was kinda like Goldilocks and the Three Bears. Yahoo's search was toooo small. Alta Vista's was toooo big. They didn't have LEXIS-NEXIS at the office, but Myron tried a less powerful media engine. He typed in the same three words and pressed the return key, and bammo.

http://www.nyherald.com/archives/9800322

Myron hit the link and the article came up:

New York Herald
THE MIND OF TERROR – YOUR DARKEST FEAR
by Stan Gibbs

Whoa, hold the phone. Myron knew the name. Stan Gibbs had been a big-time newspaper columnist, the kind of guy who regularly pontificated (read: pimped) on the cable news talk shows, though he'd been less annoying than most, which is like saying syphilis is less annoying than gonorrhea. But that had all been before the scandal gutted him like Ted Nugent over a fallen moose. Myron read:

> The phone call comes out of the blue.
> 'What is your darkest fear?' the voice whispers. 'Close your eyes now and picture it. Can you see it? Do you have it yet? The very worst agony you can imagine?'
> After a long pause, I say, 'Yes.'
> 'Good. Now imagine something worse, something far, far worse . . .'

Myron took a deep breath. He remembered the series of articles. Stan Gibbs had broken a story about a bizarre kidnapper. He'd told the heart-wrenching tale of three abductions that the police had supposedly wanted to keep quiet, out of, Stan Gibbs claimed, embarrassment. No names were mentioned. He had spoken with the families under the condition of anonymity. And, the coup de grâce, the kidnapper had granted Gibbs access:

> I ask the kidnapper why he does it. Is it for the ransom?
> 'I never pick up the ransom money,' he says. 'I usually leave explosives at the spot and burn it. But sometimes money helps me sow the seeds. That is what I'm trying to do. Sow the seeds.'

Myron felt his blood stop.

> 'You all think you're safe,' he continues, 'in your technological cocoon. But you're not. Technology has made us expect easy answers and happy endings. But with me, there is no answer and there is no end.'
> He has kidnapped at least four people: the father of two young children, age 41; a female college student, age 20; and a young couple, newlyweds ages 28 and 27. All were abducted while in the New York City area.
> 'The idea,' he says, 'is to keep the terror going. Let it grow, not with gore or obvious bloodletting, but with your own imagination. Technology is trying to destroy our ability to imagine. But when someone you love is taken away, your mind can conjure up horrors

darker than any machine – than anything even I can do. Some minds won't go that far. Some minds stop and put up a barrier. My job is to push them through that barrier.'

I ask him how he does that.

'Sow the seeds,' he repeats. 'You sow the seeds over time.'

He explains that sowing the seeds means giving hope and taking it away over a sustained period of time. His first call to the victim's family is naturally devastating, but merely the beginning of a long and torturous ordeal.

He begins the call, he claims, with a normal hello and asks the family member to please hold. After a pause, the family member hears their loved one give a blood-curdling shriek. 'Just one,' he says, 'and it's very short. I cut them off in mid-scream.

'This is the last they'll ever hear from their loved one,' he continues. 'Imagine how that scream echoes.'

But for the victim's family, it does not end there. He demands a ransom that he has no intention of claiming. He calls after midnight and asks the family to imagine their darkest fear. He convinces them that this time, he will really let their loved one go, but he is only extending hope to those who no longer have it, rekindling their agony.

'Time and hope,' he says, 'sow the seeds of despair.'

The father of two has been missing for three years. The young premed college student has been missing for twenty-seven months. The newlyweds were married almost two years ago this weekend. To date, not a trace of any of them has been found. Rarely does a week pass when the families don't get a call from their tormentor.

When I ask him if his victims are alive or dead, he is coy. 'Death is closure,' he explains, 'and closure stops the sowing.'

He wants to talk about society, how computers and technology are doing our thinking for us, how what he does lets us see the power of the human brain.

'That is where God exists,' he says. 'That is where all things valuable exist. True bliss can only be found inside of you. The meaning of life is not in your new home entertainment system or sports car. People must see their limitless potential. How do you make them see? Right now imagine what these families are going through.'

His voice soft, he invites me to try.

'Technology could never conjure up the horrors you are now imagining. Sow the seeds. Sowing the seeds shows us the potential.'

Myron's heart pounded in big thuds. He sat back, shook his head, started reading again. The crazed kidnapper ranted on, his theories feverishly demented, sort of Symbionese Liberation Army by way of Ted Kaczynski. Stan Gibbs's column continued into the next day's paper. Myron hit the link and read on. During the second day, Gibbs opened with some heartbreaking quotes from the family of the victims. Then he questioned the kidnapper some more:

I ask him how he has managed to keep these kidnappings out of the media.

'By sowing the seeds,' he repeats yet again.

I ask for an example.

'I tell his wife to go to the garage and open the red Stanley toolbox on the third shelf. I tell her to pick out the black pliers with the bubble grip. Then I send her to the basement. I tell her to stand in front of the Mission chair they bought the previous summer at that tag sale on the Cape. Imagine, I say, your husband tied naked to that chair. Imagine those pliers in my hand. And finally, imagine what I'll do if I see anything about him in the newspaper.'

But he does not stop there.

'I ask her about the children. I mention their names. I mention their schools and their teachers and their favorite breakfast cereal.'

I ask him how he knows these things.

His answer is simple. 'Daddy tells me.'

Myron fell back. 'Jesus,' he uttered.

Deep breaths, he told himself again. In and out. That's it. Think it through. Slowly now. Carefully. Okay, first off: Horrible as this is, what does it have to do with Davis Taylor né Dennis Lex? Probably nothing. The worst sort of long shot. And again, horrible as this is, Myron knew that there was more to the story. More – and in a sense, less.

The Gibbs columns drew weeks' worth of nationwide attention and criticism – until, Myron remembered, it all blew up in the most public way possible. What had happened exactly? Myron hit some keys and clicked the mouse. He started a search of articles where Stan Gibbs was the subject. They came up in date order:

FEDS DEMAND GIBBS'S SOURCE

The Federal Bureau of Investigation, which in recent weeks has been denying the allegations listed in Stan Gibbs's columns, took a new tack today. They demanded his notes and information.

Dan Conway, a spokesman for the FBI, began by saying, 'We know nothing about these crimes,' then added, 'But if Mr Gibbs is being truthful, he has important information on a possible serial kidnapper and killer, perhaps even harboring or aiding him. We have a right to that information.'

Stan Gibbs, a popular columnist and television journalist, has refused to reveal his sources. 'I'm not protecting a killer here,' Mr Gibbs said. 'The families of the victims as well as the perpetrator of the crimes spoke to me under the strict condition of confidentiality. It's a cry as old as our country: I will not reveal my sources.'

The *New York Herald* and American Civil Liberties Union have already denounced the FBI and plan on backing Mr Gibbs. The judge has ordered the case sealed from the public.

Myron read on. The arguments on both sides were pretty standard. Gibbs's attorneys naturally wrapped themselves in the First Amendment, while the feds equally naturally countered that the First Amendment was not an absolute, that you can't yell 'Fire!' in a crowded theater, and that freedom of expression does not include protecting possible criminals. The country also argued the issue. It played well on CNBC and MSNBC and CNN and a bunch of other cable letters, lighting up the phone lines like a radio giveaway. The judge was about to render a verdict when the whole story exploded in a way no one expected.

Myron hit the link:

GIBBS FIBS?
Reporter accused of plagiarism

Myron read the endgame shocker: Someone had found a

mystery novel published by a tiny press with a minuscule print run in 1978. The novel, *Whisper to a Scream*, by F. K. Armstrong, closely mirrored Gibbs's story. Too closely. Certain snippets of dialogue were pretty much copied verbatim. The crimes in the novel – kidnappings with no resolution – were too similar to what Gibbs had written to be dismissed as coincidence.

The plagiaristic spectres of Mike Barnicle and Patricia Smith and the like rose from the grave and would not disperse. Heads rolled. There were resignations and hand-wringing. For his part, Stan Gibbs refused to comment, which didn't look good. Gibbs ended up 'taking a leave of absence,' a modern-day euphemism for *getting fired*. The ACLU issued an ambiguous statement and retreated. The *New York Herald* quietly retracted the story, saying that the matter 'was under internal review.'

After some time passed, Myron reached for the phone and dialed.

'News desk. Bruce Taylor speaking.'

'How about meeting me for a drink?'

'I know this is out nowadays, Myron, but I'm strictly hetero.'

'I have the ability to change you.'

'I don't think so, pal.'

'Several women I've dated started out hetero,' Myron said. 'But one date with me and whammo, they switched teams.'

'I love it when you're self-deprecating, Myron. It's just so real.'

'So what do you say?'

'I'm on deadline.'

'You're always on deadline.'

'You buying?'

'To quote my brethren during Passover seders, why should this night be different from any other night?'

'I buy sometimes.'

'Do you even own a wallet?'

'Hey, I'm not the one asking for favors,' Bruce said. 'Four o'clock. The Rusty Umbrella.'

15

The Lex Building's wrought-iron gates lined a Fifth Avenue façade with vegetation so dense you wouldn't see light through it if a supernova burst on the other side. The famed edifice was a converted Manhattan mansion with a European courtyard and a regal art deco exterior and enough security to handle a Tyson boxing match. The building had wonderful old lines and detailed Venetian touches, except that for the sake of privacy, the windows had been converted into the smoky-limo variety. It made for a distracting and unnatural mix.

Four blue-blazered, gray-slacked guards stood at the entrance – real guards, Myron noted, with cop eyes and KGB facial tics, not the rent-a-uniforms you saw at department stores or airports. The four of them stood silently, eyeing Myron like he was wearing a tube top in the Vatican.

One of the guards stepped forward. 'May I see some ID please?'

Myron took out his wallet and showed him a credit card and driver's license.

'There's no photo on the driver's license,' the guard said.

'New Jersey doesn't require them.'

'I need a photo ID.'

'I have my picture on my health club membership card.'

Cop-patient sigh. 'That won't do, sir. Do you have a passport?'

'In midtown Manhattan?'

'Yes, sir. For the purposes of ID.'

'No,' Myron said. 'Besides, it's a terrible picture. Doesn't fully capture the radiant blue in my eyes.' Myron batted them for emphasis.

'Wait here, sir.'

He waited. The other three guards frowned, crossed their arms, studied him as though he might start drinking from a toilet. Myron heard a whirring noise and looked up. A security camera was on him now, focusing in. Myron waved, smiled into the lens, performed a few flexes he had picked up from watching he-man events on ESPN 2. He ended with a pretty dramatic back lat spread and waved to the appreciative crowd. The blue-blazers looked unimpressed.

'All natural,' Myron said. 'I've never taken steroids.'

No replies.

The first guard came back. 'Follow me, please.'

Stepping into the courtyard was like stepping into C. S. Lewis's wardrobe, another world, the other side of the shrubbery, so to speak. Here in the middle of Manhattan, the street noises were suddenly very far away, muted. The garden was lush, the tile walkways forming a pattern not unlike an Oriental carpet. There was a sprouting fountain in the middle with a statue of a horse rearing back its head.

A new set of blue-blazers greeted him by the ornate front door. This place, Myron thought, must rack up a hell of a dry-cleaning bill. They made him empty his pockets, confiscated his cell phone, frisked him by hand, ran a metal wand over his person so thoroughly he almost asked for a condom, walked him through a metal detector twice, again frisked him with a little too much gusto.

'If you touch my wee-wee one more time,' Myron said, 'I'm telling my mommy.'

More no replies. Maybe the Lexes demanded not only confidentiality but a discriminating sense of humor.

'Follow me, sir,' the talking blue-blazer said.

The stillness of the place – a building in the middle of Manhattan, for chrissake – was unnerving, the only sound now the steady echo of their footsteps against the cool marble. It was like walking through an old museum at night, the whole experience like something out of *From the Mixed-up Files of Mrs Basil E. Frankweiler*. The guards formed a poor man's presidential motorcade – the talking blue-blazer and a buddy three paces in front of him, two other blue-blazers three paces back. Just for fun, Myron would slow down or speed up and watch the guards do likewise.

Like a really bad line dance, which was something of a redundancy. At one point he almost did a moonwalk, à la Michael Jackson, but these guys were already viewing him as a potential pedophile.

The mahogany staircase was wide and smelled a bit like lemon Pledge. There were enormous tapestries on the wall, the kind with swords and horses and hedonistic feasts of suckling pig. There were two more blue-blazers on the second floor. Now it was their turn to inspect Myron as though they'd never seen a man before. Myron twirled for their benefit. They too seemed unimpressed.

'You should have seen me flex before,' Myron said.

The double doors opened and Myron entered a room slightly larger than a sports arena. Two guards followed him and took up positions in the back corners. There was a big man sitting to the right in a wing chair. At least he looked big in the chair. Or maybe the chair was tiny. The man was probably in his mid-forties. His head and neck formed a near-perfect trapezoid, the top buzzed into a military crew cut. He had a flat nose and ham-hock hands and knockwurst fingers. Ex-boxer or ex-marine or probably both. A man of ninety-degree angles and granite blocks.

Granite Man gave Myron more hard eyes, though his were more relaxed, as though Myron amused him in the way a little kitty nipping at his pant leg might. He didn't stand, choosing instead to stare at Myron and crack his knuckles one at a time.

Myron looked at Granite Man. Granite Man cracked another knuckle.

'Shiver,' Myron said.

No one asked him to take a seat. Hell, no one spoke. Myron stood there and waited with the three sets of eyes weighing on him.

'Okay,' Myron said. 'I'm intimidated. Can we get past this, please?'

Granite Man nodded at the two blazers. They both left. Almost simultaneously, a door on the other side of the room opened and two women appeared. They were pretty far away, but Myron guessed that the first one was Susan Lex. Her hair was done up in an impossibly neat, semi-shellacked bun, and her lips were pursed as if she'd just swallowed a live beetle. The other woman – she looked no more than eighteen or nineteen – had to be her daughter, a carbon copy with the same pursed lips and twenty-five years less wear and tear, not to mention better hair.

Myron started to cross the room with his hand extended, but Susan Lex held up her palm in a stop gesture. Granite Man sat forward, nearly leaning into Myron's path. He gave Myron a small shake of the head, which was no easy task when you have no neck. Myron stayed where he was.

'I don't like being threatened,' Susan Lex called from across the room.

'I apologize for that. But I had to see you.'

'And that makes it right to threaten and blackmail me?'

Myron had no quick answer to that. 'I need to talk to you about your brother Dennis.'

'So you said on the phone.'

'Where is he?'

Susan Lex looked at Granite Man. Granite Man frowned and cracked his knuckles again. 'Just like that, Mr Bolitar?' Susan Lex said. 'You call my office. You threaten me. You insist I alter my schedule to accommodate you. And then you come in here and make demands?'

'I don't mean to be abrupt,' Myron said. 'But this is a matter of life and death.'

Whenever he said 'a matter of life and death,' he expected to hear that melodramatic *dum-dum-duuuummm* music.

'That's hardly an explanation,' Susan Lex said.

'Your brother registered with the national bone marrow center,' Myron said. 'His marrow matched a sick child's.' After the creepy say-good-bye-to-the-boy conversation last night, Myron had decided to stop being gender specific. 'Without that transplant, the child will die.'

Susan Lex arched an eyebrow. The rich are really good at that, at arching eyebrows without altering anything else on their face. Myron wondered if they learned it at rich-people summer camp. Susan Lex looked at Granite Man again. Granite Man was trying to smile now. 'You're mistaken, Mr Bolitar,' she said.

Myron waited for her to say more. When she didn't, he said, 'Mistaken how?'

'If you're telling the truth, you've made a mistake. I will say no more.'

'With all due deference,' Myron said, 'that's not good enough.'

'It will have to be.'

'Where is your brother, Ms Lex?'

'Please leave, Mr Bolitar.'

'I can still go to the press.'

Granite Man crossed his legs and started cracking his knuckles again.

Myron turned to him. 'Yes, but can you do this?' Myron patted his head with one hand and rubbed his belly with the other.

Granite Man didn't like that one.

'Look,' Myron said, 'I don't want to cause any trouble here. You're private people. I understand that. But I need to find this donor.'

'It's not my brother,' Susan Lex said.

'Then where is he?'

'He's not your donor. More than that is none of your concern.'

'Does the name Davis Taylor mean anything to you?'

Susan Lex repursed the lips as though a fresh beetle had sneaked through. She turned and walked out. Her daughter did likewise. Again on cue, the door behind Myron opened and the two blue-blazers filled it. More glares. They stepped fully into the room. Granite Man finally stood, which took some time. He was indeed big. Very big.

The men approached Myron.

'Let's go to the judges,' Myron said. 'Charles Nelson Reilly, your score?'

Granite Man stepped in front of him, shoulders square, eyes calm.

'The not introducing yourself,' Myron said, doing his best Charles Nelson Reilly lisp, which was not very good. 'I thought that was really very macho. And that whole silent persona combined with the amused glare. Very nicely done, really. Professional. But – and here's where you kinda lost me – the knuckle cracking, well, Gene, that was overkill, don't you think? Overall score: an 8. Comment: stick with the subtle.'

Granite Man said, 'You finished?'

'Yes.'

'Myron Bolitar. Born in Livingston, New Jersey. Mother Ellen, father Al—'

'They like to be called El-Al,' Myron interjected. 'Like the Israeli airline.'

'Basketball All-American at Duke University. Picked eighth in the NBA draft by the Boston Celtics. Blew out your knee in your first preseason game, ending your career. Currently owns MB SportsReps, a sports representation firm. Dated the novelist Jessica Culver since you graduated college, but you two recently parted ways. Should I go on?'

'You left off the part about my being a snazzy dancer. I can demonstrate if you like.'

Granite Man smirked. 'You want my score on you now?'

'Suit yourself.'

'You wisecrack too much,' Granite Man said. 'I know you do it to look confident, but you're trying too hard. And since you raised the issue of subtlety, your story about a dying kid needing a bone marrow transplant was touching. The only thing missing was the string quartet.'

'You don't believe me?'

'No, I don't believe you.'

'So why am I here, then?'

Granite Man spread his satellite-dishes excuse for hands. 'That's what I'd like to know.'

The three men formed a triangle, Granite in front, the two blue-blazers in back. Granite made a small nod. One of the blazers produced a gun and aimed at Myron's head.

This was not good.

There are ways of disarming a man with a gun, but there's an inherent problem: It might not work. If you miscalculate or if your opponent is better than you think – something not unlikely in an opponent who knows how to handle a gun – you could get shot. That's a serious drawback. And in this particular situation there were two other opponents, both of whom looked good and were probably armed. There is a word expert fighters use for a sudden move at this juncture: *suicide*.

'Whoever did your research on me left something out,' Myron said.

'What might that be?'

'My relationship with Win.'

Granite Man didn't flinch. 'You mean Windsor Horne Lockwood the Third? Family owns Lock-Horne Security and Investments on Park Avenue. Your college roommate from Duke. Since moving out of the Spring Street loft you shared with Jessica Culver, you've been living at his apartment in the Dakota. You have close business and personal ties, might even be called best friends. That relationship?'

'That would be the one,' Myron said.

'I am aware of it. I am also aware of Mr Lockwood's' – he paused, searching for the word – 'talents.'

'Then you know that if that bozo gets itchy' – Myron head-gestured toward the blazer with the gun – 'you die.'

Granite Man wrestled with his facial muscles and this time he achieved a smile, though not without effort. Heart's song 'Barracuda' played in Myron's head. 'I am not without my own, uh, talents, Mr Bolitar.'

'If you really believe that,' Myron said, 'then you don't know enough about Win's, uh, talents.'

'I won't debate the point. But I will point out that he doesn't have an army like this at his disposal. Now, are you going to tell me why you're asking about Dennis Lex?'

'I told you,' Myron said.

'You're really going to stick with the dying-child story?'

'It's the truth.'

'And how did you get Dennis Lex's name?'

'From the bone marrow center.'

'They just gave it to you?'

Myron's turn. 'I too am not without my own, uh, talents.' It somehow didn't sound right when he said it about himself.

'So you're saying that the bone marrow center told you that Dennis Lex was a donor – that about right?'

'I'm not saying anything,' Myron said. 'Look, this is a two-way street here. I want some information.'

'Wrong,' Granite Man said. 'It's a one-way street. I'm a Mack truck. You're like an egg in the road.'

Myron nodded. 'Cutting,' he said. 'But if you're not going to give me anything, I'm not giving you anything.'

The guy with the gun stepped closer.

Myron felt a quiver in his legs, but he didn't blink. Maybe he did overplay the wisecracks, but you don't show fear. Ever. 'And let's not pretend you're going to shoot me over this. We both know you won't. You're not that stupid.'

Granite Man smiled. 'I might beat on you a bit.'

'You don't want trouble, I don't want trouble. I don't care about this family or its fortune or any of that. I'm just trying to save a kid's life.'

Granite Man played air violin for a moment. Then he said, 'Dennis Lex is not your salvation.'

'And I'm just supposed to believe you?'

'He's not your donor. That much I personally guarantee.'

'Is he dead?'

Granite Man folded his arms across his paddleball-court chest. 'If you're telling the truth, the bone marrow people either lied to you or made a mistake.'

'Or you're lying to me,' Myron said. Then added, 'Or you're making a mistake.'

'The guards will show you out.'

'I can still go to the press.'

Granite Man walked away then. 'We both know you won't,' he said. 'You're not that stupid either.'

16

Bruce Taylor was in print-journalist garb – like he'd gone to his laundry hamper and dug out whatever was on the bottom. He sat at the bar, scooped up the free pretzels, and pushed them into his mouth as though he were trying to swallow his palm.

'Hate these things,' he said to Myron.

'Yeah, I can see that.'

'I'm at a bar, for crying out loud. I gotta eat something. But nobody serves peanuts anymore. Too fattening or some such crap. Pretzels instead. And not real pretzels. Little tiny buggers.' He held one up for Myron to see. 'I mean, what's up with that?'

'And the politicians,' Myron said. 'They spend all that time on gun control.'

'So what do you want to drink? And don't ask for that Yoo-Hoo crap here. It's embarrassing.'

'What are you having?'

'The same thing I always have when you pay. Twelve-year-old Scotch.'

'I'll just have a club soda with lime.'

'Wuss.' He ordered it. 'What do you want?'

'You know Stan Gibbs?'

Bruce said, 'Whoa.'

'What whoa?'

'I mean, whoa, you get involved in some hairy-ass shit, Myron. But Stan Gibbs? What the hell could you possibly have to do with him?'

'Probably nothing.'

'Uh-huh.'

'Just tell me about him, okay?'

Bruce shrugged, took a sip of Scotch. 'Ambitious s.o.b. who went too far. What else do you need to know?'

'The whole story.'

'Starting with?'

'What exactly did he do?'

'He plagiarized a story, the dumbass. That's not unusual. But to be so stupid about it.'

'Too stupid?' Myron asked.

'What do you mean?'

'I mean we both agree that stealing from a published novel is not only unethical but idiotic.'

'So?'

'So I'm asking if it's *too* idiotic.'

'You think he's innocent, Myron?'

'Do you?'

He chucked down a few more pretzels. 'Hell no. Stan Gibbs is guilty as sin. And as stupid as he was, I know plenty stupider. How about Mike Barnicle? The guy steals jokes from a George Carlin book. George Carlin, for chrissake.'

'Does seem pretty stupid,' Myron agreed.

'And he's not the only one. Look, Myron, every profession's got their dirty laundry, right? The stuff they want swept under the rug. Cops got their blue line when one of them pounds a suspect into the earth. Doctors cover each other's asses when they take out the wrong gallbladder or whatever. Lawyers . . . well, don't even get me started on their dirty little secrets.'

'And plagiarism is yours?'

'Not just plagiarism,' Bruce said. 'Wholesale fabrication. I know reporters who make up sources. I know guys who make up dialogue. I know guys who make up whole conversations. They run stories about crack mothers and inner-city gang leaders who never existed. Ever read those columns? Ever wonder why so many drug addicts, say, sound so friggin' poignant when they can't even watch *Teletubbies* without a tutor?'

'And you're saying this happens a lot?'

'Truth?'

'Preferably.'

'It's epidemic,' Bruce said. 'Some guys are lazy. Some are too ambitious. Some are just pathological liars. You know the type.

They'll lie to you about what they had for breakfast just because it comes so naturally.'

The drinks came. Bruce pointed at the empty pretzel bowl. The bartender replaced it.

'So if it's so epidemic,' Myron said, 'how come so few get caught?'

'First off, it's hard to catch. People hide behind anonymous sources and claim people moved, stuff like that. Second, it's like I said before. It's our dirty little secret. We keep it buried.'

'I'd think you'd want to clean house.'

'Oh, right. Like cops want to. Like doctors want to.'

'You're not the same thing, Bruce.'

'Let me give you a scenario, Myron, okay?' Bruce finished up his drink, and now he pointed to his glass for a refill. 'You're an editor with, say, *The New York Times*. A story is written for you. You print it. Now it's brought to your attention that the story was fabricated or plagiarized or maybe just totally inaccurate, whatever. What do you do?'

'Retract it,' Myron said.

'But you're the editor. You're the dumbass responsible for its publication. You're probably the dumbass who hired the writer in the first place. Who do you think the higher-ups are going to blame? And do you think the higher-ups are going to be happy to hear that their paper printed something false? You think the *Times* wants to lose business to the *Herald* or the *Post* or whatever? And hell, the other papers don't even want to hear about it. The public already doesn't trust us as an institution, right? If the truth gets out, who gets hurt? Answer: everyone.'

'So you quietly fire the guy,' Myron said.

'Maybe. But, again, you're this editor for *The New York Times*. You fire, say, a columnist. Don't you think a higher-up is going to want to know why?'

'So you just let it go?'

'We're like the church used to be with pedophiles. We try to control the problem without hurting ourselves. We transfer the guy to another department. We pass the problem to someone else. Maybe we team him up with another writer. Harder to make shit up with someone looking over your shoulder.'

Myron took a sip of his club soda. Flat. 'Okay, let me ask the obvious question then. How did Stan Gibbs get caught?'

'He was dumb, dumber and dumbest. It was too high profile a piece to plagiarize like that. Not only that, but Stan rubbed the feds' face in a public crapper and flushed. You don't do that if you don't have the facts, especially to the feds. My guess is he thought he was safe because the novel had a negligible print run from some shitass vanity press in Oregon. I don't think they published more than five hundred copies of the thing, and that was more than twenty years ago. And the author was long dead.'

'But someone dug it up.'

'Yup.'

Myron thought about it. 'Strange, don't you think?'

'Most of the time I'd say yes, but not when it's this high-profile. And once the truth was uncovered, boom, Stan was done. Every media outlet got an anonymous press release about it. The feds held a press conference. I mean, there was almost a campaign against him. Someone – probably the feds – were out for their pound of flesh. And they got it.'

'So maybe the feds were so pissed they set him up.'

'How do you figure?' Bruce countered. 'The novel exists. The passages Stan copied exist. There is no way around that.'

Myron mulled that one over, looking for a way around it. Nothing came to him. 'Did Stan Gibbs ever defend himself?'

'He never commented.'

'Why not?'

'The guy's a reporter. He knew better. Look, stories like these become the worst kind of brushfire. Only way to get the fire out is to stop feeding the flame. No matter how bad, if there's nothing new to report – nothing new to feed the flame – it dies out. People always make the mistake of thinking they can douse the flame with their words, that they're so smart, their explanations will work like water or something. It's always a mistake to talk to the press. Everything – even wonderfully worded denials – feed the flames and keep it stoked.'

'But doesn't silence make you look guilty?'

'He *is* guilty, Myron. Stan could only get himself in more trouble by talking. And if he hung around and tried to defend himself, someone would dig into his past too. Mainly his old columns. All of them. Every fact, every quote, everything. And if you've plagiarized one story, you've plagiarized others. You don't do it for the first time when you're Stan's age.'

'So you think he was trying to minimize the damage?'

Bruce smiled, took a sip. 'That Duke education,' he said. 'It wasn't wasted on you.' He grabbed more pretzels. 'Mind if I order a sandwich?'

'Suit yourself.'

'It'll be worth it,' Bruce said with a suddenly big smile. 'Because I haven't yet mentioned the last little tidbit that convinced him to keep quiet.'

'What's that?'

'It's big, Myron.' The smile slid off his face. 'Very big.'

'Fine, order fries too.'

'I don't want this to become public knowledge, you understand?'

'Come on, Bruce. What?'

Bruce turned back to the bar. He picked up a cocktail napkin and tore it in half. 'You know the feds took Stan to court to find his sources.'

'Yes.'

'The court documents were kept sealed, but there was a bit of nastiness. See, they wanted Stan to provide some sort of corroboration. Something to show he didn't totally make the story up. He wouldn't offer any. For a while he claimed that only the families could back him and he wouldn't give them up. But the judge pressed. He finally admitted that there was one other person who could back his story.'

'Back up his made-up story?'

'Yes.'

'Who?'

'His mistress,' Bruce said.

'Stan was married?'

'Guess the word "mistress" gave it away,' Bruce said. 'Anyway, he was. Still is, technically, but now they're separated. Naturally Stan was hesitant about naming her – he loved his wife, had two kids, the backyard, whatever – but in the end he gave the judge her name under the condition that it stay sealed.'

'Did the mistress back him?'

'Yes. This mistress – one Melina Garston – claimed to have been with him when he met the Sow the Seeds psycho.'

Myron's brow creased. 'Why does that name ring a bell?'

'Because Melina Garston is dead now. Tied and tortured and you don't want to know what.'

'When?'

'Three months ago. Right after the shit hit Stan's fan. Worse, the police think Stan did it.'

'To keep her from telling the truth?'

'Again that Duke education.'

'But that makes no sense. She was killed after the plagiarism was discovered, right?'

'Right after, yeah.'

'So it was too late by then. Everyone thinks he's guilty already. He's lost his job. He's disgraced. If his mistress now comes out and says "Yeah, I lied," it wouldn't really change a thing. What would Stan have gained by killing her?'

Bruce shrugged. 'Maybe her retraction would have removed any doubt.'

'But there's not much doubt there anyway.'

The bartender came over. Bruce ordered a sandwich. Myron shook him off. 'Can you find out where Stan Gibbs is hiding?'

Bruce waved down the bartender again. 'I already know.'

'How?'

'He was my friend.'

'Was or is?'

'Is, I guess.'

'You like him?'

'Yeah,' Bruce said. 'I like him.'

'Yet, you still think he did it.'

'Murder, probably not. Plagiarize ...' He shrugged. 'I'm a cynical guy. And just because a guy is a friend of mine doesn't mean he can't do dumb things.'

'Will you give me his address?'

'Will you tell me why?'

Myron sipped his flat club soda. 'Okay, this is the part where you say you want to know what I have. Then I say I have nothing and when I do, you'll be the first to know. Then you get kinda huffy and say I owe you and that's not good enough, but in the end you take the deal. So why don't we skip all that and just give me the address?'

'Will I still get my sandwich?'

'Sure.'

'Fine, then,' Bruce said. 'Doesn't matter. Stan hasn't talked to anyone since he resigned – not even his close friends. What makes you think he'll talk to you?'

'Because I'm a witty dinner companion and natty dresser?'

'Yeah, that.' He turned to Myron and looked at him heavily. 'Now, this is the part where I tell you that if you find anything, anything, that suggests that Stan Gibbs is being set up, you tell me because I'm his friend and I'm a reporter hungry for a big story.'

'Not to mention a sandwich.'

No smile. 'You got me?'

'Got you.'

'Anything you want to tell me now?'

'Bruce, I got less than nothing. It's just a thread I need to snip away.'

'You know Cross River in Englewood?'

'A mid-eighties condo development that looks like something out of *Poltergeist*.'

'Twenty-four Acre Drive. Stan just came back to the area. He's renting there.'

17

The Morning Mosh was not really the establishment's name. Located in a converted warehouse downtown on the West Side, the Mosh had a neon sign that changed as the day went on. The word *Mosh* stayed lit all the time, but in the morning it blinked *Morning Mosh*, then *Mid-Day Mosh* (as it now read) and later on, *Midnight Mosh*. And that's *Mosh*, not *Nosh*. Myron had expected a bagel store. But the letter was *M*, not *N*, and this place was *Mosh*. As in *Mosh Pit*. As in some retro heavy-metal band minus the talent blaring sounds that could strip paint while kids danced – and we're using that term in its loosest form here – in a pit, careening off one another like a thousand pinballs released into the machine at the same time.

A sign by the front door read FOUR BODY PIERCE MINIMUM TO ENTER (EARS DON´T COUNT).

Myron stayed on the sidewalk and used his cell phone. He called the Mosh's number. A voice answered, 'Go for it, dude.'

'Suzze T please.'

'Dig.'

Dig?

Suzze came on two minutes later. 'Hello?'

'It's Myron. I'm out on the curb.'

'Come in. No one bites. Well, except for that guy who bit the legs off a live frog last night. Man, that was so cool.'

'Suzze, please meet me out here, okay?'

'What-ev-er.'

Myron hung up, feeling old. Suzze came out less than a minute later. She wore bell-bottom jeans with a gravity-defying waist that stayed up south of her hips. Her top was pink and much too small, revealing not only a flat stomach but a bottom-side hint of what

113

interested the fine folks at Rack Enterprises. Suzze sported only one tattoo (a tennis racket with a snake's head grip) and no piercings, not even her ears.

Myron pointed to the sign. 'You don't meet the minimum piercing requirement.'

'Yeah, Myron, I do.'

Silence. Then Myron said, 'Oh.'

They started walking down the street. Another strange Manhattan neighborhood. Kids and the homeless hung out together. There were bars and nightclubs alongside daycare centers. The modern city. Myron passed a storefront with a sign: TATTOOS WHILE U WAIT. He reread the sign and frowned. Like how else would you do it?

'We got a weird endorsement offer,' Myron said. 'You know the Rack Bars?'

Suzze said, 'Like, upscale topless, right?'

'Well, topless anyway.'

'What about them?'

'They're opening up a chain of topless coffee bars.'

Suzze nodded. 'Cool,' she said. 'I mean, taking the popularity of Starbucks and mixing it with Scores and Goldfingers, well, it's totally wise.'

'Uh, right. Anyway, they're having this big grand opening and they're trying to generate excitement and media attention and all that. So they want you to make a, uh, guest appearance.'

'Topless?'

'Like I said on the phone, I had an offer I wanted you to refuse.'

'Totally topless?'

Myron nodded. 'They insist on nipple visibility.'

'How much they willing to pay?'

'Two hundred thousand dollars.'

She stopped. 'Are you shitting me?'

'I shit you not.'

She whistled. 'Lots of cha-ching.'

'Yes, but I still think—'

'This was, like, their first offer?'

'Yes.'

'Do you think you could get them up?'

'No, that would be your job.'

She stopped and looked at him. Myron shrugged his apology. 'Tell them yes,' she said.

'Suzze . . .'

'Two hundred grand for flashing a bit of booby? Christ, last night I think I did it in there for free.'

'That isn't the same thing.'

'Did you see what I wore in *Sports Illustrated*? I might as well have been naked.'

'That isn't the same thing either.'

'This is Rack, Myron, not some sleazoid place like Buddy's. It's upscale topless.'

'Saying "upscale topless" is like saying "good toupee," ' Myron said.

'Huh?'

'It might be good,' he said, 'but it's still a toupee.'

She cocked her head. 'Myron, I'm twenty-four years old.'

'I know that.'

'That's like 107 in women-tennis years. I'm ranked thirty-one in the world right now. I haven't made two hundred grand over the past two years on tour. This is a big score, Myron. And man, will it change my image.'

'Exactly my point.'

'No, listen up, tennis is looking for draws. I'll be controversial. I'll get tons of attention. I'll suddenly be a big name. Admit it, my appearance fees will quadruple.'

Appearance fees are the money paid to the big names just to show up, win or lose. Most name players make far more in appearance fees than prize money. It's where the potential major *dinero* is, especially for a player ranked thirty-first.

'Probably,' Myron said.

She stopped and grabbed his arm. 'I love playing tennis.'

'I know that,' he said softly.

'Doing this will extend my career. That means a lot to me, okay?'

Christ, she looked so young.

'All of what you're saying may be true,' Myron said. 'But at the end of the day, you're still appearing at a topless bar. And once it's done, it's done. You will always be remembered as the tennis player who appeared topless.'

'There are worse things.'

'Yes. But I didn't become an agent to get in the stripping business. I'll do what you want. You're my client. I want what's best for you.'

'But you don't think this is best for me?'

'I have trouble advising a young woman to appear topless.'

'Even if it makes sense?'

'Even if it makes sense.'

She smiled at him. 'You know something, Myron? You're cute when you're being a prude.'

'Yeah, adorable.'

'Tell them yes.'

'Think about it for a few days, okay?'

'It's a no-brainer, Myron. Just do what you do best.'

'What's that?'

'Get the number up. And tell them yes.'

18

Cross River Condos was one of those complexes that looked like a movie façade, like whole buildings might topple over if you pushed against any one wall. The development was sprawlingly cramped, with every building looking exactly the same. Walking through it was like something out of *Alice in Wonderland*, all avenues mirroring the others, until you got dizzy. Have too much drink and you're bound to stick your key in the wrong lock.

Myron parked near the complex pool. The place was nice but too close to Route 80, the major artery that ran from, well, here in New Jersey to California. The traffic sounds sloshed over the fence. Myron located the door to 24 Acre Drive and then tried to figure out which windows belonged to it. If he had it right, the lights were on. So was the television. He knocked on the door. Myron saw a face peer through the window next to the door. The face did not speak.

'Mr Gibbs?'

Through the glass, the face said, 'Who are you?'

'My name is Myron Bolitar.'

A brief pause. 'The basketball player?'

'At one time, yes.'

The face looked through the window for a few more seconds before opening the door. The odor of too many cigarettes wafted through the opening and happily nested inside Myron's nostrils. Not surprisingly, Stan Gibbs had a cigarette in his mouth. He had a gray stubble-to-beard going, too far gone for retro *Miami Vice*. He wore a yellow Bart Simpson sweatshirt, dark green sweatpants, socks, sneakers, and a Colorado Rockies baseball cap – the standard fashion fare shared with equal fervor by joggers and couch potatoes. Myron suspected the latter here.

'How did you find me?' Stan Gibbs asked.

'It wasn't difficult.'

'That's not an answer.'

Myron shrugged.

'It doesn't matter,' Stan said. 'I have no comment.'

'I'm not a reporter.'

'So what are you?'

'A sports agent.'

Stan took a puff of the cigarette, didn't remove it from his mouth. 'Sorry to disappoint you, but I haven't played competitive football since high school.'

'May I come in?'

'No, I don't think so. What do you want?'

'I need to find the kidnapper you wrote about in your article,' Myron said.

Stan smiled with very white teeth, especially when you considered the smoking. His skin was sort of clumpy and winter-colorless, his hair thin and tired, but he had those bright eyes, superbright eyes, the kind that look like supernatural beacons are shining out from within. 'Don't you read the papers?' he asked. 'I made the whole thing up.'

'Made it up or copied it from a book?'

'I stand corrected.'

'Or maybe you were telling the truth. In fact, maybe the subject of your articles called me on the phone last night.'

Stan shook his head, the growing ash on the cigarette holding on like a kid on an amusement park ride. 'This is not something I want to revisit.'

'Did you plagiarize the story?'

'I already said I wouldn't comment—'

'This isn't for public consumption. If you did – if the story was a fake – just tell me now and I'll go away. I don't have time to waste on false leads.'

'Nothing personal,' Stan said, 'but you're not making a whole lot of sense here.'

'Does the name Davis Taylor mean anything to you?'

'No comment.'

'How about Dennis Lex?'

That threw him. The dangling cigarette started to slip from

Stan's lips, but he caught it with his right hand. He dropped it on the walkway and watched it sizzle for a moment.

'Maybe you better come in.'

The condo was a duplex centered with that staple of new American contruction, the cathedral ceiling. Plenty of light came in from the big windows, splashing down on a decor straight out of a Sunday circular. A blond-wood entertainment center took up one wall, a matching coffee table not far from it. There was also a white-and-blue-striped couch – Myron would bet his lunch money it was a Serta Sleeper – and matching love seat. The carpeting was the same neutral as the exterior, a sort of inoffensive tan, and the place was clean yet disorderly in a divorcé way, newspapers and magazines and books piled here and there, nothing really put in a specific place.

He had Myron sit on the couch. 'Want something to drink?'

'Sure, whatever,' Myron said. The coffee table had one photograph on it. A man had his arms around two boys. All three were smiling too hard, like they'd just come in second place and didn't want to appear disappointed. They were standing in a garden of some sort. Behind them loomed a marble statue of a woman with a bow and arrow over her shoulder. Myron picked up the frame and studied it. 'This you?'

Gibbs lifted his head while scooping a handful of ice into a glass. 'I'm on the right,' he said. 'With my brother and my father.'

'Who's that a statue of?'

'Diana the Huntress. You familiar with her?'

'Didn't she turn into Wonder Woman?'

Stan chuckled. 'Sprite okay?'

Myron put the photograph down. 'Sure.'

Stan Gibbs poured the drink, brought it out to Myron, handed it to him. 'What do you know about Dennis Lex?'

'Just that he exists,' Myron said.

'So why mention his name to me?'

Myron shrugged. 'Why did you react so strongly to hearing it?'

Gibbs took out another cigarette, lit it. 'You're the one who came to me.'

'True.'

'Why?'

No secret. 'I'm looking for a man named Davis Taylor. He's a bone marrow donor who matched a kid and then vanished. I traced him to an address in Connecticut, but he's not there. So I dug a little more and found out that Davis Taylor is a name change. His real name is Dennis Lex.'

'I still don't see what this has to do with me.'

'This might sound a little nutty,' Myron said. 'But I left a voice mail message for Davis Taylor né Dennis Lex. When he called back, he made little sense. But he kept telling me to "sow the seeds." '

A small quake ran through Stan Gibbs. It passed quickly. 'What else did he say?'

'That was pretty much it. I should sow the seeds. I should say good-bye to the child. Stuff like that.'

'It's probably nothing,' Gibbs said. 'He probably just read my article and decided to have a little fun at your expense.'

'Probably,' Myron said. 'Except that wouldn't really explain your reaction to Dennis Lex's name.'

Stan shrugged, but there wasn't much behind it. 'The family is famous.'

'If I said Ivana Trump, would you have reacted the same?'

Gibbs stood. 'I need some time to think about this.'

'Think out loud,' Myron said.

Stan just shook his head.

'Did you make up the story, Stan?'

'Another time.'

'Not good enough,' Myron said. 'You owe me something here. Did you plagiarize the story?'

'How do you expect me to answer that?'

'Stan?'

'What?'

'I don't care about your situation. I'm not here to judge you or tell on you. I don't give a rat's ass if you made up the story or not. All I care about is finding the bone marrow donor. Period. End of story. *El Fin.*'

Stan's eyes started to well up. He took another puff of the cigarette. 'No,' he said. 'I never plagiarized. I never saw that book in my life.'

It was like the room had been holding its breath and finally let go.

'How do you explain the similarities between your article and that novel?'

He opened his mouth, stopped, shook his head.

'Your silence makes you look guilty.'

'I don't have to explain anything to you.'

'Yeah, you do. I'm trying to save a kid's life here. You're not that wrapped up in your problems, are you, Stan?'

Stan moved back into the kitchen. Myron stood and followed him. 'Talk to me,' Myron said. 'Maybe I can help.'

'No,' he said. 'You can't.'

'How do you explain the similarities, Stan? Just tell me that, okay? You must have thought about it.'

'I don't need to think about it.'

'Meaning?'

He opened the refrigerator and grabbed another can of Sprite. 'Do you think all psychotics are original?'

'I'm not following you.'

'You received a call from a guy who told you about sowing the seeds.'

'Right.'

'There are two possibilities that explain why he did that,' Stan said. 'One, he is the same killer I wrote about. Or two?' Stan looked at Myron.

'He just repeated what he'd read in the article,' Myron said.

Stan snapped and pointed at Myron.

'So you're saying that the kidnapper you interviewed read this novel and it, what, influenced him somehow? That he copied it?'

Stan took a swig from the can. 'That's a theory,' he said.

And a damn good one, Myron thought. 'So why didn't you say that to the press? Why didn't you defend yourself?'

'None of your goddamn business.'

'Some people say it's because you were afraid they'd look closer at your work. That they'd find other fabrications.'

'And some people are morons,' he finished.

'So why didn't you fight?'

'I spent my whole life being a journalist,' Stan said. 'Do you know what it means for a journalist to be called a plagiarist? It's like a daycare worker being called a child molester. I'm done. No words can change that. I've lost everything to this scandal. My wife, my kids, my job, my reputation—'

'Your mistress?'

He shut his eyes suddenly, tightly, like a child trying to make the bogeyman go away.

'The police think you killed Melina,' Myron said.

'I'm well aware of that.'

'Tell me what's going on here, Stan.'

He opened his eyes and shook his head. 'I have to make some calls, check out some leads.'

'You can't just cut me loose.'

'I have to,' he said.

'Let me help.'

'I don't need your help.'

'But I need yours.'

'Not right now,' Stan said. 'You'll have to trust me on this.'

'I'm not big on trust,' Myron said.

Stan smiled. 'Neither am I,' he said. 'Neither am I.'

19

Myron pulled out. So, too, he noticed, did two men in a black Oldsmobile Ciera. Hmm.

The cell phone rang.

'Have you learned anything?' It was Emily.

'Not really,' Myron said.

'Where are you?'

'Englewood.'

'Do you have any plans for dinner?' Emily asked.

Myron hesitated. 'No.'

'I'm a good cook, you know. We dated in college, so I didn't have much chance to demonstrate my culinary skills.'

'I remember you cooking for me once,' Myron said.

'I did?'

'In my wok.'

Emily chuckled. 'That's right, you had an electric wok in your dorm, right?'

'Yep.'

'I almost forgot about that,' Emily said. 'Why did you have one, anyway?'

'To impress chicks.'

'Really?'

'Sure. I thought I'd invite a girl up to my room, slice up some vegetables, add a little soy sauce—'

'To the vegetables?' she asked.

'For starters.'

'So how come you never pulled that one on me?'

'Didn't have to.'

'You calling me easy, Myron?'

123

'How exactly does one answer that,' Myron asked, 'and maintain possession of both testicles?'

'Come on over,' Emily said. 'I'll make us some dinner. No soy sauce.'

Another hesitation.

'Please don't make me ask again,' Emily said.

He wanted very much to say no. 'Okay.'

'Just take Route 4—'

'I know the way, Emily.'

He hung up then and checked the rearview mirror. The black Oldsmobile Ciera was still following. Better safe than sorry. Myron hit the preprogrammed number on his cell phone. After one ring, Win answered.

'Articulate,' Win said.

'Got a tail, methinks.'

'License plate?'

Myron read it off to him.

'Where should we coordinate?'

'Garden State Plaza mall,' Myron said.

'On my way, fair maiden.'

Myron stayed on Route 4 until he saw a sign for the Garden State Plaza. He took a rather complicated cloverleaf overpass and veered into the mall's lot. The black Olds followed, dropping back a bit. Stall time. Myron circled a few times before finding a parking space. The Olds kept its distance. He turned off the car and headed for the 'Northeast Entrance.'

The Garden State Plaza had all the artificial elements endemic in malls – the mall ear-pop when you enter, the stale mall air, the mall hollow acoustics, as though all sound were traveling through a high-volume distorter – the audial equivalent of a shower door, voices somehow rendered both loud and incomprehensible. Too much with the high ceilings and faux marble, nothing soft to cushion the sound.

He strolled through the nouveau riche section of the Garden State Plaza, past several barren shoe stores, the kind that display maybe three pairs of shoes on the ends of what look like deer antlers. He reached a store called Aveda, which sold wildly overpriced cosmetics and lotions. The Aveda saleswoman, a starving young thang in tourniquet-tight black, informed Myron that they were having a sale on face moisturizers. Myron refrained from crying out 'Yippee!' and went on his way. Victoria's Secret was next, and Myron did that male surreptitious glance at the lingerie window displays. Most of your more sophisticated heterosexual males are well versed in this art, awarding the racily clad supermodels the most casual of once-overs, feigning a lack of interest in the blown-up, blown-clear images of Stephanie and Frederique in Miracle Bras. Myron, of course, did the same thing – and then he thought, why pretend? He stopped short, squared his shoulders, ogled in earnest. Honesty. Shouldn't a woman respect that in a man too?

He checked his watch. Not yet. More stall. The plan, as it were, was fairly simple. Win drives to the Garden State Plaza. When he arrives, he calls Myron on the cell phone. Myron then goes back to his car. Win looks for the black Olds and follows the followee. Super clever, no?

Myron hit Sharper Image, one of the few places in the world where people use the words *shiatsu* and *ionic* and nobody laughs. He tried out a massage chair (setting: Knead) and debated purchasing a $5,500 life-size statue of a *Star Wars* storm-trooper that had been reduced to a mere $3,499. Talk about redefining nouveau riche. Here's a little tip for you: If you've purchased a Sharper Image life-size *Star Wars* storm-trooper, take out your platinum-est charge card, hand it to the nearest cashier, and buy a life.

The cell phone rang. Myron picked it up.

'They're feds,' Win said.

'Yikes.'

'Yes.'

'No reason to follow them, then.'

'No.'

Myron spotted two men in suits and sunglasses behind him. They were studying the fruit-flavored shampoos in the Garden Botanica store window a little too closely. Two men in suits and sunglasses. Oh, like that happens. 'I think they're following me in here too.'

'If they arrest you with lingerie,' Win said, 'tell them it's for your wife.'

'That what you do?'

'Keep the phone on,' Win said.

Myron did as he asked. An old trick of theirs. Myron kept his cell phone on, thereby freeing Win to listen in. Okay, fine, now what? He kept strolling. Two more men in business suits were window-shopping up ahead. They turned as Myron approached, both staring him down. Some tail. Myron glanced behind him. The first two feds were right there.

The two feds in front of him stepped directly into his path. The other two came up behind him, boxing him in.

Myron stopped, looked at all four feds. 'Did you guys check out the facial moisturizer sale at Aveda?'

'Mr Bolitar?'

'Yes.'

One of them, a short guy with a severe haircut, flashed a badge. 'I'm Special Agent Fleischer with the Federal Bureau of Investigation. We'd like a word with you, sir.'

'What about?'

'Would you mind coming with us?'

They had the standard-issue stone expressions; Myron would get nothing out of them. Probably didn't even know anything themselves. Probably just delivery boys. Myron shrugged and followed them out. Two got into a white Olds Ciera. The other two stayed with Myron. One opened the back door of the black Ciera and head-gestured for Myron to get in. He did so. The interior was very clean. Nice, smooth seats. Myron ran his hand over it.

'Corinthian leather?' he asked.

Special Agent Fleischer turned around. 'No, sir, that would be the Ford Granada.'

Touché.

No one spoke. No radio played. Myron settled back. He debated calling Emily and postponing their soy-sauce-less encounter, but he didn't want the feds to hear him. He sat tight and kept his mouth shut. He didn't do that often. It felt odd and somehow right.

Thirty minutes later, he was in the basement of a modest high-rise in Newark. He sat at a table with his hands on a semi-sticky table. The room had one barred window and cement walls the color and texture of dried oatmeal. The feds excused themselves and left Myron alone. Myron sighed and sat back. He'd figured that this was the old soften-him-up-by-making-him-wait bit, when the door flew open.

The woman was first. She wore a pumpkin-orange blazer, blue jeans, sneakers, and ball-and-chain earrings. The word that came to mind was *husky*. Not big really. Husky. Everything was husky – even her hair, a sort of canned-corn yellow. The guy riding in on her fumes was geeky thin with a pointy head and a small, greased shock of black hair. He looked like an upside-down pencil. He spoke first.

'Good afternoon, Mr Bolitar,' Pencil said.

'Good afternoon.'

'I'm Special Agent Rick Peck,' he said. 'This is Special Agent Kimberly Green.'

The orange-blazered Green did a caged-lion pace. Myron nodded at her. She nodded back but grudgingly, like her teacher had just told her to apologize for something she didn't do.

Pencil Peck continued. 'Mr Bolitar, we'd like to ask you a few questions.'

'What about?'

Peck kept his eyes on his notes and spoke like he was reading. 'Today you visited one Stan Gibbs at 24 Acre Drive. Is that correct?'

'How do you know I didn't visit two Stan Gibbs?'

Peck and Green exchanged a glance. Then Peck said, 'Please, Mr Bolitar, we'd appreciate your cooperation. Did you visit Mr Gibbs?'

'You know I did,' Myron said.

'Fine, thank you.' Peck wrote something down slowly. Then he looked up. 'We'd very much like to know the nature of your visit.'

'Why?'

'You are the first visitor Mr Gibbs has had since moving to his current residence.'

'No, I mean, why do you want to know?'

Green crossed her arms. She and Peck looked at each other again. Peck said, 'Mr Gibbs is part of an ongoing investigation.'

Myron waited. No one said anything. 'Well, that pretty much clears it up.'

'That's all I can say for the moment.'

'Same here.'

'Pardon?'

'If you can't say any more, I can't say any more.'

Kimberly Green put her hands on the table, gave a toothy grimace – husky teeth? – and leaned down like she might take a bite out of him. The canned-corn hair smelled like Pert Plus. She eyeballed him – must have read a memo on intimidating glares – and then spoke for the first time. 'Here's how we're going to play it, asshole. We're going to ask you questions. You're going to listen to them and then you're going to answer them. You got it?'

Myron nodded. 'I want to make sure I got this straight,' he said to her. 'You're playing bad cop, right?'

Peck picked up the ball. 'Mr Bolitar, no one is interested in making trouble here. But we'd very much like your cooperation in this matter.'

'Am I under arrest?' Myron asked.

'No.'

'Bye then.'

He started to stand. Kimberly Green gave him a shove mid-rise and he fell back into the chair. 'Sit down, asshole.' She looked over at Peck. 'Maybe he's part of it.'

'You think so?'

'Why else would he be so reluctant to answer questions?'

Peck nodded. 'Makes sense. An accomplice.'

'We can probably arrest him now,' Green said. 'Lock him up for the night, maybe leak it to the press.'

Myron looked up at her. 'Gasp,' he said. 'Now. I. Am. Really. Scared. Second gasp.'

She narrowed her eyes. 'What did you say?'

'Don't tell me,' Myron said. 'Maybe I'm guilty of aiding and abetting. That's my personal favorite. Does anyone actually get prosecuted for that?'

'You think we're playing games here?'

'I do. And by the way, how come you're all called "special" agent? Doesn't that sound like something someone made up one day? Like a kid's game to raise self-esteem. "We're promoting you from agent to special agent, Barney," and then what, super-special agent?'

Green grabbed his lapels and leaned his chair back. 'You're not funny.'

Myron looked at her hands gripping him. 'Are you for real?'

'You want to try me?' she said.

Peck said, 'Kim.'

She ignored him and kept her glare on Myron. 'This is serious,' she said.

Her tone aimed for angry but came out more like a frightened plea. Two more agents entered. With the four delivery boys, that made eight. This was something big. What, Myron had no idea. The murder of Melina Garston maybe. But that was doubtful. The locals usually handled murders. You don't call in the feds.

The new guys came at Myron in different ways, but there were only so many routes to travel and Myron knew them all. Threatening, friendly, flattering, insulting, building up, belittling, hard, soft, every sell. They denied him the bathroom, they made excuses to keep him longer, all the while they're working him and he's working them and neither one is giving. Sweat started flowing, mostly from them, the stains and stench filling the air, metastasizing into something Myron could swear was genuine fear.

Kimberly Green came in and out and she kept shaking her head at him. Myron wanted to cooperate, but here's the pertinent cliché: Once the genie is out of the bottle, you can't put it back in. He didn't know what they were investigating. He didn't know if it would benefit Jeremy to talk or hurt him. But once he spoke, once his words were in the public domain, he couldn't take them back. Any leverage he might later be able to apply would be gone. So, for now, even if he might want to help, he wouldn't. Not until he learned more. He had the contacts. He could find out quickly enough, make an informed decision.

Sometimes, negotiating meant shutting up.

When things wound down, Myron got up to leave. Kimberly Green blocked his path. 'I'm going to make your life hell,' she said.

'That your way of asking me out?'

She leaned back as if he'd slapped her. When she recovered,

she shook her head slowly. 'You have no idea, do you?'

Shutting up, he reminded himself. Myron pushed past her and headed outside.

20

He called Emily from the car.

'I thought I was being stood up,' she said.

Myron checked out the rearview mirror and spotted what might be another fed tail. No matter. 'Sorry,' he said. 'Something came up.'

'Involving the donor?'

'I don't think so.'

'You still in Jersey?' Emily asked.

'Yes.'

'Come on over. I'll reheat dinner.'

He wanted to say no. 'Okay.'

Franklin Lakes was about sprawling. Everything sprawled. The houses were mostly new construction, big brick mansions on eternal cul-de-sacs, little gates at the front of the driveways that opened with push-button or intercom, like that would really protect the owners from what lay outside the lush lawns and pedicure-clipped hedges. The interiors were sprawling too, dining rooms big enough to house helicopters, remote-controlled blinds, Sub-Zero/Viking Stove kitchens with marble islands that over-looked family rooms the size of movie theaters, always with complicated state-of-the-art entertainment centers.

Myron rang the bell and the door opened and for the first time in his life, Myron was face-to-face with his son.

Jeremy smiled at him. 'Hi.'

Strong, totally alien surges ricocheted haphazardly through Myron, his nervous system melting down and in overdrive all at once. His diaphragm contracted and his lungs stopped. So, he was sure, did his heart. His mouth weakly opened and closed like a dying fish on a boat deck. Tears headed up and pushed toward the eyes.

'You're Myron Bolitar, right?' Jeremy said.

An ocean-shell rushing filled Myron's ears. He managed a nod.

'You played ball against my dad,' Jeremy said, still with the smile that ripped at the corners of Myron's heart. 'In college, right?'

Myron found his voice. 'Yes.'

The kid nodded back. 'Cool.'

'Yeah.'

A horn honked. Jeremy leaned to the right and looked behind Myron. 'That's my ride. Later.'

Jeremy leaped past Myron. Myron numbly turned and watched the boy jog down the driveway. Imagination maybe, but that gait was oh-so-familiar. From Myron's old game films. More surges. *Oh Christ . . .*

Myron felt a hand on his shoulder, but he ignored it and watched the boy. The car door opened and swallowed Jeremy into the darkness. The driver's window slid down and a pretty woman called out, 'Sorry I'm late, Em.'

From behind him, Emily said, 'No problem.'

'I'll take them to school in the morning.'

'Great.'

A wave and the pretty woman's window slid back into place. The car started on its way. Myron watched it disappear down the road. He felt Emily's eyes on him. He slowly turned to her.

'Why did you do that?'

'I thought he'd be gone by now,' Emily said.

'Do I really look that stupid?'

She stepped back into the house. 'I want to show you something.'

Trying to get his legs back, his head wobbly and his internal referee still giving him the eight count, Myron followed her silently up the stairway. She led him down a darkened corridor lined with modern lithographs. She stopped, opened a door, and flipped on the lights. The room was teenage-cluttered, as if someone had put all the belongings in the center of the room and dropped a hand grenade on them. The posters on the walls – Michael Jordan, Keith Van Horn, Greg Downing, Austin Powers, the words

YEAH, BABY! across his middle in pink tie-dye lettering – had been hung askew, all tattered corners and missing pushpins. There was a Nerf basketball hoop on the closet door. There was a computer on the desk and a baseball cap dangling from a desk lamp. The corkboard had a mix of family snapshots and construction-paper crayons signed by Jeremy's sister, all held up by oversized pushpins. There were footballs and autographed baseballs and cheap trophies and a couple of blue ribbons and three basketballs, one with no air in it. There were stacks of computer-game CD-ROMs and a Game Boy on the unmade bed and a surprising amount of books, several opened and facedown. Clothes littered the floor like war wounded; the drawers were half open, shirts and underwear hanging out like they'd been shot mid-escape. The room had the slight, oddly comforting smell of kids' socks.

'He's a slob,' she said. Leaving off the obvious 'like you.'

Myron stayed still.

'He keeps Oxy 10 in his desk drawer,' Emily said. 'He thinks I don't know. He's at that age where crushes keep him up all night, but he's never even kissed a girl.' She walked over to the corkboard and snatched up a photograph of Jeremy. 'He's beautiful, don't you think?'

'This isn't helping, Emily.'

'I want you to understand.'

'Understand what?'

'He's never been kissed. He is going to die and he's never even kissed a girl.'

Myron held up his hands. 'I don't know what you want me to say here.'

'Try to understand, okay?'

'I don't need melodrama. I understand.'

'No, Myron, you don't. You look back at the night and see it as some sort of Gothic blunder. We did something sinful and for that we all paid a heavy price. If we could just go back and erase that tragic mistake, well, it's all so *Hamlet* and *Macbeth*, isn't it? Your ruined basketball career, Greg's future, our marriage – all laid to waste in that one moment of lust.'

'It wasn't lust.'

'Let's not go through that argument again. I don't care what it was. Lust, stupidity, fear, fate. Call it whatever the hell you want to – but I would never want to go back. That "mistake" was the best thing that ever happened to me. Jeremy, our son, came out of that mess. Do you hear what I'm saying? I'd destroy a million careers and marriages for him.'

She looked at him, challenging. He said nothing.

'I'm not religious and I don't believe in fate or destiny or any of that,' she went on. 'But maybe, just maybe, there had to be a balance. Maybe the only way to produce something so wonderful was to surround the event with so much destruction.'

Myron started backing out of the room. 'This isn't helping,' he said again.

'Yes,' she said, 'it is.'

'You want me to find the donor. I'm trying to do that. But this kind of distraction doesn't help. I need to stay detached.'

'No, Myron, you need attachment. You need to get emotional. You have to understand the stakes – sour son, that beautiful boy who opened the door – is going to die before he's even kissed a girl.' She moved closer to him and looked into his eyes and Myron thought that her eyes had never looked so clear before.

'I watched you play every game at Duke,' she said. 'I fell in love with you on that court – not because you were the team star or because you were graceful or athletic. You were so open out there, so raw and emotional. And the more emotional you got, the more pressure there was, the better you played. If the game was a blowout, you lost interest. You needed it to matter. You needed to be double-teamed with only a few seconds on the clock. You needed to lose control a little.'

'This isn't a game, Emily.'

'Right,' she said. 'The stakes are higher. The emotion should be higher. I want you desperate, Myron. That's when you're at your best.'

He looked at the photograph of Jeremy, and he knew that he was feeling something that he had never felt before. He blinked, caught the expression on his face in the closet-door mirror, and for a moment he saw his own father staring back.

Emily hugged him then. She buried her face in his shoulder and started to cry. Myron held on tight. They stood that way for several minutes before making their way downstairs. Over dinner,

Emily told him about Jeremy, and he soaked in every story. They moved to the couch and broke out the photo albums. Emily tucked her legs under her, her elbow on the top of the couch, her head leaning on the heel of her hand, and told him more. It was nearly two in the morning when she walked him to the door. They were holding hands.

'I know you spoke to Dr Singh,' she said in the open door.

'Yes.'

She let loose a deep breath. 'I'm just going to say this, okay?'

'Okay.'

'I've been keeping track. I bought one of those home tests. The, uh, optimum conception day will be Thursday.'

He opened his mouth but she stopped him with her hand.

'I know all the arguments against this, but it might be Jeremy's only chance. Don't say anything. Just think about it.'

She closed the door. Myron stared at it for a few moments. He tried to conjure up the moment Jeremy had opened it, the crooked smile on the boy's face, but already the image was hazy and fading fast.

21

First thing in the morning, Myron called Terese. Still no answer. He frowned at the phone. 'Am I getting the big kiss-off?' he asked Win.

'Doubtful,' Win said. He was reading the newspaper and wearing silk pajamas with a matching bathrobe and slippers. Give him a pipe and he could have been something Noël Coward created on an off day.

'What makes you say that?'

'Our Ms Collins appears to be rather direct,' Win said. 'If you were being tossed into the dung heap, you'd know the smell.'

'And then there's the part about my being irresistible to women,' Myron said.

Win turned the page.

'So what's she up to?'

Win tapped his chin with his index finger. 'What's the term you relationship people use? Oh, yes. Space. Perhaps she needs some space.'

' "Needing space" is usually a code phrase for the big kiss-off.'

'Yes, well, whatever.' Win crossed his legs. 'You want me to look into it?'

'Into what?'

'What Ms Collins might be up to.'

'No.'

'Fine,' Win said. 'Let's move on, shall we? Tell me about your encounter with the Federal Bureau of Investigation.'

Myron recapped the interrogation.

'So we don't know what they wanted,' Win said.

'Correct.'

'Not a clue?'

136

'Nothing. Except that they were scared.'

'Curious.'

Myron nodded.

Win took a sip of tea, pinky up. Oh, the horrors that pinky had witnessed, partaken in, even. They sat in Win's formal dining room and used a silver tea set. Victorian mahogany table with lion-paw feet, silver tea set, silver milk pitcher, boxes of Cap'n Crunch and some new cereal called Oreo, which is exactly what you would imagine. 'Theorizing at this juncture is a waste of time. I'll make some calls, see what I can find out.'

'Thanks.'

'I'm still not sure I see a connection between Stan Gibbs and our blood donor.'

'It's a long shot,' Myron agreed.

'More than that. A newspaper columnist makes up a story about a serial kidnapper and now – what? – we think the fictional character is the donor?'

'Stan Gibbs claims the story is real.'

'Does he now?'

'Yes.'

Win rubbed his chin. 'Pray tell, why does he not defend himself?'

'No clue.'

'Presumably because he is guilty,' Win said. 'Man is, above all, selfish. He's into self-preservation. It's instinctive. He does not martyr himself. He cares about one thing above all else: saving his hide.'

'Assuming I agree with your sunny view of human nature, wouldn't you agree that man would lie to save himself?'

'Of course,' Win said.

'So armed with this pretty decent defense – the idea that the serial kidnapper copycatted the novel – why wouldn't Stan use it to defend himself, even if he was guilty of plagiarism?'

Win nodded. 'I like the way you're thinking.'

'Cynically, yes.'

The intercom buzzed. Win pressed the button, and the doorman announced Esperanza. A minute later, she swept into the room, grabbed a chair, and poured herself a bowl of Oreo cereal.

'Why do they always say it's "part of this complete breakfast"?' Esperanza asked. 'Every single time, every single cereal. What's all that about?'

Nobody replied.

Esperanza took a spoonful, looked at Win, head-gestured toward Myron. 'I hate it when he's right,' she said to Win.

'A bad omen,' Win agreed.

Myron said, 'I was right?'

She turned her gaze to Myron. 'I did that school check on Dennis Lex. I tracked down any and all educational institutions any of his siblings or parents had gone to. Nothing. College, high school, middle school – even grammar school. No trace of Dennis Lex.'

'But?' Myron said.

'Preschool.'

'You're kidding me.'

'Nope.'

'You found his preschool?'

'I'm more than just a great piece of ass,' Esperanza said.

Win said, 'Not to me, my dear.'

'You're sweet, Win.'

Win bowed his head slightly.

'Miss Peggy Joyce,' Esperanza said. 'She still teaches and runs the Shady Wells Montessori School for Children in East Hampton.'

'And she remembers Dennis Lex?' Myron said. 'From thirty years ago?'

'Apparently.' Esperanza shoved in another spoonful and tossed Myron a sheet of paper. 'This is her address. She's expecting you this morning. Drive safely now, ya hear?'

22

The car phone rang.

'The old man is a lying sack of shit.' It was Greg Downing.

'What?'

'The geezer is lying.'

'You mean Nathan Mostoni?'

'Jesus Christ, what other old man have I been watching?'

Myron switched ears. 'What makes you think he's lying, Greg?'

'Lots of things.'

'Like?'

'Like starting with Mostoni never hearing from the bone marrow center. Does that sound logical to you?'

He thought of Karen Singh and her dedication and the stakes. 'No,' Myron said, 'but it's like we said before – he might be confused.'

'I don't think so.'

'Why not?'

'Nathan Mostoni goes out plenty on his own, for one thing. Sometimes he acts loony, but other times, he seems just fine. He shops himself. He talks to people. He dresses like a normal person.'

'That doesn't mean anything,' Myron said.

'No? An hour ago he went out, right? So I got close to the house, right up against the back window, and I dialed that number, the one you got for the donor.'

'And?'

'And I hear a phone inside the house ringing.'

That made Myron pause.

'So what do you think we should do?' Greg asked.

'I'm not sure. Have you seen anybody else at the house?'

'Nobody. Mostoni goes out but nobody's been here. And I tell you something else. He looks younger now. I don't know how else to explain it. It's weird. You making any headway on your end?'

'I'm not sure.'

'That's some answer, Myron.'

'The only one I got.'

'So what do you think we should do about Mostoni?'

'I'll have Esperanza do a background check. In the meantime, stay on him.'

'Time's a-ticking away here, Myron.'

'I know that. I'll be in touch.'

He disconnected the call and flipped on the radio. Chaka Khan was singing 'Ain't Nobody Love You Better.' If you can listen to that one without moving your feet, you got some serious rhythm issues. He took the Long Island Expressway east, which was shockingly clear today. Usually the road was more or less a parking lot that swayed forward every couple of minutes.

People always tell you that the Hamptons, the swanky Long Island summer spot where Manhattanites get away from it all by being with other Manhattanites, is best in the off season. You always hear that about vacation spots. People, mostly vacationers themselves, whine through the high-season months, waiting to reach this apex of a theoretically swarmless nirvana. But – and this was the part Myron never understood – no one is ever in the Hamptons in the off months. No one. Downtown is dead to the point of craving tumbleweeds. Shop owners sigh and discount nothing. The restaurants are less crowded, sure, but they're also closed. And hey, let's be honest here, the weather and beaches and even the people-watching are big draws here. Who goes to a Long Island beach in the winter?

The school was in a residential neighborhood with older, more modest homes – a place where the true Long Island regulars, none of whom hang out with Alec and Kim at Nick and Toni's, resided. Myron parked in a church lot and followed the signs down the steps into the rectory's basement. A young woman, a hall monitor of sorts, greeted Myron at the landing. He gave her his name and said he was here to see Ms Joyce. The young woman nodded and told him to follow her.

The corridor was silent. Strange when one considered that this was a preschool. *Preschool.* Another new term. In Myron's day, they had called them nursery schools. Myron wondered when the name had changed and what group had considered the term *nursery school* somehow discriminatory. Professional RNs? Breast-feeding mothers? Bottle-fed infants maybe?

Still silent. Perhaps it was vacation or naptime. Myron was about to ask the young hall monitor when she opened a door. He looked in. Wrong-a-mundo. The room was chock full of small children, probably twenty give or take, and they were all working independently and in total silence. The older teacher smiled at Myron. She whispered to the little boy she was working with – he was doing something with blocks and letters – and stood.

'Hello,' she said to Myron, speaking softly.

'Hi,' Myron whispered back.

She leaned toward the young monitor. 'Miss Simmons, will you help Mrs McLaughlin?'

'Of course.'

Peggy Joyce wore an open yellow sweater over a buttoned-at-the-neck blouse. The collar was frilly. She had half-moon glasses dangling from a chain around her neck. 'We can chat in my office.'

'Okay.' He followed her. The place was silent as, well, a place without children. Myron asked, 'Do you give those kids Valium?'

She smiled. 'Just a little Montessori.'

'A little what?'

'You don't have children, do you?'

The question caused a pang, but he answered in the negative. 'It's a teaching philosophy created by Dr Maria Montessori, Italy's first female physician.'

'It seems to work.'

'I suppose.'

'Do the children act like this at home?'

'Good Lord, no. Truth be told, it doesn't translate into the real world. But few things do.'

They moved into the office, which consisted of a wooden desk, three chairs, one file cabinet.

'How long have you taught here?' Myron asked.

'I'm in my forty-third year.'

'Wow.'

'Yes.'

'I guess you've seen lots of changes?'

'In kids? Almost none. Children don't change, Mr Bolitar. A five-year-old is still a five-year-old.'

'Still innocent.'

She cocked her head. ' "Innocent" isn't the word I would use. Children are total id. They are perhaps the most naturally vicious creatures on God's green earth.'

'Strange outlook for a preschool teacher.'

'Just an honest one.'

'So what word would you use?'

She thought about it. 'If pressed, I'd say "unformed." Or maybe "undeveloped." Like a picture you've already taken but haven't processed yet.'

Myron nodded, though he had no idea what she meant. There was something about Peggy Joyce that was a little, well, scary.

'Do you remember that book *All I Really Need to Know I Learned in Kindergarten*?' she asked him.

'Yes.'

'It's true, but not in the way you think. School removes children from their warm parental cocoon. School teaches them to bully or be bullied. School teaches them how to be cruel to one another. School teaches them that Mommy and Daddy lied to them when they told them that they were special and unique.'

Myron said nothing.

'You don't agree?'

'I don't teach preschool.'

'That's sidestepping, Mr Bolitar.'

Myron shrugged. 'They learn socialization. That's a hard lesson. And like every hard lesson, you have to get it wrong before you can get it right.'

'They learn boundaries, in other words?'

'Yes.'

'Interesting. And perhaps true. But you remember when I was giving the film-processing example earlier?'

'Yes.'

'School only processes the picture. It doesn't snap it.'

'Okay,' Myron said, not wanting to follow her train of thought.

'What I mean is, everything is pretty much decided by the time

142

these children leave here and enter kindergarten. I can tell who will be successful and who will fail, who will end up happy and who will end up in prison, and ninety per cent of the time I'm right. Maybe Hollywood and video games have an influence, I don't know. But I can usually tell which kid will be watching too many violent movies or playing too many violent games.'

'You can tell all this by the time they're five years old?'

'Pretty much, yes.'

'And you feel that's it? That they don't have the ability to change?'

'The ability? Oh, probably. But they're already on a path, and while they may still be able to change it, the majority do not. Staying on the path is easier.'

'So let me ask you the eternal question: Is it nature or nurture?'

She smiled. 'I get asked that all the time.'

'And?'

'I answer nurture. Know why?'

Myron shook his head.

'Believing in nurture is like believing in God. You might be wrong, but you might as well cover your bases.' She folded her hands and leaned forward. 'Now, what can I do for you, Mr Bolitar?'

'Do you remember a student named Dennis Lex?'

'I remember all my students. Does that surprise you?'

Myron didn't want her going off on another tangent. 'Did you teach the other Lex children?'

'I taught them all. Their father made a lot of changes after his book became a bestseller. But he kept them here.'

'So what can you tell me about Dennis Lex?'

She sat back and regarded him as though seeing him for the first time. 'I don't want to be rude, but I'm wondering when you're going to tell me what this is all about. I'm talking to you, Mr Bolitar – and breaching confidences, I suspect – because I think you're here for a very specific reason.'

'What reason is that, Ms Joyce?'

Her eyes had a steely glint. 'Don't play games with me, Mr Bolitar.'

She was right. 'I'm trying to find Dennis Lex.'

Peggy Joyce kept still.

'I know this sounds weird,' he went on. 'But as far as I can tell, he fell off the earth after preschool.'

She stared straight ahead, though Myron had no idea at what. There were no photographs on the walls, no diplomas, no drawings by little hands. Just cold wall. 'Not after,' she said finally. 'During.'

There was a knock on the door. Peggy Joyce said, 'Come in.' The young hall monitor, Miss Simmons, entered with a little boy. His head was down and he'd been crying. 'James needs a little time,' Miss Simmons said.

Peggy Joyce nodded. 'Let him lie on the mat.'

James eyed Myron and left with Miss Simmons.

Myron turned to Peggy Joyce. 'What happened to Dennis Lex?'

'It's a question I've been waiting for someone to ask for more than thirty years,' she said.

'What's the answer?'

'First, tell me why you're looking for him.'

'I'm trying to find a bone marrow donor. I think it might be Dennis Lex.' He gave her as few details as he could. When he finished, she put a bony hand to her face.

'I don't think I can help you,' she said. 'It was so long ago.'

'Please, Ms Joyce. A child will die if I don't find him. You're my only lead.'

'You spoke to his family?'

'Only his sister Susan.'

'What did she tell you?'

'Nothing.'

'I'm not sure what I can add.'

'You could start by telling me what Dennis was like.'

She sighed and neatly arranged her hands on her thighs. 'He was like the other Lex children – very bright, thoughtful, contemplative, perhaps a bit too much so for so young a child. With most students, I try to get them to grow up a bit. With the Lex children, that was never an issue.'

Myron nodded, trying to encourage.

'Dennis was the youngest. You probably know that. He was here the same time as his brother Bronwyn. Susan was older.' She stopped, looked lost.

'What happened to him?'

'One day he and Bronwyn didn't come to school. I got a call from their father saying that he was taking them on an unplanned vacation.'

'Where?'

'He didn't say. He wasn't being very specific.'

'Okay, go on.'

'That's pretty much it, Mr Bolitar. Two weeks later, Bronwyn came back to school. I never saw Dennis again.'

'You called his father?'

'Of course.'

'What did he say?'

'He told me that Dennis wouldn't be coming back.'

'Did you ask him why?'

'Of course. But . . . did you ever meet Raymond Lex?'

'No.'

'You didn't question a man like that. He mentioned something about home schooling. When I pressed, he made it clear it was none of my concern. Over the years, I've tried to keep track of the family, even when they moved out of the area. But like you, I never heard anything about Dennis.'

'What did you think happened?'

She looked at him. 'I assumed he was dead.'

Her words, though not all that surprising, worked like a vacuum, sucking the room dry, forcing out the air.

'Why?' Myron asked.

'I figured that he was ill, and that was why he was pulled out of school.'

'Why would Mr Lex try to hide something like that?'

'I don't know. After his novel became a bestseller, he became private to the point of paranoia. Are you sure this donor you're looking for is Dennis Lex?'

'Not sure, no.'

Peggy Joyce snapped her fingers. 'Oh, wait, I have something you may find interesting.' She stood and opened a file drawer. She sifted through it, pulled something out, studied it for a moment. Her elbow smacked the drawer closed. 'This was taken two months before Dennis left us.'

She handed him an old class photograph, the color not so much fading as greening from age. Fifteen kids flanked by two teachers, one a far younger Peggy Joyce. The years had not been unkind to her, but they'd passed anyway. A small black sign with the white lettering read SHADY WELLS MONTESSORI SCHOOL and the year.

'Which one is Dennis?'

She pointed to a boy sitting in the front row. He had a Prince Valiant cut and a face-splitting smile that never quite hit his eyes. 'Can I have this?'

'If you think it will help.'

'It might.'

She nodded. 'I better get back to my students.'

'Thank you.'

'Do you remember your preschool, Mr Bolitar?'

Myron nodded. 'Parkview Nursery School in Livingston, New Jersey.'

'How about your teachers? Do you remember them at all?'

Myron thought about it. 'No.'

She nodded as though he'd answered correctly. 'Good luck,' she said.

23

AgeComp. Or age-progression software, if you prefer.

Myron had learned a bit about it when searching for a missing woman named Lucy Mayor. The key was in the digital imaging. All Myron had to do – or in the case of their office, all Esperanza had to do – was take the class photograph and scan it into the computer. Then, using common software programs like Photo-shop or Picture Publisher, you blow up the face of young Dennis Lex. AgeComp, a software program constantly being retooled and perfected by missing-children organizations, does the rest. Using advanced mathematical algorithms, AgeComp stretches, merges, and blends digital photographs of missing children and produces a color image of what they might look like today.

Naturally, a lot is left to chance. Scarring, facial fractures, facial hair, cosmetic surgery, hairstyle or, in the case of some of the older ones, male pattern baldness. Still, the class photo could be a serious lead.

When he was back in Manhattan, the cell phone rang.

'I spoke to the feds,' Win said.

'And?'

'Your impression is correct.'

'What impression?'

'They are indeed frightened.'

'Did you speak to PT?'

'I did. He put me onto the right person. They requested a face-to-face.'

'When?'

'Pretty pronto. We are, in fact, waiting in your office.'

'The feds are in my office right now?'

'Affirmative.'

'Be there in five.'

More like ten. When the elevator opened, Esperanza was sitting at Big Cyndi's desk.

'How many?' he asked.

'Three,' Esperanza said. 'One blond woman, one extra-strength dork, one nice suit.'

'Win's with them?'

'Yep.'

He handed her the photograph and pointed to Dennis Lex's face. 'How long before we could get an age progression on this?'

'Jesus, when was this taken?'

'Thirty years ago.'

Esperanza frowned. 'You know anything about age progression?'

'Some.'

'It's mostly used to find missing kids,' she said. 'And it's usually used to age them five, maybe ten years.'

'But we can get something, right?'

'Something very rough, yeah maybe.' She flicked on the scanner and placed the photo facedown. 'If they're in the lab, we'll probably have it by the end of the day. I'll crop it and e-mail it over.'

'Do it later,' he said, gesturing toward the door. 'Mustn't keep the feds waiting. Our tax dollars and all that.'

'You want me in there?'

'You're a part of everything that goes on here, Esperanza. Of course I want you in there.'

'I see,' she said. Then: 'Is this the part where I blink back tears because you're making me feel oh-so-special?'

Wiseass.

Myron opened his office door. Esperanza followed. Win sat behind Myron's desk, probably so that none of the feds would. Win could be territorial – just one of the ways he was like a Doberman. Kimberly Green and Rick Peck rose with lack-of-sleep-luggage eyes and squared-off smiles. The third fed stayed in his seat, not moving, not even turning to see who'd entered. Myron saw his face and felt a jolt.

Whoa.

Win watched Myron, an amused smile curling the ends of his

mouth. Eric Ford, deputy director of the Federal Bureau of Investigation, was the man in the suit. His presence meant one thing: This was serious big-time.

Kimberly Green pointed at Esperanza. 'What's she doing in here?'

'She's my partner,' Myron said. 'And it's not polite to point.'

'Your partner? You think this is a business transaction?'

'She stays,' Myron said.

'No,' Kimberly Green said. She was still wearing the ball-and-chain earrings, still the jeans and black turtleneck, but the jacket now was spearmint green. 'We're not exactly thrilled talking to you and Cheekbones boy over there' – she gestured toward Win – 'but at least you have some clearance. We don't know her. She goes.'

Win's smile spread and his eyebrows did a quick up-and-down. Cheekbones. He liked that.

'She goes,' Green said again.

Esperanza shrugged. 'No biggie,' she said.

Myron was about to say something, but Win shook his head. He was right. Save it for the important battles.

Esperanza left. Win got up and gave Myron the chair. He stood on Myron's right, arms crossed, totally at ease. Green and Peck fidgeted. Myron turned to Eric Ford. 'I don't think we've met.'

'But you know who I am,' Ford said. He had one of those smooth soft-rock-DJ voices.

'Yes.'

'And I know who you are,' he said. 'So what would be the point?'

Oookay. Myron glanced back at Win. Win shrugged.

Ford nodded at Kimberly Green. She cleared her throat. 'For the record,' she said, 'we don't think we should have to go through this.'

'Through what?'

'Telling you about our investigation. Debriefing you. As a good citizen, you should be willing to cooperate with our investigation because it's the right thing to do.'

Myron looked at Win and said, 'Oh boy.'

'Some aspects of an investigation need to be contained,' she continued. 'You and Mr Lockwood should understand that better

149

than most. You should be anxious to cooperate with any federal investigation. You should respect what we're trying to do here.'

'Right, okay, we respect. Can we skip ahead, please? You looked us up. You know we'll keep our mouths shut. Otherwise none of us would be here.'

She folded her hands and put them in her lap. Peck kept his head down and scribbled notes, Lord knew on what. Myron's decor maybe. 'What we say here cannot leave this room. It is classified to the highest—'

'Skipping,' Myron said with an impatient hand roll. 'Skipping.'

Green slid her eyes toward Ford. He nodded again. She took a deep breath and said, 'We have Stan Gibbs under surveillance.'

She stopped, settled back. Myron waited a few seconds and then said, 'Label me surprised.'

'That information is classified,' she said.

'Then I'll leave it out of my diary.'

'He isn't supposed to know.'

'Well, that's usually implied with words like "classified" and "surveillance."'

'But Gibbs does know. He loses us whenever he really wants. Because when he's out in public, we can't get too close.'

'Why can't you get too close?'

'He'll see us.'

'But he already knows you're there?'

'Yes.'

Myron looked up at Win. 'Wasn't there an Abbott and Costello skit that went like this?'

'Marx Brothers,' Win said.

'If we were out in the open about tailing him,' Green said, 'the fact that he's a target could become public knowledge.'

'And you're trying to contain that?'

'Yes.'

'How long has he been under surveillance?'

'Well, it's not that simple. He's been out of range a lot—'

'How long?'

Again Green looked at Ford. Again Ford nodded. She balled her hands into fists. 'Since the first article on the kidnappings appeared.'

Myron sat back, feeling something akin to a head rush. He

shouldn't have been surprised, but damned if he wasn't. The article came flooding back to him – the sudden disappearances, the awful phone calls, the constant, eternal anguish, the picket-fenced lives suddenly bulldozed over by inexplicable evil.

'My God,' Myron said. 'Stan Gibbs was telling the truth.'

'We never said that,' Kimberly Green said.

'I see. So you've been tailing him because you don't like his syntax?'

Silence.

'The articles were true,' Myron said. 'And you've known it all along.'

'What we did or did not know is not your concern.'

Myron shook his head. 'Unbelievable,' he said. 'So let me see if I got this straight. You have a serial psycho out there who snatches people out of the blue and torments their families. You want to keep a lid on it because if word got out to the public, you'd have a panic situation. Then the psycho goes directly to Stan Gibbs and suddenly the story is in the public domain . . .' Myron's voice died off, seeing that his logic trail had hit a major pothole. He frowned and forged ahead. 'I don't know how that old novel or the plagiarism charges tie in. But either way, you decided to ride it. You let Gibbs get fired and disgraced, probably in part because you were pissed off that he upset your investigation. But mostly' – he spotted what he thought was a clearing – 'but mostly you did it so you could watch him. If the psycho contacted him once, you figured, he'd probably do it again – especially if the articles had been discredited.'

Kimberly Green said, 'Wrong.'

'But close.'

'No.'

'The kidnappings Gibbs wrote about took place, right?'

She hesitated, gave Ford an eye check. 'We can't verify all of his facts.'

'Jesus, I'm not taking a deposition here,' Myron said. 'Was his column true, yes or no?'

'We've told you enough,' she said. 'It's your turn.'

'You haven't told me squat.'

'And you've told us less.'

Negotiating. Life is being a sports agent – constant negotiating.

He had learned the importance of leverage, of doling out, of being fair. People forget that last one, and it always costs you in the end. The best negotiator isn't the one who gets the whole pie while leaving scant crumbs behind. The best negotiator is the one who gets what he wants while keeping the other side happy. So normally, Myron would dole out a little something here. Classic give-and-take. But not this time. He knew better. Once he told them the reason for his visit to Stan Gibbs, his leverage would be zippo.

The best negotiator, like the best species, also knows how to adapt.

'First answer my question,' Myron said. 'Yes or no, was the story Stan Gibbs wrote true?'

'There is no yes-or-no answer to that,' she said. 'Parts were true. Parts were not true.'

'For example?'

'The young couple was from Iowa, not Minnesota. The missing father had three children, not two.' She stopped, folded her hands.

'But there have been kidnappings?'

'We knew about those two,' she said. 'We had no information about the missing college student.'

'Probably because the psycho got to her parents. They probably never reported it.'

'That's our theory,' Kimberly Green said. 'But we don't know for sure. Still, there are major discrepancies. The families swear they never spoke to him, for example. Many of the phone calls and events don't match what we know to be true.'

Myron saw more clearing. 'So you asked Gibbs about it? About his sources?'

'Yes.'

'And he refused to tell you anything.'

'That's right.'

'So you destroyed him.'

'No.'

'The one part I don't get is the plagiarism,' Myron said. 'I mean, did you guys somehow set that up? I can't see how. Unless you made up a book and . . . no, that's too far-fetched. So what's the deal with that?'

Kimberly Green leaned forward. 'Tell us why you went to his apartment.'

'Not until—'

'For several months we couldn't find Stan Gibbs,' she interrupted. 'We think maybe he left the country. But since he's moved into that condo, he's always alone. As I said before, he loses us sometimes. But he never accepts visitors. Several people have tracked him down. Old friends even. They come to his door or they call on the phone. And you know what always happens, Myron?'

Myron didn't like her tone of voice.

'He sends them away. Every single time. Stan Gibbs sees no one. Except you.'

Myron looked up at Win. Win nodded very slowly. Myron took a look at Eric Ford before going back to Kimberly Green. 'You think I'm the kidnapper?'

She leaned back with a partial shrug, looking satiated. Turning the tables and all that. 'You tell us,' she said.

Win started for the door. Myron rose and followed.

'Where the hell are you two going?' Green asked.

Win grabbed the knob. Myron headed around the desk and said, 'I'm a suspect. I'm not talking until I have an attorney present. If you'll excuse me.'

'Hey, we're just talking here,' Kimberly Green said. 'I never said I thought you were the kidnapper.'

'Sounded that way to me,' Myron said. 'Win?'

'He snatches hearts,' Win told her, 'not people.'

'You got something to hide?' Green said.

'Just his fondness for cyber pornography,' Win said. Then: 'Oops.'

Kimberly Green stood and blocked Myron's path. 'We think we know about the missing college student,' she said, her eyes locked hard on his. 'Do you want to know how we found out about it?'

Myron kept still.

'Through her father. He got a call from the kidnapper. I don't know what was said. He hasn't said a word since. He's catatonic. Whatever that psycho said to that girl's father put him in a padded room.'

Myron felt the room shrink, the walls closing in.

'We haven't found any bodies yet, but we're pretty sure he kills them,' she went on. 'He kidnaps them, does Lord knows what, and makes the families suffer interminably. And you know he won't stop.'

Myron kept his eyes steady. 'What's your point?'

'This isn't funny.'

'No,' he said. 'It's not. So stop playing stupid games.'

She said nothing.

'I want to hear it from your mouth,' Myron said. 'Do you think I'm involved in this, yes or no?'

Eric Ford took this one. 'No.'

Kimberly Green slid back into her chair, her eyes never leaving Myron's. Eric Ford made a big hand gesture. 'Please sit down.'

Myron and Win moved back to their original positions.

Eric Ford said, 'The novel exists. So do the passages Stan Gibbs plagiarized. The book was sent to our office anonymously – more specifically, to Special Agent Green here. We admit that we found that issue confusing at first. On the one hand, Gibbs knows about the kidnappings. On the other hand, he doesn't know everything and he clearly copied excerpts from an old, out-of-print mystery novel.'

'There's an explanation,' Myron said. 'The kidnapper might have read the book. He might have identified with the character, become a copycat of sorts.'

'We considered that possibility,' Eric Ford said, 'but we don't believe that's the case here.'

'Why not?'

'It's complicated.'

'Does it involve trigonometry?'

'You still think this is a joking matter?'

'You still think it's smart to play games?'

Ford closed his eyes. Green looked on edge. Peck continued scribbling notes. When Ford opened his eyes, he said, 'We don't believe Stan Gibbs made up the crimes,' he said. 'We believe he perpetrated them.'

Myron felt a pow. He looked up at Win. Nothing.

'You have some background in the criminal mind, do you not?' Ford asked.

Myron might have nodded.

'Well, here we have an old pattern with a new twist. Arsonists love to watch firemen put out the blaze. Oft-times they're even the ones who report the fire. They play the good Samaritan. Murderers love to attend the funerals of their victims. We videotape funerals. I'm sure you know this.'

Myron nodded again.

'Sometimes killers make themselves part of the story.' Eric Ford was gesturing a lot now, his knotted hands rising and falling as though this were a press conference in too big a room. 'They claim to be witnesses. They become the innocent bystanders who happened to find the body in the brush. You're familiar with this moth-near-the-flame phenomenon, are you not?'

'Yes.'

'So what could be more enticing than being the only columnist to report the story? Can you imagine the high? How mind-bogglingly close to the investigation you'd be. The brilliance of your deception – for a psychotic, it's almost too delicious. And if you are perpetrating these crimes to get attention, then here you get a double dose. Attention as the serial kidnapper, one. Attention as the brilliant reporter with the scoop and possible Pulitzer, two. You even get the bonus attention of a man bravely defending the First Amendment.'

Myron was holding his breath. 'That's a hell of a theory,' he said.

'You want more?'

'Yes.'

'Why won't he answer any of our questions?'

'You said it yourself. First Amendment.'

'He's not a lawyer or psychiatrist.'

'But he is a reporter,' Myron said.

'What kind of monster would continue to protect his source in this situation?'

'I know plenty.'

'We spoke to the victims' families. They swore they never spoke to him.'

'They could be lying. Maybe the kidnapper told them to say that.'

'Okay, then why hasn't Gibbs done more to defend himself against the charges of plagiarism? He could have fought them. He could have even provided some detail that would have proved he was telling the truth. But no, instead he goes silent. Why?'

'You think it's because he's the kidnapper? The moth flew too close to the flame and is licking his wounds in darkness?'

'Do you have a better explanation?'

Myron said nothing.

'Lastly, there's the murder of his mistress, Melina Garston.'

'What about it?'

'Think it through, Myron. We put the screws to him. Maybe he expected that, maybe he didn't. Either way, the courts don't see everything his way. You don't know about the court findings, do you?'

'Not really, no.'

'That's because they were sealed. In part, the judge demanded that Gibbs show some proof he had been in contact with the killer. He finally said that Melina Garston would back him.'

'And she did, right?'

'Yes. She claimed to have met the subject of his story.'

'I still don't understand. If she backed him up, why would he kill her?'

'The day before Melina Garston died, she called her father. She told him that she lied.'

Myron sat back, tried to take it all in.

Eric Ford said, 'He's back now, Myron. Stan Gibbs has finally surfaced. While he was gone, the Sow the Seeds kidnapper was gone too. But this brand of psycho never stops on his own. He's going to strike again and soon. So before that happens, you better talk to us. Why were you at his condominium?'

Myron thought about it but not for long. 'I was looking for someone.'

'Who?'

'A missing bone marrow donor. He could save a child's life.'

Ford looked at him steadily. 'I assume that Jeremy Downing is the child in question.'

So much for being vague, but Myron was not surprised. Phone records probably. Or maybe there had indeed been a tail when he visited Emily's. 'Yes. And before I go on, I want your word that you will keep me in the loop.'

Kimberly Green said, 'You're not a part of this investigation.'

'I'm not interested in your kidnapper. I'm interested in my donor. You help me find him, I'll tell you what I know.'

'We agree,' Ford said, waving Kimberly Green silent. 'So how does Stan Gibbs fit in with your donor?'

Myron reviewed it for them. He started with Davis Taylor and then moved on to Dennis Lex and then the cryptic phone call. They kept their faces steady, Green and Peck scratching on their pads, but there was a definite jolt when he mentioned the Lex family.

They asked a few follow-up questions, like why he got involved in the first place. He said that Emily was an old friend. He wasn't about to go into the patrimony issue. Myron could see Green getting antsy. He had served his purpose. She was anxious to get out and start tracking things down.

A few minutes later, the feds snapped their pads closed and rose. 'We're on it,' Ford said. He looked straight at Myron. 'And we'll find your donor. You stay out.'

Myron nodded and wondered if he could. After they left, Win took a seat in front of Myron's desk.

'Why do I feel like I was picked up at a bar and now it's the next morning and the guy just handed me the "I'll call you" line?' Myron asked.

'Because that's precisely what you are,' Win said. 'Slut.'

'Think they're holding something back?'

'Without question.'

'Something big?'

'Gargantuan,' Win said.

'Not much we can do about it now.'

'Nope,' Win said. 'Nothing at all.'

24

Myron's mom met him at the front door.

'I'm picking up the takeout,' Mom said.

'You?'

She put her hands on her hips and shot him her best wither. 'There a problem with that?'

'No, it's just . . .' He decided to drop it. 'Nothing.'

Mom kissed his cheek and fished through her purse for the car keys. 'I'll be back in a half hour. Your father is in the back.' She gave him the imploring eyes. 'Alone.'

'Okay,' he said.

'No one else is here.'

'Uh-huh.'

'If you catch my drift.'

'It's caught.'

'You'll be alone.'

'Caught, Mom. Caught.'

'It'll be an opportunity—'

'Mom.'

She put her hands up. 'Okay, okay, I'm going.'

He walked around the side of the house, past the garbage cans and recycling bins, and found Dad on the deck. The deck was sanded redwood with built-in benches and resin furniture and a Weber 500 barbecue, all brought to being during the famed Kitchen Expansion of 1994. Dad was bent over a railing with a screwdriver in his hand. For a moment, Myron fell back to those 'weekend projects' with Dad, some of which lasted almost an entire hour. They would go out with toolbox in tow, Dad bent over like he was now, muttering obscenities under his breath. Myron's sole task consisted of handing Dad tools like a scrub nurse in the operating room, the whole exercise boring as hell, shuffling his feet in the sun, sighing heavily, finding new angles from which to stand.

'Hey,' Myron said.

Dad looked up, smiled, put down the tool. 'Screw loose,' he said. 'But let's not talk about your mother.'

Myron laughed. They found molded-resin chairs around a table impaled by a blue umbrella. In front of them lay Bolitar Stadium, a small patch of green-to-brown grass that had hosted countless, oft-solo football games, baseball games, soccer games, Wiffle ball games (probably the most popular sport at Bolitar Stadium), rugby scrums, badminton, kickball, and that favorite pastime for the future sadist, bombardment. Myron spotted Mom's former vegetable garden – the word *vegetable* here being used to describe three annual soggy tomatoes and two flaccid zucchinis; it was now slightly more overgrown than a Cambodian rice paddy. To their right were the rusted remnants of their old tetherball pole. Tetherball. Now, there was a really dumb game.

Myron cleared his throat and put his hands on the table. 'How you feeling?'

Dad gave a big nod. 'Good. You?'

'Good.'

The silence floated down, puffy and relaxed. Silence with a father can be like that. You drift back and you're young and you're safe, safe in that all-encompassing way only a child can be with his father. You still see him hovering in your darkened doorway, the silent sentinel to your adolescence, and you sleep the sleep of the naive, the innocent, the unformed. When you get older, you realize that this safety was just an illusion, another child's perception, like the size of your backyard.

Or maybe, if you're lucky, you don't.

Dad looked older today, the flesh on his face more sagged, the once-knotted biceps spongy under the T-shirt, starting to waste. Myron wondered how to start. Dad closed his eyes for a three count, opened them, and said, 'Don't.'

'What?'

'Your mother is about as subtle as a White House press release,' Dad said. 'I mean, when was the last time she picked up the takeout instead of me?'

'Has she ever?'

'Once,' Dad said. 'When I had a fever of a hundred and four. And even then she whined about it.'

'Where's she going?'

'She has me on a special diet now, you know. Because of the chest pains.' *Chest pains.* Euphemism for *heart attack.*

'Yeah, I figured that.'

'She's even tried cooking a little. She told you?'

Myron nodded. 'She baked something for me yesterday.'

Dad's body went stiff. 'By God,' he said. 'Her own son?'

'It was pretty scary.'

'The woman has many, many talents, but they could airdrop that stuff into starving African nations and no one would eat it.'

'So where's she going?'

'Your mother is high on some crazy Middle Eastern health food place. Just opened in West Orange. Get this, it's called Ayatollah Granola.'

Myron gave him flat eyes.

'Hand to God, that's the name. Food is almost as dry as that Thanksgiving turkey your mother made when you were eight. You remember that?'

'At night,' Myron said. 'It still haunts my sleep.'

Dad looked off again. 'She left us alone so we could talk, right?'

'Right.'

He made a face. 'I hate when she does stuff like that. She means well, your mother. We both know that. But let's not do it, okay?'

Myron shrugged. 'You say so.'

'She thinks I don't like growing old. News flash: No one does. My friend Herschel Diamond – you remember Heshy?'

'Sure.'

'Big guy, right? Played semipro football when we were young. So Heshy, he calls me and he says now that I'm retired, I can do tai chi with him. I mean, tai chi? What the hell is that anyway? If I want to move slowly, I have to drive down to the Y to do it with a bunch of old yentas? I mean, what's that about? I tell him no. So then Heshy, this great athlete, Myron, he could hit a softball a country mile, this marvelous big ox, he tells me we can walk together. Walk. At the mall. Speed-walk, he calls it. At the mall, for chrissake. Heshy always hated the place – now he wants us to trot around like a bunch of jackasses in matching sweatsuits and expensive walking shoes. Pump our arms with these little *faigelah* barbells. Walking shoes, he calls them. What the hell is that anyway? I never had a pair of shoes I couldn't walk in, am I right?'

He waited for an answer. Myron said, 'As rain.'

Dad stood up. He grabbed a screwdriver and feigned working. 'So now, because I don't want to move like an old Chinaman or walk around a godforsaken mall in overpriced sneakers, your mother thinks I'm not adjusting. You hear what I'm saying?'

'Yes.'

Dad stayed bent, fiddling a little more with the railing. In the distance, Myron heard children playing. A bike bell rang. Someone laughed. A lawn mower purred. Dad's voice, when he finally spoke again, was surprisingly soft. 'You know what your mother really wants us to do?' he said.

'What?'

'She wants you and I to reverse roles.' Dad finally looked up through his heavy-lidded eyes. 'I don't want to reverse roles, Myron. I'm the father. I like being the father. Let me stay that, okay?'

Myron found it hard to speak. 'Sure, Dad.'

His father put his head back down, the gray wisps upright in the humidity, his breathing tool-work heavy, and Myron again felt something open up his chest and grab hold of his heart. He looked at this man he'd loved for so long, who'd gone without complaint to that damn muggy warehouse in Newark for more than thirty years, and Myron realized that he didn't know him. He didn't know what his father dreamed about, what he wanted to be when he was a kid, what he thought about his own life.

Dad kept working on the screw. Myron watched him.

Promise me you won't die, okay? Just promise me that.

He almost said it out loud.

Dad straightened himself out and studied his handiwork. Satisfied, he sat back down. They started talking about the Knicks and the recent Kevin Costner movie and the new Nelson DeMille book. They put away the toolbox. They had some iced tea. They lounged side by side in matching molded-resin chaises. An hour passed. They fell into a comfortable silence. Myron fingered the

161

condensation on his glass. He could hear his father's breathing, moderately wheezy. Dusk had settled in, bruising the sky purple, the trees going a burnt orange.

Myron closed his eyes and said, 'I got a hypothetical for you.'

'Oh?'

'What would you do if you found out you weren't my real father?'

Dad's eyebrows went skyward. 'You trying to tell me something?'

'Just a hypothetical. Suppose you found out right now that I wasn't your biological son. How would you react?'

'Depends,' Dad said.

'On?'

'How you reacted.'

'It wouldn't make a difference to me,' Myron said.

Dad smiled.

'What?' Myron said.

'Easy for both of us to say it wouldn't matter. But news like that is a bombshell. You can't predict what someone will do when a bomb lands. When I was in Korea—' Dad stopped, Myron sat up. 'Well, you never knew how someone would react . . .' His voice tailed off. He coughed into his fist and then started up again. 'Guys you were sure would be heroes completely lost it – and vice versa. That's why you can't ask stuff like this as a hypothetical.'

Myron looked at his father. His father kept his eyes on the grass, taking another deep sip. 'You never talk about Korea,' Myron said.

'I do,' Dad said.

'Not with me.'

'No, not with you.'

'Why not?'

'It's what I fought for. So we wouldn't have to talk about it.'

It didn't make sense and Myron understood.

'There a reason you raised this particular hypothetical?' Dad asked.

'No.'

Dad nodded. He knew it was a lie, but he wouldn't push it. They settled back and watched the familiar surroundings.

'Tai chi isn't so bad,' Myron said. 'It's a martial art. Like tae kwon do. I've been thinking of taking it up myself.'

Dad took another sip. Myron sneaked a glance. Something on his father's face began to quiver. Was Dad indeed getting smaller, more fragile – or was it like the backyard and safety, again the shifting perception of a child turned adult?

'Dad . . . ?'

'Let's go inside,' his father said, standing. 'We stay out much longer, one of us is going to get misty and say, "Wanna play catch?" '

Myron bit off a laugh and followed him inside. Mom came home not long after that, lugging two bags of food as though they were stone tablets. 'Everybody hungry?' she called out.

'Starving,' Dad said. 'I'm so hungry I could eat a vegetarian.'

'Very funny, Al.'

'Or even your cooking . . .'

'Ha-ha,' Mom said.

'. . . though I'd prefer the vegetarian.'

'Stop it, Al, I'm going to phlegm up, you keep making me laugh like this.' Mom dropped the bags onto the kitchen counter. 'See, Myron? It's a good thing your mother is shallow.'

'Shallow?' Myron asked.

'If I judged a man on brains or sense of humor,' Mom continued, 'you'd have never been born.'

'Right-o,' Dad said with a hearty smile. 'But one look at your old man in a bathing suit and whammo – all mine.'

'Oh please,' Mom said.

'Yes,' Myron said. 'Please.'

They both looked at him. Mom cleared her throat. 'So did you two, uh, have a nice talk?'

'We talked,' Dad said. 'It was very life-affirming. I see the errors of my ways.'

'I'm being serious.'

'So am I. I see everything differently now.'

She put her arms around his waist and nuzzled him. 'So you'll call Heshy?'

'I'll call Heshy,' he said.

'Promise.'

'Yes, Ellen, I promise.'

'You'll go to the Y and do jai alai with him?'

'Tai chi,' Dad corrected.

'What?'

'It's called tai chi, not jai alai.'

'I thought it was jai alai.'

'Tai chi. Jai alai is the game with the curved rackets down in Florida.'

'That's shuffleboard, Al.'

'Not shuffleboard. The other thing with the sticks. And the gambling.'

'Tai chi?' Mom said, testing it for sound. 'Are you sure?'

'I think so.'

'But you're not positive?'

'No, I'm not positive,' Dad said. 'Maybe you're right. Maybe it is called jai alai.'

The name debate continued for a while. Myron didn't bother correcting them. Never cut in on that strange dance known as marital discourse. They ate the health food. It was indeed nasty. They laughed a lot. His parents must have said 'You don't know what you're talking about' to each other fifty times; maybe it was a euphemism for 'I love you.'

Eventually Myron said good night. Mom kissed his cheek and made herself scarce. Dad walked him to the car. The night was silent save a lone dribbling basketball somewhere on Darby Road or maybe Coddington Terrace. A nice sound. When he hugged his father goodbye, Myron again noticed that his father felt smaller, less substantial. Myron held on a little longer than usual. For the first time he felt like the bigger man, the stronger man, and he suddenly remembered what Dad had said about reversing roles. So he held on in the dark. Time passed. Dad patted his back. Myron kept his eyes closed and held on tighter. Dad stroked his hair and shushed him. Just for a little while. Just until the roles reversed themselves again, returning both of them to where they belonged.

25

Granite Man was waiting outside the Dakota.

Myron spotted him from his car. He picked up the cell phone and called Win. 'I have company.'

'A rather large gentleman, yes,' Win said. 'Two cohorts are parked across the street in a corporate vehicle owned by the Lex family.'

'I'll leave the cell phone on.'

'They confiscated it last time,' Win said.

'Yes.'

'Likely they'll do the same.'

'We'll improvise.'

'Your funeral,' Win said, and hung up.

Myron parked in the lot and approached Granite Man.

'Mrs Lex would like to see you,' Granite Man said.

'Do you know what she wants?' Myron asked.

Granite Man ignored the question.

'Maybe she saw me flexing on the security tape,' Myron said. 'Wanted to get to know me better.'

Granite Man did not laugh. 'You ever think about doing this comedy thing professionally?'

'There have been offers.'

'I bet. Get in the car.'

'Okay, but I have a curfew, you know. And I never French-kiss on the first date. Just so we understand each other.'

Granite Man shook his head. 'Man, I'd like to waste you.'

They got in the car. Two blue-blazers sat in front. The car ride was silent except for Granite Man and His Magic Cracking Knuckles. The Lex building emerged grudgingly through the dark. Myron traveled through the security travail again. As Win predicted, they confiscated his phone. Granite Man and the two blazers turned left this time instead of right. They escorted him into an elevator. It opened into what appeared to be living quarters.

Susan Lex's office had been done sort of Renaissance palatial, but the apartment up here – it looked like an apartment anyway – did a one-eighty. Modern and minimalism were the major themes. The walls were painted stark white and had nothing on them. The floors were a pigeon-gray wood. There were black and white bookshelves made of fiberglass, most empty, some with indistinct figurines. The couch was red and shaped like two lips. There was a well-stocked see-through bar constructed out of Lucite. Two metallic swivel stools were painted red on the base, looking about as inviting as rectal thermometers. A fire danced lazily in the fireplace, fake logs casting an unnatural glow over the black mantel. The whole place had a feel and aura about as warm as a cold sore.

Myron strolled, feigning interest. He stopped at a crystal statue with a marble base. Something modern or cubist or what-have-you. Symmetrical Bowel Movement maybe. Myron put his hand on it. Substantial. He looked out the one-way glass. Too low for much of a view beyond the hedges lining the front gate. Hmm.

The two blue-blazers did the Buckingham Palace Guard thing on either side of the door. Granite Man followed Myron, his hands clasped behind his lower back. A door on the other side of the room opened. Myron was not surprised to see Susan Lex enter, again keeping her distance. There was a man with her this time. Myron did not bother approaching.

'And you are?' he called out.

Susan Lex answered this one. 'This is my brother Bronwyn.'

'Not the brother I'm interested in,' Myron said.

'Yes, I know. Please sit down.'

Granite Man gestured toward the lips-couch. Myron sat on the lower lip, waiting to be swallowed. Granite Man sat right next to him. Cozy.

'Bronwyn and I would like you to answer some questions, Mr Bolitar,' Susan Lex said.

'Could you move a little closer?'

She smiled. 'I think not.'

'I showered.'

She ignored the remark. 'I understand that you occasionally do some investigative work,' Susan Lex said.

Myron did not reply.

'Is that correct?'

'Depends on what you mean by investigative work.'

'I'll take that as a yes,' Susan Lex said.

Myron gave her a suit-yourself shrug.

'Is that why you're searching for our brother?' she asked.

'I already told you why I was searching for him.'

'That bit about him being a bone marrow donor?'

'It's not a bit.'

'Please, Mr Bolitar,' Susan Lex said with that rich-people air. 'We both know that's a lie.'

Myron started to rise. Granite Man put a hand on Myron's knee. It felt like a cinder block. Granite Man shook his head. Myron stayed where he was. 'It's not a lie,' he said.

'We're wasting time,' Susan Lex said. She flicked her eyes at Granite Man. 'Show him the pictures, Grover.'

Myron turned to him. 'Grover is the name of my very favorite *Sesame Street* character. I want you to know that.'

'We've been following you, *Myron*.' Granite Man handed him a pile of photographs. Myron looked at them. They were eight-by-tens of him at the condo with Stan Gibbs. The first one showed him knocking on the door. The second one showed Stan sticking his head out. The third one showed them both heading inside the condo.

'Well?'

Myron frowned. 'I have no knack for accessorizing.'

'We know that you're working for Stan Gibbs,' Susan Lex said.

'Doing what exactly?' Myron asked.

'Investigating. As I stated earlier. So now that we understand your true motive, tell me how much it will cost for you to go away.'

'I don't know what you're talking about.'

'Simply put, how much will it cost to have you cease and desist?' Susan Lex asked. 'Or are you going to force us to destroy you too?'

Too?

Brain click.

Myron turned his attention to the silent brother. 'Let me ask you something, Bronwyn,' he said. 'You and Dennis were both going to nursery school. You both disappeared. Two weeks later, only you came back. How come? What happened to your brother?'

Bronwyn's mouth opened and closed, marionette style. He looked to his sister for help.

'It's like he disappeared off the face of the earth after that,' Myron went on. 'For thirty years, he's totally off the radar. But now, well, it's like he's come back for some reason. He changed his name, opened a small checking account, donated blood to a bone marrow center. So what gives, Bron? You got a clue?'

Bronwyn said, 'That simply cannot be!'

His sister silenced him with a look. But Myron felt something in the air. He mulled the feeling over and another thought hit him: Maybe the Lex siblings didn't know the answer themselves. Maybe they were looking for Dennis too.

It was while he was lost in that thought that Granite Man punched him deep in the stomach. The fist followed through to the point where it seemed the knuckles must have reached the fabric of the couch. Myron snapped closed at the waist. He dropped to the floor, struggled to regain a breath, suffocating from within. He lowered his head to his knees, consumed with one thought: air. He needed air.

Susan Lex's voice boomed in his ears. 'Stan Gibbs knows the truth. His father is a disgusting liar. His accusations are totally without merit. But I'll defend my family, Mr Bolitar. You tell Mr Gibbs he has not yet begun to suffer. What has happened to him so far is nothing compared to what I will do to him – and you – if he doesn't stop. Do you understand?'

Air. Gulps of air. Myron managed not to throw up. He took his time, looked up, met her eye. 'Not even a little,' he said.

Susan Lex looked at Grover. 'Then make him.'

With that, she left the room. Her brother took one last look and followed.

Myron gathered his breath a hitch at a time. 'Nice sucker punch, Grover,' he said.

Grover shrugged. 'I went easy on you.'

'Next time, go easy when I'm looking, tough guy.'

'Won't change the outcome.'

'We'll see.' Myron sat up. 'So what the hell is she talking about?'

'I thought Ms Lex made herself very clear,' he said. 'But because you appear to be a little vacant between the ears, I'll restate her position. She doesn't like people interfering with her affairs. Stan Gibbs, for example, interfered. You can see what happened to him. You interfered. You're about to see what's going to happen to you.'

Myron struggled to his feet. The blue-blazers stayed by the door. Granite Man started cracking his knuckles again. 'Listen closely, please,' he said. 'I'm going to break your leg. Then you're going to limp your sorry ass out of here and tell Gibbs that if he sniffs around again, I will exterminate you both. Any questions?'

'Just one,' Myron said. 'Don't you think leg breaking is a tad cliché?'

Grover smiled. 'Not the way I do it.'

Myron looked around the room.

'Nowhere to run, my friend.'

'Who wants to run?' Myron countered.

Without warning, he grabbed the heavy bowel-movement statue. The blue-blazers drew their guns. Granite Man ducked. But Myron wasn't going for them. He heaved the statue, straightened his arms, spun around like a discus thrower, and hurled it marble-base-forward at the plate-glass window. The window exploded.

And that was when the gunfire began.

'Hit the deck!' Myron shouted.

The blue-blazers obeyed. Myron dove. The bullets continued. Sniper fire. One took out the overhead light. One hit the lamp.

Gotta love that Win.

'You want to live,' Myron shouted, 'stay down.'

The bullets stopped. One of the blue-blazers started rising. A bullet sang out, nearly parting the man's hair. The blazer dropped back down, flattening himself into a bearskin rug.

'I'm getting up now,' Myron said. 'And I'm leaving. I'd advise you guys to stay down. And, Grover?'

'What?'

'Radio downstairs. Tell them not to stop me. I can't be certain

169

but I'm pretty sure my friend will lob in grenades if I'm unduly delayed.'

Granite Man made the call. No one moved. Myron stood up. He almost whistled as he walked out.

26

It was midnight when Myron knocked on the door of Stan Gibbs's condo.

'Let's take a walk,' Myron said to him.

Stan threw down his cigarette, smothered it with his toe. 'A drive might be better,' he countered. 'The feds use long-range amplifiers.'

They got into Myron's Ford Taurus, aka the Chick Trawler. Stan Gibbs flicked on the radio and started playing with the stations. Commercial for Heineken. Does anyone really care that it's imported by Van Munchin and Company?

'Are you wearing a wire, Myron?'

'No.'

'But the FBI spoke to you,' Stan said. 'After you left.'

'How did you know?'

'They're watching me,' he said with a shrug. 'It would only be logical to assume they questioned you.'

'Tell me about your connection with Dennis Lex,' Myron said.

'I already told you. I don't have one.'

'A big guy named Grover picked me up tonight. He and Susan Lex gave me a very stern warning not to play with you anymore. Bronwyn was there too.'

Stan Gibbs closed his eyes and rubbed them. 'They knew about your visit here.'

'Had eight-by-ten glossies.'

'And they concluded that you're working for me.'

'Bingo.'

Stan shook his head. 'Get out of this, Myron. You don't want to mess with these people.'

'Is that advice you wished someone had given you earlier?'

His smile had nothing behind it. Exhaustion came off him like heat squiggles on a hot sidewalk. 'You have no idea,' he said.

'Tell me about it.'

'No.'

'I can help,' Myron said.

'Against the Lexes? They're too powerful.'

'And being powerful, you wanted to do a story on them, right?'

He said nothing.

'And they didn't like that. In fact, they took exception.'

More nothing.

'You started digging where they didn't want you to. You learned that there was another brother named Dennis.'

'Yes.'

'And that really pissed them off.'

Stan started biting a hangnail.

'Come on, Stan. Don't make me drag this out of you.'

'You've pretty much got it.'

'Then tell me.'

'I wanted to do a story on them. An exposé, really. I even had a publisher all lined up for a book deal. But then the Lexes got wind of it. They warned me to stay away. A big man came to my apartment. I didn't catch his name. Looked like Sergeant Rock.'

'That would be Grover.'

'He told me that I could stop or I could be destroyed.'

'And that only made you more curious.'

'I guess.'

'So you found out about Dennis Lex.'

'Just that he existed. And that he vanished into thin air when he was a young child.' Stan turned to him. Myron slowed the car and felt something creep along the top of his scalp.

'Like the Sow the Seeds victims,' Myron finished.

'No.'

'Why not?'

'It's different.'

'How?' Myron asked.

'This is going to sound silly,' Stan said, 'but the family doesn't have that same sense of terror that the other families have.'

'The rich are good with façades.'

'It's more than that,' Stan said. 'I can't put my finger on it.

exactly. But I'm sure Susan and Bronwyn Lex know what happened to their brother.'

'But they want to keep it a secret.'

'Yes.'

'Do you have a guess why?'

'No,' Stan said.

Myron glanced back. The feds were following at a discreet enough distance.

'Do you think Susan Lex is responsible for that novel surfacing?'

'The thought has crossed my mind.'

'But you never looked into it?'

'I started to. After the scandal hit. But I got a call from the big guy. He told me that it was just the beginning. That he was just flicking his finger and next time he would crush me between both palms.'

'He can be a poetic fellow,' Myron said.

'Yes.'

'But I still don't get something.'

'What?'

'You don't scare easily. When they warned you away the first time, you ignored it. After what they did to you, I'd have thought you'd fight back even harder.'

'You're forgetting something,' Stan said.

'What?'

'Melina Garston.'

Silence.

'Think about it,' Stan said. 'My mistress, the only person who can back up my meeting with the Sow the Seeds kidnapper, ends up dead.'

'Her father claims she retracted that.'

'Oh, right. In some bizarre before-death confession.'

'You think the Lexes arranged that too?'

'Why not? Look at what happened here. Who's the lead suspect in Melina's murder? I am, right? That's what the feds told you. They think I killed her. We know that the Lexes have enough juice to dig up this novel I supposedly plagiarized. Who knows what else they can do?'

'You think they could frame you for the murder?'

'At the very least.'

'Are you saying they killed Melina Garston?'

'Maybe. Or it could have been the Sow the Seeds kidnapper. I don't know.'

'But you think Melina was a warning.'

'She was definitely a warning,' Stan Gibbs said. 'I just don't know who sent it.'

On the radio, Stevie sang out about a landslide coming down. Oh yeah.

'You're leaving something out, Stan.'

Stan kept his eyes forward. 'What's that?'

'There's a personal connection here,' Myron said.

'What do you mean?'

'Susan Lex mentioned your father. She said he was a liar.'

Stan shrugged. 'She might be right.'

'What does he have to do with this?'

'Take me back.'

'Don't hold back on me now.'

'What do you really want here, Myron?'

'Excuse me?'

'What's your interest here?'

'I told you.'

'That boy who needs a bone marrow transplant?'

'He's thirteen years old, Stan. He'll die without it.'

'And what if I don't believe you? I did a little research of my own. You used to do government work.'

'A long time ago.'

'And maybe now you're helping the FBI. Or even the Lex family.'

'No.'

'I can't take that chance.'

'Why not? You're telling me the truth, right? The truth can't hurt you.'

He snorted. 'You really believe that?'

'Why did Susan Lex mention your father?'

Nothing.

'Where is your father?' Myron said.

'That's just it.'

'What?'

Stan looked at him. 'He vanished. Eight years ago.'

Vanished. That word again.

'I know what you're thinking and you're wrong. My father wasn't a well man. He had been in and out of institutions all his life. We've always assumed he ran off.'

'But you never heard from him.'

'That's right.'

'Dennis Lex vanishes. Your father vanishes—'

'More than twenty years apart,' Stan interjected. 'It's not connected.'

'So I still don't get it,' Myron said. 'What does your father or his disappearance have to do with the Lexes?'

'They think he's the reason I wanted to do the story. But they're wrong.'

'Why would they think that?'

'My father was a student of Raymond Lex's. Before *Midnight Confessions* came out.'

'So?'

'So my father claimed the novel was his. He said that Raymond Lex stole it from him.'

'Jesus Christ.'

'No one believed him,' Stan added quickly. 'Like I said, he wasn't right in the head.'

'Yet you suddenly decided to investigate the family?'

'Yes.'

'And you're telling me that's just a coincidence? That your own investigation had nothing to do with your father's accusations?'

Stan leaned his head against the car window like a little kid longing for home. 'No one believed my father. That includes me. He was a sick man. Delusional even.'

'So?'

'So at the end of the day, he was still my father,' Stan said. 'Maybe I owed it to him to at least give him the benefit of the doubt.'

'Do you think Raymond Lex plagiarized your father?'

'No.'

'Do you think your father is still alive?'

'I don't know.'

'There has to be a connection here,' Myron said. 'Your story, the Lex family, your father's accusations—'

Stan closed his eyes. 'No more.'

Myron switched tracks. 'How did the Sow the Seeds kidnapper get in touch with you?'

'I never reveal sources.'

'Come on, Stan.'

'No,' he said firmly. 'I may have lost a lot. But not that part of me. You know I can't say anything about my sources.'

'You know who it is, don't you?'

'Take me home, Myron.'

'Is it Dennis Lex – or did the same kidnapper take Dennis Lex?'

Stan crossed his arms. 'Home,' he said.

His face closed down. Myron saw it. There would be no more give tonight. He took a right and started heading back. Neither man spoke again until Myron stopped the car in the front of the condominium.

'Are you telling the truth, Myron? About the bone marrow donor?'

'Yes.'

'This boy is someone close to you?'

Myron kept both hands on the wheel. 'Yes.'

'So there's no way you'll walk away from this?'

'None.'

Stan nodded, mostly to himself. 'I'll do what I can. But you have to trust me.'

'What do you mean?'

'Give me a few days.'

'To do what?'

'You won't hear from me for a little while. Don't let that shake your faith.'

'What are you talking about?'

'You do what you have to,' he said. 'I'll do the same.'

Stan Gibbs stepped out of the car and disappeared into the night.

27

Greg Downing woke Myron early the next morning with a phone call. 'Nathan Mostoni left town,' he said. 'So I came back to New York. I get to pick up my son this afternoon.'

Goody-goody for you, Myron thought. But he kept his tongue still.

'I'm going to the Ninety-second Street Y to shoot around,' Greg said. 'You want to come?'

'No,' Myron said.

'Come anyway. Ten o'clock.'

'I'll be late.' Myron hung up and rolled out of bed. He checked his e-mail and found a JPEG image from Esperanza's contact at AgeComp. He clicked the file and an image slowly appeared on the screen. The possible face of Dennis Lex as a man in his mid to late thirties. Weird. Myron looked at the picture. Not familiar. Not familiar at all. Remarkable work, these age-enhanced images. So lifelike. Except in the eyes. The eyes always looked like the eyes of the dead.

He clicked on the print icon and heard his Hewlett-Packard go to work. Myron checked the clock on the bottom right-hand corner of the screen. Still early in the morning, but he didn't want to wait.

He called Melina Garston's father.

George Garston agreed to meet Myron at his penthouse at Fifth Avenue and Seventy-eighth Street, overlooking Central Park. A dark-haired woman answered the door. She introduced herself as Sandra and led him silently down the corridor. Myron looked out a window. He could see the Gothic outline of the Dakota all the way across the park. He remembered reading somewhere how

Woody and Mia would wave towels from their respective apartments on either side of Central Park. Happier days, no doubt.

'I don't understand what you have to do with my daughter,' George Garston said to him. Garston wore a collared blue shirt nicely offset by a shock of white neck-to-chest hairs sprouting out like a troll doll's. His bald head was an almost perfect sphere jammed between two boulder-excuses for shoulders. He had the proud, burly build of a successful immigrant, but you could see that he'd taken a hit. There was a slump there now, the stoop of the eternally grieving. Myron had seen it before. Grief like his breaks your back. You go on, but you always stoop. You smile, but it never really reaches the eyes.

'Probably nothing,' Myron said. 'I'm trying to find someone. He may be connected to your daughter's murder. I don't know.'

The study was too-dark cherry-wood with drawn curtains and one lamp giving off a faint yellow glow. George Garston turned to the side, staring at the rich paisley wallpaper, showing Myron his profile. 'We've worked together once,' he said. 'Not us personally. Our companies. Did you know that?'

'Yes,' Myron said.

George Garston had made his fortune with a chain of Greek quasi-restaurants, the kind that work best as mall stands in crowded food courts. The chain was called Achilles Meals. For real. Myron had a Greek hockey player who endorsed the chain regionally, in the upper Midwest.

'So a sports agent is interested in my daughter's murder,' Garston said.

'It's a long story.'

'The police aren't talking. But they think it's her boyfriend. This reporter. Do you agree?'

'I don't know. What do you think?'

He made a scoffing noise. Myron could barely see his face anymore. 'What do I think?' he said. 'You sound like one of those grief counselors.'

'Didn't mean to.'

'Spewing all that sensitivity garbage. They're just trying to distract you from reality. They say they want you to face it. But really, it's the opposite. They want you to dig so far into yourself you won't be able to see how terrible your life is now.' He grunted and shifted in his chair. 'I don't have an opinion on Stan Gibbs. I never met him.'

'Did you know he and your daughter were dating?'

In the dark, Myron saw the big head silently go back and forth. 'She told me she had a boyfriend,' he said. 'She didn't tell me his name. Or that he was married.'

'You wouldn't have approved?'

'Of course I wouldn't have approved,' he said, trying to sound snappish, but he was beyond petty indignation. 'Would you approve if it was your daughter?'

'I guess not. So you knew nothing about her relationship with Stan Gibbs?'

'Nothing.'

'I understand that you spoke to her not long before she died.'

'Four days before.'

'Can you tell me about the conversation?'

'Melina had been drinking,' he said in that pure monotone you get when the words have been ricocheting around your brain too long. 'A lot. She drank too much, my daughter. Got that from her papa – who got it from his papa. The Garston family legacy.' He made a chuckling sound that sounded far closer to a sob than anything in the neighborhood of a laugh.

'Melina talked to you about her testimony?'

'Yes.'

'Could you tell me what she said exactly?'

'"I made a mistake, Papa." That's what she said. She said that she lied.'

'What did you say?'

'I didn't even know what she was talking about. It's as I told you before – I didn't know about this boyfriend.'

'Did you ask her to explain?'

'Yes.'

'And?'

'And she didn't. She said to forget about it. She said she'd take care of it. Then she told me she loved me and hung up.'

Silence.

'I had two children, Mr Bolitar. Did you know that?'

Myron shook his head.

'A plane crash killed my Michael three years ago. Now an animal has tortured and killed my girl. My wife, her name was Melina too, passed away fifteen years ago. There is no one. Forty-eight years ago, I thought I came to this country with nothing. I made a lot of money. And now I truly have nothing. You understand?'

'Yes,' Myron said.

'Is that all, then?'

'Your daughter had an apartment on Broadway.'

'Yes.'

'Are her personal belongings still there?'

'Sandra – that's my daughter-in-law – she's been packing her things. But it's all still there. Why?'

'I'd like to go through them, if it's okay with you.'

'The police already did that.'

'I know.'

'You think you might find something they didn't?'

'I'm almost positive I won't.'

'But?'

'But I'm attacking this thing from a different perspective. It gives me a fresh set of eyes.'

George Garston flicked on his desk lamp. The yellow from the bulb painted his face a dark jaundice. Myron could see that his eyes were too dry, brittle like fallen acorns in the sun. 'If you find whoever killed my Melina, you will tell me first.'

'No,' Myron said.

'Do you know what he did to her?'

'Yes. And I know what you want to do. But it won't make you feel any better.'

'You say this like you know it for a fact.'

Myron kept silent.

George Garston flicked off the light and turned away. 'Sandra will take you over now.'

'He sits in that study all day,' Sandra Garston told him, pressing the elevator button. 'He won't go out anymore.'

'It's still new,' Myron said.

She shook her head. Her blue-black hair fell in big, loose curls, like thermal fax paper fresh out of the machine. But despite the hair color, her overall effect was almost Icelandic, the face and build of a world-class speed skater. Her features were sharp and ended rather abruptly. Her skin had the red of raw cold.

'He thinks he has no one,' she said.

'He has you.'

'I'm a daughter-in-law. He sees me and it's like a tether to Michael. I don't have the heart to tell him I finally started dating.'

When they reached the street, Myron asked, 'Were you and Melina close?'

'I think so, yes.'

'Did you know about her relationship with Stan Gibbs?'

'Yes.'

'But she never told her father.'

'Oh, she would never. Papa didn't approve of most men. A married one would have sent him off the ledge.'

They crossed the street and into the mid-city wonder known as Central Park. The park was packed on this rather spectacular day. Asian sketch artists hustled business. Men jogged by in those shorts that look suspiciously like diapers. Sunbathers lazed around on the grass, crowded together yet totally alone. New York City is like that. E. B. White once said that New York bestows the gift of loneliness and the gift of privacy. Damn straight. It was like everyone was plugged into their own internal Walkman, each playing a different tune, bopping obliviously to his or her own beat.

A yah-dude with a bandanna around his head tossed a Frisbee and yelled 'Fetch,' but he had no dog. Hard-bodied women skated by in black jogging bras. Lots of men with various builds had their shirts off. Examples: A guy thick with flab that looked like wet Play-Doh jiggled past him. Behind him, a well-built guy skidded to a stop and arrogantly flexed a bicep. Actually flexed. In public. Myron frowned. He didn't know which was worse: guys who shouldn't take their shirts off and do, or guys who should take their shirts off and do.

When they reached Central Park West, Myron asked, 'Did you have a problem with her dating a married man?'

Sandra shrugged. 'I worried, of course. But he told Melina he would leave his wife.'

'Don't they all?'

'Melina believed it. She seemed happy.'

'Did you ever meet Stan Gibbs?'

'No. Their relationship was supposed to be a secret.'

'Did she ever tell you about lying in court?'

'No,' she said. 'Never.'

Sandra used her key and swung the door open. Myron stepped inside. Colors. Lots of them. Happy colors. The apartment looked like the Magical Mystery Tour meets the *Teletubbies*, all bright hues, especially greens, with hazy psychedelic splashes. The walls were covered with vivid watercolors of distant lands and ocean voyages. Some surreal stuff too. The effect was like an Enya video.

'I started throwing her stuff in boxes,' Sandra said. 'But it's hard to pack up a life.'

Myron nodded. He started walking around the small apartment, hoping for a psychic revelation or something. None came. He ran his eyes over the artwork.

'She was supposed to have her first show in the Village next month,' Sandra said.

Myron studied a painting with white domes and crystal blue water. He recognized the spot in Mykonos. It was wonderfully done. Myron could almost smell the salt of the Mediterranean, taste the grilled fish along the beach, feel the night sand clinging to a lover's skin. No clue here, but he stared another minute or two before turning away.

He started going through the boxes. He found a high school yearbook, class of 1986, and flipped through it until he found Melina's picture. She'd like to paint, it said. He glanced again at the walls. So bright and optimistic, her work. Death, Myron knew, was always ironic. Young death most ironic of all.

He turned his attention back to her photograph. Melina was looking off to the side with the hesitant, unsure smile of high school. Myron knew it well. Don't we all. He closed the book and headed to her closets. Her clothes were neatly arranged, lots of sweaters folded on the top shelf, shoes lined up like tiny soldiers. He moved back to the boxes and found her photographs in a shoebox. A shoebox of all things. Myron shook his head and started going through them. Sandra sat on the floor next to him. 'That's her mother,' she said.

Myron looked at the photograph of two women, clearly mother

and daughter, embracing. There was no sign of the unsure smile this time. This smile – the smile in her mother's arms – soared like an angel's song. Myron stared at the angel-song smile and imagined that celestial mouth crying out in hopeless agony. He thought about George Garston alone in that jaundice-lit study. And he understood.

Myron checked his watch. Time to pick up the pace. He thumbed through pictures of her father, her brother, Sandra, family outings, the norm. No pictures of Stan Gibbs. Nothing helpful.

He found makeup and perfume in another box. In another, he stumbled across a diary, but Melina hadn't written anything in it for two years. He paged through it, but it felt like too much of an unnecessary violation. He found a love letter from an old boyfriend. He found some receipts.

He found copies of Stan's columns.

Hmm.

In her address book. All the columns. There were no markings on them. Just the clippings themselves, held together by a paper clip. So what did that mean? He checked them again. Just clippings. He put them aside and did some more flipping. Something fell out near the back. Myron picked up a piece of cream-colored or aged-white paper torn along the left edge, more a card really, folded in half. The outside was totally blank. He opened it. On the upper half, the words *With Love, Dad* had been written in script. Myron thought again about George Garston sitting alone in that room and felt a deep burn flush his skin.

He sat on the couch now and tried again to conjure up something. That might sound weird – sitting in this too empty room, the sweet smell of a dead woman still hovering, feeling not unlike that tiny old lady in the *Poltergeist* movies – but you never knew. The victims didn't speak to him or anything like that. But sometimes he could imagine what they'd been thinking and feeling and some spark would hit the edges and start to flame. So he tried it again.

Nothing.

He let his eyes wander across the canvases and the burn under his skin started up again. He scanned the bright colors, let them assault him. The brightness should have protected her. Nonsense, but there you have it. She'd had a life. Melina worked and she painted and she loved bright colors and had too many sweaters and stored her precious memories in a shoebox and someone had snuffed that life away because none of that meant anything to him. None of that was important. It made Myron mad.

He closed his eyes and tried to turn the anger down a notch. Anger wasn't good. It clouded reason. He'd let that side of him out before – his Batman complex, as Esperanza had called it – but being a hero seeking justice or vengeance (if they weren't the same thing) was unwise, unhealthy. Eventually you saw things you didn't want to. You learned truths you never should have. It stings and then it deadens. Better to stay away.

But the heat in his blood would not leave him. So he stopped fighting it, let the heat soothe him, relax his muscles, settle gently over him. Maybe the heat wasn't such a bad thing. Maybe the horrors he'd seen and the truths he'd learned hadn't changed him, hadn't deadened him, after all.

Myron closed the boxes, took one last, lingering look at the sunkissed isle of Mykonos, and made a silent vow.

28

Greg and Myron met up on the court. Myron strapped on his knee brace. Greg averted his eyes. The two men shot for half an hour, barely speaking, lost in the pure strokes. People ducked in and pointed at Greg. Several kids came up to him and asked him for autographs. Greg acquiesced, glancing at Myron as he took pen in hand, clearly uncomfortable getting all this attention in front of the man whose career he had ended.

Myron stared back at him, offering no solace.

After some time, Myron said, 'There a reason you wanted me here, Greg?'

Greg kept shooting.

'Because I have to get back to the office,' Myron said.

Greg grabbed the ball, dribbled twice, took a turnaround jumper. 'I saw you and Emily that night. You know that?'

'I know that,' Myron said.

Greg grabbed the rebound, took a lazy hook, let the ball hit the floor and slowly bounce toward Myron. 'We were getting married the next day. You know that?'

'Know that too.'

'And there you were,' Greg said, 'her old boyfriend, screwing her brains out.'

Myron picked up the ball.

'I'm trying to explain here,' Greg said.

'I slept with Emily,' Myron said. 'You saw us. You wanted revenge. You told Big Burt Wesson to hurt me during a preseason game. He did. End of story.'

'I wanted him to hurt you, yes. I didn't mean for him to end your career.'

'You say tomato, I say tomahto.'

'It wasn't intentional.'

'Don't take this the wrong way,' Myron said in a voice that sounded awfully calm in his own ears, 'but I don't give two shits about your intentions. You fired a weapon at me. You might have aimed for a flesh wound, but that didn't happen. You think that makes you blameless?'

'You fucked my fiancée.'

'And she fucked me. I didn't owe you anything. She did.'

'Are you telling me you don't understand?'

'I understand. It just doesn't absolve you.'

'I'm not looking for absolution.'

'Then what do you want, Greg? You want us to clasp hands and sing "Kumbaya"? Do you know what you did to me? Do you know what the one moment cost me?'

'I think maybe I do,' Greg said. He swallowed, put out a pleading hand as though he wanted to explain more, and then he let the hand drop to the side. 'I'm so sorry.'

Myron started shooting but he felt his throat swell.

'You don't know how sorry I am.'

Myron said nothing. Greg tried to wait him out. It didn't work.

'What else do you want me to say here, Myron?'

Myron kept shooting.

'How do I tell you I'm sorry?'

'You've already done it,' Myron said.

'But you won't accept it.'

'No, Greg. I won't. I live without playing pro ball. You live without my accepting your apology. Pretty good deal for you, you ask me.'

Myron's cell phone rang. He ran over, picked it up, said hello.

A whisper asked, 'Did you do as I instructed?'

His bones turned to solid ice. He swallowed away something thick and said, 'As you instructed?'

'The boy,' the voice whispered.

The stale air pressed against him, weighed down his lungs. 'What about him?'

'Did you say one last good-bye?'

Something inside of Myron withered up and blew away. His

knees buckled as the realization seeped into his chest. And the voice came on again:

'Did you say one last good-bye to the boy?'

29

Myron snapped his head toward Greg.

'Where's Jeremy?'

'What?'

'Where is he?'

Greg saw whatever it was on Myron's face and dropped the basketball. 'He's with Emily, I guess. I don't get him until noon.'

'Got a cell phone?'

'Yes.'

'Call her.'

Greg was already heading toward his gym bag, the athlete with the wonderful reflexes. 'What's going on?'

'Probably nothing.'

Myron explained about the call. Greg did not slow down to listen. He dialed. Myron started running toward his car. Greg followed, the phone pressed against his ear.

'No answer,' Greg said. He left a message on the machine.

'Does she have a cell phone?'

'If she does, I don't have the number.'

Myron hit a stored number as they walked. Esperanza picked up.

'I need Emily's cell phone number.'

'Give me five,' Esperanza said.

Myron hit another stored number. Win answered and said, 'Articulate.'

'Possible trouble.'

'I'm here.'

They reached the car. Greg was calm. That surprised Myron. On the court, when the pressure mounted, Greg's modus operandi was to get freaky, start screaming, psych himself into a frenzy. But of course, this was not a game. As his father had recently told him, when real bombs drop, you never know how someone will react.

Myron's phone rang. Esperanza gave him Emily's cell phone number. Myron dialed it. After six rings, Emily's voice mail picked up. Damn. Myron left a message. He turned to Greg.

'Any clue where Jeremy might be?' Myron asked.

'No,' Greg said.

'How about a neighbor we can call? Or a friend?'

'When Emily and I were married, we lived in Ridgewood. I don't know the neighbors in Franklin Lakes.'

Myron gripped the steering wheel. He hit the accelerator. 'Jeremy's probably safe,' Myron said, trying to believe it. 'I don't even know how this guy would know his name. It's probably a bluff.'

Greg started shaking.

'He'll be all right.'

'Jesus, Myron, I read those articles. If that guy has my kid . . .'

'We should call the FBI,' Myron said. 'Just in case.'

'You think that's the way to go?' Greg asked.

Myron looked at him. 'Why? You don't?'

'I just want to pay the ransom and get my boy back. I don't want anybody screwing it up.'

'I think we should call,' Myron said. 'But it's your decision.'

'There's something else we have to consider,' Greg said.

'What?'

'There's a good chance this wacko is our donor, right?'

'Yes.'

'If the FBI kills him, it's over for Jeremy.'

'First things first,' Myron said. 'We have to find Jeremy. And we have to find this kidnapper.'

Greg kept shaking.

'What do you want to do, Greg?'

'You think we should call?'

'Yes.'

Greg nodded slowly. 'Call,' he said.

Myron dialed Kimberly Green's number. He felt waves pounding in his head, the blood flowing to his ears. He tried not to think about Jeremy's face, what his smile had looked like when he opened that door.

Did you say one last good-bye to the boy?

A voice said, 'Federal Bureau of Investigation.'

'Myron Bolitar calling Kimberly Green.'

'Special Agent Green is unavailable.'

'The Sow the Seeds kidnapper may have taken somebody else. Put her on.'

The hold was longer than Myron expected.

Kimberly Green started with a bark. 'What the hell are you ranting about?'

'He just called me.' Myron filled her in.

'We're on our way,' she said.

They hit a patch of traffic where Route 4 met Route 17, but Myron went up on the grass and knocked over several orange construction buckets. He broke off at Route 208 and exited near the synagogue. Two miles later, they made the final turn onto Emily's street. Myron could see two FBI cars making the turn at the same time.

Greg, who had gone into something of a trance, woke up and pointed. 'There she is.'

Emily was putting her key in the front door. Myron started honking madly. She looked back confused. He turned the car and skidded. The FBI car followed. Myron and Greg were both out the door almost before the car had stopped.

'Where's Jeremy?' they both said in unison.

Emily had her head tilted to the side. 'What?' she called back. 'What's going on here?'

Greg took it. 'Where is he, Emily?'

'He's with a friend—'

From inside the house, the phone started ringing. Everyone froze. Emily snapped out of it first. She ran inside and picked up the phone. She put the phone to her ear, cleared her throat, and said, 'Hello.'

Through the receiver, they could all hear Jeremy's scream.

30

There were six federal agents in all. Kimberly Green was the task force leader. They set up with quiet efficiency. Myron sat on one couch, Greg the other. Emily paced between them. There was probably something symbolic in that, but Myron was not sure what. He tried to push himself past the numb so he could get to a place where he could do some good.

The phone call had been brief. After the scream, the whispery voice had said, 'We'll call back.' That was it. No warnings not to contact the authorities. No telling them to prepare funds. No setting up another time to call. Nothing.

They all sat there, the boy's scream still echoing, mauling, shredding, conjuring up images of what could have made a thirteen-year-old boy scream like that. Myron shut his eyes and pushed hard. That was what the bastard wanted. Unwise to play into that.

Greg had contacted his bank. He was not a risky investor, and so most of his assets were liquid. If ransom money was needed, he'd be ready. The various feds, all male except for Kimberly Green, put traces on all the possible phones, including Myron's. She and her men were doing a lot of sotto voce. Myron hadn't pressed them yet. But that wasn't going to last.

Kimberly caught his eyes and waved him over. He stood and excused himself. Greg and Emily paid no attention, still lost in the vortex of that scream.

'We need to talk,' she said.

'Okay,' Myron said. 'Start by telling me what happened when you checked out Dennis Lex.'

'You're not family,' she said. 'I could throw you out.'

'This isn't your house,' he said. 'What happened with Dennis Lex?'

She put her hands on her hips. 'It's a dead end.'

'How so?'

'We traced it down. He's not involved in any of this.'

'How do you know that?'

'Myron, come on. We're not stupid.'

'So where is Dennis Lex?'

'It's not relevant,' she said.

'The hell it's not. Even if he's not the kidnapper, we still have him as the bone marrow donor.'

'No,' she said. 'Your donor is Davis Taylor.'

'Who changed his name from Dennis Lex.'

'We don't know that.'

Myron made a face. 'What are you talking about?'

'Davis Taylor was an employee in the Lex conglomerate.'

'What?'

'You heard me.'

'So why did he donate blood for a bone marrow drive?'

'It was a work thing,' she said. 'The plant boss had a sick nephew. Everyone at the plant gave.'

Myron nodded. Something finally made sense. 'So if he didn't give a blood sample,' he said, 'it would have been conspicuous.'

'Right.'

'You got a description on him?'

'He worked on his own, kept to himself. All anyone remembers is a man with a full beard, glasses, and long blond hair.'

'A disguise,' Myron said. 'And we know Davis Taylor's original name was Dennis Lex. What else?'

Kimberly Green raised her hand. 'Enough.' She sort of hitched herself up, trying to alter momentum. 'Stan Gibbs is still our top suspect here. What did you talk about last night?'

'Dennis Lex,' Myron said. 'Don't you get it?'

'Get what?'

'Dennis Lex is connected into all this. He's either the kidnapper, or maybe he was the first victim.'

'Neither,' she said.

'Then where is he?'

She shook it off. 'What else did you two talk about?'

'Stan's father.'

'Edwin Gibbs?' That got her attention. 'What about him?'

'That he vanished eight years ago. But you already know about that, don't you?'

She nodded a little too firmly. 'We do,' she said.

'So what do you think happened to him?' Myron asked.

She hesitated. 'You believe that Dennis Lex may be Sow the Seeds' first victim, correct?'

'I think it's something to look into, yes.'

'Our theory,' she went on, 'is that the first victim may have been Edwin Gibbs.'

Myron made a face. 'You think Stan kidnapped his own father?'

'Killed him. And the others. We don't believe any of them are still alive.'

Myron tried not to let that sink in. 'You have any evidence or motive?'

'Sometimes the apple doesn't fall far from the tree.'

'Oh, that'll go over big with a jury. Ladies and gentlemen, the apple doesn't fall far from the tree. And you should never put the cart before the horse. Plus every dog has his day.' He shook his head. 'Are you listening to yourself?'

'On its own, I admit it doesn't make sense. But put it all together. Eight years ago, Stan was starting out on his own. He was twenty-four, his father forty-six. By all accounts, the two men did not get along. Suddenly Edwin Gibbs vanishes. Stan never reports it.'

'This is silly.'

'Maybe. But then add back everything else we already know. The only columnist to get this scoop. The plagiarism. Melina Garston. Everything that Eric Ford discussed with you yesterday.'

'It still doesn't add up.'

'Then tell me where Stan Gibbs is.'

Myron looked at her. 'Isn't he at the condo?'

'Last night, after you two talked, Stan Gibbs slipped surveillance. He's done that before. We usually pick him up a few hours later. But that hasn't happened this time. He's suddenly out of sight – and by coincidence, Jeremy Downing has been snatched by the Sow the Seeds kidnapper. You want to explain that one to me?'

Myron's mouth felt dry. 'You're searching for him?'

'We got an APB. But we know he's good at hiding. You got any clue where he went?'

'None.'

'He said nothing to you about it?'

'He mentioned that he might go away for a few days. But that I should trust him.'

'Bad advice,' she said. 'Anything else?'

Myron shook his head. 'Where is Dennis Lex?' he tried again. 'Did you see him?'

'I didn't have to,' she said. But her voice had a funny monotone to it. 'He's not involved in this.'

'You keep saying that,' Myron said. 'But how do you know?'

She slowed down. 'The family.'

'You mean Susan and Bronwyn Lex?'

'Yes.'

'What about them?'

'They gave us reassurances.'

Myron almost stepped back. 'You just took their word for it?'

'I didn't say that.' She glanced around, let loose a sigh. 'And it's not my call.'

'What?'

She looked straight through him. 'Eric Ford handled it personally.'

Myron could not believe what he was hearing.

'He told me to stay away,' she said, 'that he had it covered.'

'Or covered up,' Myron said.

'Nothing I can do about it.' She looked at him. She had stressed the word *I*. Then she walked away without another word. Myron dialed his cell phone.

'Articulate,' Win said.

'We're going to need help,' Myron said. 'Is Zorra still working freelance?'

'I'll call her.'

'Maybe Big Cyndi too.'

'Do you have a plan?'

'No time for a plan,' Myron said.

'Ooo,' Win said. 'Then we're going to get nasty.'

'Yes.'

'And here I thought you weren't going to break the rules anymore.'

'Just this once,' Myron said.

'Ah,' Win countered. 'That's what they all say.'

31

Win, Esperanza, Big Cyndi, and Zorra were all in his office.

Zorra wore a yellow monogrammed sweater (the monogram being one letter: Z), large white pearls à la Wilma Flintstone, a plaid skirt, and white bobby socks. Her – or if you want to be anatomically correct, his – wig looked like early Bette Midler or maybe Little Orphan Annie on methadone. Shiny red high-heel shoes like something stolen from a trampy Dorothy in Oz adorned the men's-size-twelve feet.

Zorra smiled at Myron. 'Zorra is happy to see you.'

'Yeah,' Myron said. 'And Myron is happy to see you too.'

'This time, we're on the same side, yes?'

'Yes.'

'Zorra pleased.'

Zorra's real name was Shlomo Avrahaim, and she was a former Israeli Mossad agent. The two had had a nasty run-in not long ago. Myron still carried the wound near his rib cage – a scar-shaped Z made by a blade Zorra hid in her heel.

Win said, 'The Lex Building is too well guarded.'

'So we go with Plan B,' Myron said.

'Already in motion,' Win said.

Myron looked at Zorra. 'You armed?'

Zorra pulled a weapon out from under her skirt. 'The Uzi,' Zorra said. 'Zorra likes the Uzi.'

Myron nodded. 'Patriotic.'

'Question,' Esperanza said.

'What?'

Esperanza settled her eyes on his. 'What if this guy doesn't cooperate?'

'We don't have time to worry about it,' Myron said.

'Meaning?'

'This psycho has Jeremy,' Myron said. 'You understand that? Jeremy has to be the priority here.'

Esperanza shook her head.

'Then stay behind,' he said.

'You need me,' she said.

'Right. And Jeremy needs *me*.' He stood. 'Okay, let's go.'

Esperanza shook her head again, but she went along. The group – a sort of cut-rate Dirty (One-Third of a) Dozen – broke off when they reached the street. Esperanza and Zorra would walk. Win, Myron, and Big Cyndi headed into a garage three blocks away. Win had a car there. Chevy Nova. Totally untraceable. Win had a bunch of them. He referred to them as disposable vehicles. Like paper cups or something. The rich. You don't want to know what he does with them.

Win drove, Myron took the front passenger seat, and Big Cyndi squeezed into the back, which was a little like watching a film of childbirth on rewind. Then they were off.

The Stokes, Layton and Grace law firm was one of the most prestigious in New York. Big Cyndi stayed in reception. The receptionist, a skinny skirt-suit of gray, tried not to stare. So Big Cyndi stared at her, daring her not to look. Sometimes Big Cyndi would growl. Like a lion. No reason. She just liked to do it.

Myron and Win were ushered into a conference room that looked like a million other big Manhattan law firm conference rooms. Myron doodled on a yellow legal pad that looked like a million other big Manhattan law firm legal pads, watched through the window the smug, pink, fresh-scrubbed Harvard grads stroll by, again all looking exactly the same as the ones at a million other big Manhattan law firms. Reverse discrimination maybe, but all young white male lawyers looked the same to him.

Then again, Myron was a white Harvard law school graduate. Hmm.

Chase Layton trolled in with his rolly build and well-fed face and chubby hands and gray comb-over, looking like, well, a name partner at a big Manhattan law firm. He wore a gold wedding band on one hand and a Harvard ring on the other. He greeted

Win warmly – most wealthy people do – and then gave a firm, I'm-your-guy hand-shake to Myron.

'We're in a rush,' Win said.

Chase Layton shoved the big smile out of the room and strapped on his best battle-ready face. Everyone sat. Chase Layton folded his hands in front of him. He leaned forward, putting a bit of a belly push on the vest buttons. 'What can I do for you, Windsor?'

Rich people always called him Windsor.

'You've been after my business for a long time,' Win said.

'Well, I wouldn't say—'

'I'm here to give it to you. In exchange for a favor.'

Chase Layton was too smart to snap-bite at that. He looked at Myron. An underling. Maybe there'd be a clue how to play on this plebeian's face. Myron kept up the neutral. He was getting better at it. Must be from hanging around Win so much.

'We need to see Susan Lex,' Win said. 'You are her attorney. We'd like you to get her to come here immediately.'

'Here?'

'Yes,' Win said. 'At your office. Immediately.'

Chase opened his mouth, closed it, checked on the underling again. Still no clue. 'Are you serious, Windsor?'

'You do that, you get the Lock-Horne business. You know how much income that would generate?'

'A great deal,' Chase Layton said. 'And yet not even a third of what we receive from the Lex family.'

Win smiled. 'Talk about having your cake and eating it too.'

'I don't understand this,' Chase said.

'It's pretty straightforward, Chase.'

'Why do you want to see Ms Lex?'

'We can't divulge that.'

'I see.' Chase Layton scratched a ham-red cheek with a manicured finger. 'Ms Lex is a very private person.'

'Yes, we know.'

'She and I are friends.'

'I'm sure,' Win said.

'Perhaps I can set up an introduction.'

'No good. It has to be now.'

'Well, she and I usually conduct business at her office—'

'Again no good. It has to be here.'

Chase rolled his neck a bit, stalling for time, trying to sort through this, find an angle to play. 'She's a very busy woman. I wouldn't even know what to say to get her here.'

'You're a good attorney, Chase,' Win said, steepling his fingers. 'I'm sure you'll come up with something.'

Chase nodded, looked down, studied his manicure. 'No,' he said. He looked back up slowly. 'I don't sell out clients, Windsor.'

'Even if it meant landing a client as big as Lock-Horne?'

'Even then.'

'And you're not doing this just to impress me with your discretion?'

Chase smiled, relieved, as though he finally got the joke. 'No,' he said. 'But wouldn't that be having my cake and eating it too?' He tried to laugh it off. Win didn't join him.

'This isn't a test, Chase. I need you to get her here. I guarantee that she won't find out you helped me.'

'Do you think that's all that concerns me here – how it would look?'

Win said nothing.

'If that's the case, you've misread me. The answer is still no, I'm afraid.'

'Thank about it,' Win said.

'Nothing to think about,' Chase said. He leaned back, crossing one leg over the other, making sure the crease sat right. 'You didn't really think I'd go along with this, did you, Windsor?'

'I hoped.'

Chase again looked at Myron, then back at Win. 'I'm afraid I can't help you, gentlemen.'

'Oh, you'll help us,' Win said.

'Pardon me?'

'It's just a matter of what we need to do to get your cooperation.'

Chase frowned. 'Are you trying to bribe me?'

'No,' Win said. 'I already did that. By offering you our business.'

'Then I don't understand—'

Myron spoke for the first time. 'I'm going to make you,' he said.

Chase Layton looked at Myron and smiled. Again he said, 'Pardon me?'

Myron rose. He kept his expression flat, remembering what he'd learned from Win about intimidation. 'I don't want to hurt you,' Myron said. 'But you will call Susan Lex and get her to come here. And you'll do it now.'

Chase folded his arms and sat them atop his belly. 'If you wish to discuss this further—'

'I don't,' Myron said.

Myron walked around the table. Chase did not back away. 'I will not call her,' he said firmly. 'Windsor, would you tell your friend to sit down?'

Win feigned a helpless shrug.

Myron stood directly over Chase. He looked back at Win. Win said, 'Let me handle it.'

Myron shook his head. He loomed over Chase and let his gaze fall. 'One last chance.'

Chase Layton's face was calm, almost amused. He probably saw this as a bizarre put-on – or perhaps he was just certain that Myron would back down. That was how it was with men like Chase Layton. Physical violence was not a part of the Layton equation. Oh, sure, those uneducated animals on the street might engage in it. They might knock him on the head for his wallet. Other people – lesser people, really – yes, they solved problems with physical violence. But that was another planet – one filled with a more primitive species. In Chase Layton's world, a world of status and position and lofty manners, you were untouchable. Men threatened. Men sued. Men cursed. Men schemed behind one another's backs. Men never engaged in face-to-face violence.

That was why Myron knew that no bluff would work here. Men like Chase Layton believed that anything remotely physical was a bluff. Myron could probably point a gun at him, and he wouldn't budge. And in that scenario, Chase Layton would be right.

But not this one.

Myron boxed Chase Layton's ears hard with his palms.

Chase's eyes widened in a way they probably never had before. Myron put his hand over the lawyer's mouth, muffling the scream. He cupped the back of the man's skull and pulled him back, knocking him off his chair and on to the floor.

Chase lay on his back. Myron looked him straight in the eye and saw a tear roll down the man's cheek. Myron felt ill. He thought about Jeremy and that helped keep his face neutral. Myron said, 'Call her.'

He slowly released his hand.

Chase's breathing was labored. Myron glanced at Win. Win shook his head.

'You,' Chase said, spitting out the word, 'are going to jail.'

Myron closed his eyes, made a fist, and punched the lawyer up and under the ribs, toward the liver. The lawyer's face fell into itself. Myron held the man's mouth again, but this time there was no scream to smother.

Win eased back in his chair. 'For the record, I am the sole witness to this event. I'll swear under oath that it was self-defense.'

Chase looked lost.

'Call her,' Myron said. He tried to keep the pleading out of his voice. He looked down at Chase Layton. Chase's shirttail was out of his pants, his tie askew, his comb-over unraveling, and Myron realized that nothing would ever be the same for this man. Chase Layton had been physically assaulted. He would always walk a little more warily now. He would sleep a little less deeply. He would always be a little different inside.

Maybe so too would Myron.

Myron punched him again. Chase made an *oof* noise. Win stood by the door. Keep your face even, Myron told himself. A man at work. A man who won't stop no matter what. Myron cocked his fist again.

Five minutes later, Chase Layton called Susan Lex.

32

'Would have been better,' Win said, 'if you let me hurt him.'

Myron kept walking. 'It would have been the same,' he said.

Win shrugged. They had an hour to set up. Big Cyndi was now in the conference room with Chase Layton, supposedly going over her new professional-wrestling contract. When she entered the room, all six-six, three hundred pounds of her wearing her Big Chief Mama costume, Chase Layton barely looked up. The pain from the punches, Myron was sure, was ebbing. He had not struck the man in any place that would do lasting damage, except maybe to the obvious.

Esperanza was set up in the lobby. Myron and Win met Zorra two levels down, on the seventh floor. Zorra had staked out the lower floors and decided that this would be the quietest and easiest to contain. The office suites on the northern side were empty, Zorra noted. Anyone entering or leaving had to do so from the west. Zorra was stationed there with one cell phone. Esperanza had the other one downstairs. Win held the third. They were on a three-way line with one another. Myron and Win were in position. In the last twenty minutes, the elevator had stopped at their floor only twice. Good. Both times the door opened, Myron and Win feigned conversation, just two guys waiting for an elevator heading in the opposite direction. Real undercover commandos.

Myron hoped like hell no one happened upon the scene when it all went down. Zorra would warn them, of course, but once the operation was under way, it couldn't be stopped. They'd have to come up with some excuse, say it was a drill maybe, but Myron was not sure he could stomach hurting any more innocents today. He closed his eyes. Can't back down now. Too far gone.

Win smiled at him. 'Wondering yet again if the ends justify the means?'

'Not wondering,' Myron said.

'Oh?'

'I know they don't.'

'And yet?'

'I'm not in the mood for introspection right now.'

'But you're so good at it,' Win said.

'Thanks.'

'And knowing you as well as I do, you'll save it for later – for when you have more time. You'll gnash your teeth over what you just did. You'll feel ashamed, remorseful, guilty – though you'll also be oddly proud that you didn't have *moi* do your dirty work. You'll end up making a clear declaration that it will never happen again. And perhaps it won't – not, at least, until the stakes are this high.'

'So I'm a hypocrite,' Myron said. 'Happy?'

'But that is my point,' Win said.

'What?'

'You're not a hypocrite. You aim toward lofty heights. The fact that your arrow cannot always reach them does not make you a hypocrite.'

'So in conclusion,' Myron said, 'the ends do not justify the means. Except sometimes.'

Win spread his hands. 'See? I just saved you hours of soul-searching. Perhaps I should consider penning one of those how-to-manage-your-time manuals.'

Esperanza broke in through the phone. 'They're here,' she said.

Win put the phone to his ear. 'How many?'

'Three coming in. Susan Lex. That granite guy Myron keeps talking about. Another bodyguard. Two more staying parked outside.'

'Zorra,' Win said into the phone. 'Please keep an eye on the two gentlemen outside.'

Zorra said, 'And if they move?'

'Detain them.'

'With pleasure.' Zorra giggled. Win smiled. Welcome to the Psycho Hotline. Only $3.99 per minute. First call is free.

Myron and Win waited now. Two minutes passed. Esperanza said, 'Middle elevator. All three are inside.'

'Anyone else with them?'

'No . . . wait. Damn, two businessmen are going in.'

Myron closed his eyes and cursed.

Win looked at him. 'Your call.'

Panic squeezed Myron's chest. Innocent people in the elevator. There was sure to be violence. Witnesses now.

'Well?'

'Hold the phone.' It was Esperanza. 'The granite guy blocked their path. Looks like he told them to wait for another elevator.'

'Top-notch security,' Win said. 'Good to see we're not dealing with amateurs.'

'Okay,' Esperanza said. 'Just the three of them are inside now.'

The relief in Myron's face was palpable.

Esperanza said, 'Elevator closing . . . now.'

Myron pressed the Up button. Win took out his forty-four. Myron pulled out a Glock. They waited. Myron kept the gun by his thigh. It felt heavy in a terrible, comforting way. Myron kept glancing down the corridor. No one. He hoped their luck would hold. He felt his pulse start to race. His mouth was dry. The room suddenly felt warmer.

A minute later, the light above the middle elevator dinged.

Win's face was in the zone, semi-euphoric. He wriggled his eyebrows and said, 'Showtime.'

Myron tensed his muscles, leaned in a bit. The elevator's whirring noise stopped. There was a delay and then the doors started sliding open. Win didn't wait. He was inside before the opening had reached a foot. He found Grover and stuck the gun in the big man's ear. Myron did the same with the other guard.

'Waxy ear buildup a problem, Grover?' Win said in his best voice-over. 'Smith and Wesson has the solution!'

Susan Lex started to open her mouth. Win cut her off with a finger against her lip and a gentle 'Shh.'

Win frisked and disarmed Grover. Myron followed his lead with the second guard. Grover glared daggers at Win. Win took them on and said, 'Please – no, pretty please – make a sudden move.'

Grover didn't budge.

Win stepped back. The elevator door started closing. Myron stopped it with his foot. He pointed the weapon at Susan Lex. 'You're coming with me,' Myron said.

'Don't you want revenge first?' Grover said.

Myron looked at him.

'Go ahead.' Grover spread his hands. 'Hit me in the gut. Go ahead, give it your best shot.'

'Pardon *moi*,' Win said. 'But does that offer apply to me too?'

Grover looked at the smaller man like a tasty left-over. 'I heard you're not bad,' he said.

Win looked back at Myron. ' "Not bad," ' he repeated. 'Monsieur Grover heard I was "not bad." '

'Win,' Myron said.

Win snapped his knee deep into Grover's groin. He followed through, driving the man's testicles all the way into his stomach. Grover did not make a sound. He simply folded like a bad hand of poker.

'Oh, wait, you said "gut," didn't you?' Win looked down at him, frowned. 'Must work on my aim. Perhaps you're right. Perhaps I am merely "not bad." '

Grover was on his knees, his hands between his legs. Win kicked him in the head with his instep. Grover toppled over like a bowling pin. Win looked over at the other guard, who was putting his hands up and backing quickly into a corner.

'Will you tell your friends I was "not bad?" ' Win asked him.

The guard shook his head.

'Enough,' Myron said.

Win picked up the cell phone. 'Zorra, report.'

'They are not moving, handsome.'

'Come back up then. You can help me clean up.'

'Clean up? Ooo, Zorra will hurry.'

Win laughed.

'No more,' Myron said. Win did not reply, but Myron hadn't really expected him to. Myron grabbed Susan Lex's arm. 'Let's go.'

He pulled her into the stairwell. Zorra bounded into view – on high heels no less. Leaving two unarmed men alone with Win and Zorra. Talk about scary. But he had no choice here. Myron turned to Susan Lex, keeping tight hold of her elbow.

'I need your help,' he said to her.

Susan Lex looked at him, head high, not backing off.

'I promise not to say anything,' he went on. 'I have no interest in hurting you or your family. But you're going to take me to see Dennis.'

'And if I say no?'

Myron just looked at her.

'You'd hurt me?' she said.

'I just beat up an innocent man,' Myron said.

'And you'd do the same to a woman?'

'I wouldn't want to be accused of sexism.'

Her expression remained defiant, but unlike Chase Layton, she seemed to understand how the real world worked. 'You know what sort of power I have.'

'I do.'

'Then you know what I'll do to you when this is all over?'

'I don't much care. A thirteen-year-old boy has been kidnapped.'

She almost smiled. 'I thought you said he needed a bone marrow transplant.'

'I don't have time to explain.'

'My brother isn't involved in this.'

'I keep hearing that.'

'Because it's true.'

'Then prove it to me.'

Something in her face shifted then, changing her features, relaxing them into something strangely approaching tranquility. 'Come,' she said. 'Let's go.'

33

Susan Lex directed him north on the FDR to the Harlem River Drive and then north again to 684. Once they were in Connecticut, the roads grew quieter. Woods thickened. Buildings grew scarce. Traffic was pretty much nonexistent.

'We're almost there,' Susan Lex said. 'I'd like the truth now.'

'I'm telling you the truth.'

'Fine,' she said. Then: 'How do you plan on getting away with this?'

'With what?'

'Are you going to kill me when this is all over?'

'No.'

'Then I'll come back after you. I'll press charges, if nothing else.'

'I told you before. I don't much care. But I've thought of something.'

'Oh?'

'Dennis will save me.'

'How?'

'If he is the Sow the Seeds kidnapper—'

'He's not.'

'—or somehow involved with him, then what I'm doing here will be small potatoes by comparison.'

'And if he's not?'

Myron shrugged. 'Either way, I'm going to learn whatever it is you want to hide. We make a deal. I never tell what I saw. In exchange, you leave me alone.'

'Or I can simply kill you.'

'I don't believe you'd do that.'

'No?'

'You're not a killer. And even if you were, it would be too complicated. I'd leave evidence behind. I have Win covering my back. It would be too messy.'

'We'll see,' she said, but there was no starch there. She pointed up ahead. 'Turn off up here.'

She pointed to a dirt road that seemed to materialize from nowhere. There was a guardhouse fifty yards down and to the left. Myron pulled up. Susan Lex leaned over and smiled. The guard waved her through. There were no signs, no identification marks, nothing. The whole setup looked like some sort of militia compound.

After the gatehouse, the dirt road stopped and a paved one began. New pavement from the looks of it colored the dark black-gray of heavy rain. Trees crowded the sides like parade watchers. Up ahead, the road narrowed. The trees closed in too. Myron veered the car to the left and passed through wrought-iron gates guarded by two stone falcons.

'What is this?' Myron asked.

Susan Lex did not reply.

A mansion seemed to push out of the green, elbowing its way forward. The exterior was classic off-white Georgian but on an oversized scale. Palladian windows, pilasters, fancy pediments, curved balconies, brick cornering and what looked like real stone masonry were all garnished with hints of green ivy. A set of oversized double doors were dead center, the entire edifice perfectly symmetrical.

'Park in the lot over there,' Susan Lex said.

Myron followed her finger. There was indeed a paved lot. Myron figured it contained close to twenty cars. Various makes. A BMW, a couple of Honda Accords, three Mercedes of different lineage, Fords, SUVs, one station wagon. Your basic American melting pot. Myron glanced back at the oversized manor. He noticed ramps now. Lots of them. He checked the cars. Several had MD license plates.

'A hospital,' he said.

Susan Lex smiled. 'Come along.'

They headed up the brick path. Gloved gardeners were on their knees, working on the flower beds. A woman walked by in the opposite direction. She smiled politely but said nothing. They passed through an arched entranceway and into a two-story foyer. A woman seated behind the desk stood, slightly startled.

'We weren't expecting you, ma'am,' she said.

'That's fine.'

'I don't have security set up.'

'That's fine too.'

'Yes, ma'am.'

Susan Lex barely broke stride. She took the sweeping staircase on her left, staying in the middle, not touching a handrail. Myron followed.

'What did she mean about security?' Myron asked.

'When I visit, they make sure the hallways are kept clear and that no one else is present.'

'To keep your secret?'

'Yes,' she said. She did not stop moving. 'Perhaps you noticed that she called me "ma'am." That's part of the discretion here. They never use names.'

When they reached the top level, Susan turned to the left. The corridor had raised wallpaper in a classic floral design and nothing else. No small tables, no chairs, no pictures in frames, no Oriental runners. They passed by maybe a dozen rooms, only two with doors open. Myron noticed that the doors were extra wide and he remembered his visit to Babies and Children's Hospital. Extra wide doors there too. For wheelchairs and stretchers and the like.

When they reached the end of the corridor, Susan stopped, took a deep breath, looked back at Myron. 'Are you ready?'

He nodded.

She opened the door and stepped inside. Myron followed. A four-poster antique bed, like something you'd see on a tour of Jefferson's Monticello, overwhelmed the room. The walls were warm green with woodwork trim. There was a small crystal chandelier, a burgundy Victorian couch, a Persian rug with deep scarlets. A Mozart violin concerto was playing a bit too loudly on the stereo. A woman sat in the corner reading a book. She too started upright when she saw who it was.

'It's okay,' Susan Lex said. 'Would you mind leaving us for a few moments?'

'Yes, ma'am,' the woman said. 'If you need anything—'

'I'll ring, thank you.'

The woman did a semi-curtsy/semi-bow and hurried out. Myron looked at the man in the bed. The resemblance to the computer rendering was uncanny, almost perfect. Even, strangely enough, the dead eyes. Myron moved closer. Dennis Lex followed him with the dead eyes, unfocused, empty, like windows over a vacant lot.

'Mr Lex?'

Dennis Lex just stared at him.

'He can't talk,' she said.

Myron turned to her. 'I don't understand,' he said.

'You were right before. It's a hospital. Of sorts. In another era, I suppose one would have called it a private sanitarium.'

'How long has your brother been here?'

'Thirty years,' she said. She moved toward the bed, and for the first time, she looked down at her brother. 'You see, Mr Bolitar, this is where the wealthy store unpleasantness.' She reached down and stroked her brother's cheek. Dennis Lex did not respond. 'We're too cultured not to give our loved ones the best. All very humane and practical, don't you know.'

Myron waited for her to say more. She kept stroking her brother's cheek. He tried to see her face, but she kept it lowered and away from him.

'Why is he here?' Myron asked.

'I shot him,' she said.

Myron opened his mouth, closed it, did the math. 'But you were only a child when he disappeared.'

'Fourteen years old,' she said. 'Bronwyn was six.' She stopped stroking the cheek. 'It's an old story, Mr Bolitar. You've probably heard it a thousand times. We were playing with a loaded gun. Bronwyn wanted to hold it, I said no, he reached for it, it went off.' She said it all in one breath, staring down at her brother, still stroking the cheek. 'This is the end result.'

Myron looked at the still eyes in the bed. 'He's been here since?'

She nodded. 'For a while I kept waiting for him to die. So I could officially be a murderer.'

'You were a child,' Myron said. 'It was an accident.'

She looked at him and smiled. 'My, that means so much coming from you, thank you.'

Myron said nothing.

'No matter,' she said. 'Daddy took care of it. He arranged for my brother to have the best care. He was a very private person, my father. It was his gun. He'd left it where his children could play with it. His business and reputation were both growing. He had political aspirations at the time. He just wanted it all to go away.'

'And it did.'

She tilted her head back and forth. 'Yes.'

'What about your mother?'

'What about her?'

'What did she say?'

'My mother hated unpleasantness, Mr Bolitar. After the incident, she never saw her son again.'

Dennis Lex made a sound, a guttural scrape, nothing remotely human. Susan gently shushed him.

'Did you and Bronwyn ever get help?' Myron asked.

She cocked an eyebrow. 'Help?'

'Counseling. To help you through it.'

She made a face. 'Oh please,' she said.

Myron stood there, his mind circling nowhere over nothing.

'So now you know the truth, Mr Bolitar.'

'I guess,' he said.

'Meaning?'

'I wonder why you told me all this. You could have just shown Dennis to me.'

'Because you won't talk.'

'How can you be so sure?'

She smiled. 'After you shoot your own brother, shooting strangers becomes so easy.'

'You don't really believe that.'

'No, I suppose not.' Susan Lex turned and faced him. 'The fact is, you really don't have much to tell. As you said earlier, we both have reasons to keep our mouths shut. You'll be arrested for kidnapping and Lord knows what. The evidence of my crime – if indeed it was a crime – is nonexistent. You'd be worse off than I.'

Myron nodded, but his mind still whirred. Her story might be true or just something she told him to gain sympathy, to contain the damage. Still, there was the ring of truth in her words. Maybe her reason for talking was simpler. Maybe, after all this time, she just needed someone who'd listen to her confession. Didn't matter.

None of it mattered. There was nothing here. Dennis Lex was truly a dead end.

Myron looked out the window. The sun was starting to dip away. He checked his watch. Jeremy had been missing five hours now – five hours alone with a madman – and Myron's best lead, his *only* lead, was lying brain-damaged in a hospital room.

The sun was still strong, bathing the expansive garden in white. Myron saw what looked like a maze made of shrubbery. He spotted several patients in wheelchairs, legs covered with blankets, sitting by a fountain. Serene. The rays reflected off a pool of water and a statue in the middle of—

He stopped. The statue.

Myron felt the blood in his veins turn to crystal. He shaded his eyes with his hand and squinted again.

'Oh Christ,' he said.

Then he sprinted toward the stairs.

34

Susan Lex's helicopter was starting to descend toward the sanitarium's landing pad when Kimberly Green called him on the cell phone.

'We've caught Stan Gibbs,' she said. 'But the boy wasn't with him.'

'That's because he isn't the kidnapper.'

'You know something I don't?'

Myron ignored the question. 'Has Stan told you anything?'

'Nope. He lawyered up already. Says he won't talk to anyone but you. You, Myron. Why don't I find that particularly surprising?'

Had Myron responded, the helicopter's rotor would have drowned it out. He backed off a few steps. The copter touched down. The pilot stuck his head out and waved to him.

'I'm on my way,' Myron shouted into the phone. He switched it off and turned to Susan Lex. 'Thank you.'

She nodded.

He ducked and ran toward the helicopter. As they rose, Myron looked back down. Susan Lex's chin was tilted up, her eyes still on him. He waved. And she waved back.

Stan was not in a holding cell because they had nothing to hold him on. He sat in a waiting room with his eyes on the table and let his attorney, Clara Steinberg, do the talking. Myron had known Clara – he called her Aunt Clara though there was no familial relationship – since he was too young to remember. Aunt Clara and Uncle Sidney were Mom and Dad's closest friends. Dad had gone to elementary school with Clara. Mom had roomed with her in law school. Aunt Clara, in fact, had set up Mom and Dad on their first date. She liked to remind Myron with a wink that 'you wouldn't be here if it weren't for your aunt Clara.' Then she'd wink again. Subtle, that Clara. During the holidays, she always pinched Myron's cheeks in admiration of his *punim*.

'Let me set up the ground rules, *bubbe*,' she said to him. Clara had gray hair and a pair of oversized glasses that magnified her eyes to Ant-Man size. She looked up at him and the giant eyes seemed to reel in everything all at once. She wore a white blouse with a gray vest, matching skirt, a kerchief around her neck, and teardrop pearl earrings. Think Shtetl Barbara Bush.

'One,' she said, 'I am Mr Gibbs's attorney of record. I have requested that this conversation not be overheard. I have changed rooms four times to make sure the authorities don't listen in. But I don't trust them. They think your aunt Clara is an old dodo bird. They think we're going to chat right here.'

'We're not?' Myron said.

'We're not,' she repeated. There was little hint of the cheek pincher here; if she were an athlete, you'd say that she'd strapped on her game face. 'What we're going to do first is stand up. Got me?'

'Stand up,' Myron repeated.

'Right. Then I'm going to lead you and Stan outside, across the street. I'm going to remain on the other side of the street with all those friendly agents. We do this right now, quickly, so they won't have a chance to set up surveillance. Understood?'

Myron nodded. Stan kept his eyes on the Formica.

'Good, just so we're all on the same page here.' She knocked on the door. Kimberly Green opened it. Clara walked past her without speaking. Myron and Stan followed. Kimberly rushed up behind them.

'Where do you think you're going?'

'Change of plans, doll.'

'You can't do that.'

'Sure I can. I'm a sweet little old lady.'

'I don't care if you're the Queen Mother,' Kimberly said. 'You're not going anywhere.'

'You married, hon?'

'What?'

'Never mind,' Clara said. 'Try this on for size. See how it fits. My client demands privacy.'

'We already promised—'

'Shh, you're talking when you should be listening. My client demands privacy. So he and Mr Bolitar are going to take a little walk somewhere. You and I will watch from a distance. We will not listen in.'

'I already told you—'

'Shh, you're giving me a headache.' Aunt Clara rolled her eyes and kept walking. Myron and Stan followed. They reached the doorway. Clara pointed to a bus depot across the street. 'Sit over there,' she said to them. 'On the bench.'

Myron said okay. Clara put a hand on his elbow.

'Cross at the corner,' she said. 'And wait for the light.'

The two men walked to the corner and waited for the light before crossing the street. Kimberly Green and her fellow agents fumed. Clara took them by the hand and led them back toward the building's entrance. Stan and Myron sat on the bench. Stan watched a New Jersey Transit bus go by like it carried the secret to life.

'We don't have time to enjoy the scenery, Stan.'

Stan leaned forward, put his elbows on his knees. 'This is difficult for me.'

'If it makes it any easier,' Myron said, 'I know that the Sow the Seeds kidnapper is your father.'

Stan's head fell into his hands.

'Stan?'

'How did you find out?'

'Through Dennis Lex. I found him in a private sanitarium in Connecticut. He's been there for thirty years. But you already knew that, didn't you?'

Gibbs said nothing.

'At the sanitarium, there's a big garden in the back. With this statue of Diana the Huntress. There's a picture in your condo of you and your father standing in front of that same statue. He was a patient there. You don't have to confirm or deny it. I was just there. Susan Lex has pull. An administrator told us Edwin Gibbs had been in and out of there for fifteen years. The rest is fairly obvious. Your father was there a long time. It'd be easy to learn who else was there, no matter how strict the so-called security. So he knew about Dennis Lex. And he stole his identity. It's a hell of a twist, I'll give him that. Fake IDs used to be somewhat pretty easy to come by. You'd visit a graveyard, find a child who died, request his social security card, bingo. But that doesn't work anymore. Computers closed down that loophole. Nowadays when you die, your social security number dies with you. So your father took the identity of someone still alive, someone who has no use for it, someone committed permanently. In other words, he used the ID of a living person who has no life. And to go deeper undercover, he changed the person's name. Dennis Lex became Davis Taylor. Untraceable.'

'Except you traced it.'

'I got lucky.'

'Go on,' Stan said. 'Tell me what else you know.'

'We don't have time for this, Stan.'

'You don't understand,' he said.

'What?'

'If you're the one who says it – if you figure it out on your own – it's not as much a betrayal. You see?'

No time to argue. And maybe Myron did see. 'Let's start with the question every reporter wanted to know: why you? Why did the Sow the Seeds kidnapper choose you? The answer: because the kidnapper was your father. He knew you wouldn't turn him in. Maybe part of you hoped someone would figure it out. I don't know. I also don't know if you found him or he found you.'

'He found me,' Stan said. 'He came to me as a reporter. Not as a son. He made that clear.'

'Sure,' Myron said, 'double protection. He gets you with the fact that you'd be turning in your own father – plus he gives you an ethical foundation for remaining silent. The beloved First Amendment. You couldn't name a source. It gave you a very neat out – you could be both moralistic and the good son.'

Stan looked up. 'So you see that I had no choice.'

'Oh, I wouldn't be so easy on myself,' Myron said. 'You weren't being totally altruistic. Everyone says you were ambitious. That played a part here. You got fame out of this. You were handed a monster story – the kind that propels careers into the stratosphere. You were on TV and got your own cable show. You got a big raise and invited to fancy parties. You want to tell me that wasn't a part of it?'

'It was a by-product,' Stan said. 'It wasn't a factor.'

'You say so.'

'It's like you said – I couldn't turn him in, even if I wanted to. There was a constitutional principle here. Even if he wasn't my father, I had an obligation—'

'Save it for your minister,' Myron said. 'Where is he?'

Stan did not reply. Myron looked across the street. Lots of traffic. The cars started blurring and through them, standing on the other side of the street with Kimberly Green, he saw Greg Downing.

'That man over there,' Myron said, pointing with his chin. 'That's the boy's father.'

Stan looked, but his face didn't change.

'There's a kid in danger,' Myron said. 'That trumps your constitutional cover.'

'He's still my father.'

'And he's kidnapped a thirteen-year-old boy,' Myron said.

Stan looked up. 'What would *you* do?'

'What?'

'Would you give up your father? Just like that?'

'If he was kidnapping children? Yeah, I would.'

'Do you really think it's that easy?'

'Who said anything about easy?' Myron said.

Stan put his head back in his hands. 'He's sick and he needs help.'

'And there's also an innocent boy out there.'

'So?'

Myron looked at him.

'I don't mean to sound callous, but I don't know this boy. He has no connection to me. My father does. That's what matters here. You hear about a plane crash, right? You hear about how two hundred people die and you sigh and you go on with your life and you thank God it wasn't your loved one in the plane. Don't you do that?'

'What's your point?'

'You do that because the people on the plane are strangers. Like this boy. We don't care about strangers. They don't count.'

'Speak for yourself,' Myron said.

'Are you close to your father, Myron?'

'Yes.'

'And in your heart of hearts, in your deepest, most honest moments, if you could sacrifice his life to save those two hundred people on the airplane, would you do it? Think about it. If God came down to you and said, "Okay, that plane never crashed. Those people all arrive safely. In exchange, your father will die." Would you make that trade?'

'I'm not into playing God.'

'But you're asking me to,' Stan said. 'I turn my father in, they'll kill him. He'll get the lethal injection. If that's not playing God, I don't know what is. So I'm asking you. Would you trade those two hundred lives for your father's?'

'We don't have time—'

'Would you?'

'Okay, if it was my father shooting down the plane,' Myron said, 'yes, Stan, I would make that trade.'

'And suppose your father wasn't culpable? If he was sick or deranged?'

'Stan, we don't have time for this.'

Something in Stan's face dropped. He closed his eyes.

'There's a boy out there,' Myron said. 'We can't let him die.'

'And if he's already dead?'

'I don't know.'

'You'll want my father dead.'

'Not by my hand,' Myron said.

Stan took a deep breath and looked over at Greg Downing. Greg stared back, stared right through him. 'Okay,' he said at last. 'But we go alone.'

'Alone?'

'Just you and me.'

Kimberly Green had a major conniption. 'Are you insane?'

They were back inside, sitting around the Formica table. Kimberly Green, Rick Peck, and two other faceless feds were hunched together as one. Clara Steinberg sat with her client. Greg sat next to Myron. Jeremy's kidnapping had siphoned all the blood from Greg's face. His hands looked sucked dry, his skin

218

almost crisp, his eyes too solid and unblinking. Myron put a hand on his shoulder. Greg didn't seem to notice.

'You want my client to cooperate or not?' Clara asked.

'I'm supposed to let my number one suspect go?'

'I'm not running away,' Stan said.

'How am I supposed to know that?' Kimberly countered.

'It's the only way,' Stan said, his voice a plea. 'You'll go in with guns blazing. Someone is going to get hurt.'

'We're professionals,' Green countered. 'We don't go in with guns blazing.'

'My father is unstable. If he sees a lot of cops, I can guarantee there will be bloodshed.'

'Doesn't have to be that way,' she said. 'It's up to him.'

'Exactly,' Stan said. 'I'm not taking that chance with my father's life. You let us go. You don't follow us. I'll have him surrender to you. Myron will be with me the whole time. He's armed and he has a cell phone.'

'Come on,' Myron said. 'We're wasting time here.'

Kimberly Green chewed on her lower lip. 'I don't have the authorization—'

'Forget it,' Clara Steinberg said.

'Excuse me?'

Clara pointed a meaty finger at Kimberly Green. 'Listen up, missy, you haven't arrested Mr Gibbs, correct?'

Green hesitated. 'That's correct.'

Clara turned to Stan and Myron and waved the backs of both hands at them. 'So shoo, go, good-bye. We're talking nonsense here. Hurry along. Shoo.'

Stan and Myron slowly rose.

'Shoo.'

Stan looked down at Kimberly. 'If I spot a tail, I'm calling this off. You got me?'

She stewed in silence.

'You've been trailing me for three weeks now. I know what one of your tails looks like.'

'She won't tail you.'

It was Greg Downing. He and Stan locked eyes again. Greg stood. 'I want to go with you too,' Greg said. 'And I probably have the strongest interest in keeping your father alive.'

'How do you figure?'

'Your father's bone marrow can save my son's life. If he dies, so does my son. And if Jeremy has been hurt . . . well, I'd like to be there for him.'

Stan didn't waste a lot of time thinking about it. 'Let's hurry.'

35

Stan drove. Greg sat in the front passenger seat, Myron in the back.

'Where are we going?' Myron asked.

'Bernardsville,' Stan said. 'It's in Morris County.'

Myron knew the town.

'My grandmother died three years ago,' Stan said. 'We haven't sold the house yet. My father sometimes stays there.'

'Where else does he stay?'

'Waterbury, Connecticut.'

Greg looked back at Myron. The old man, the blond wig. It clicked for both of them at the same time.

'He's Nathan Mostoni?'

Stan nodded. 'That's his main alias. The real Nathan Mostoni is another patient at Pine Hills – that's what we call that fancy loony bin, Pine Hills. Mostoni was the one who came up with the idea of using the identification of the committed, mostly for scams. He and my father became close friends. When Nathan slipped into total delirium, my father took his identity.'

Greg shook his head, made two fists. 'You should have turned the crazy bastard in.'

'You love your son, don't you, Mr Downing?'

Greg gave Stan a look that could have bored holes through titanium. 'What the hell does that have to do with anything?'

'Would you want your son to turn you in one day?'

'Don't hand me that. If I'm a raving psychopathic maniac, yeah, my son can turn me in. Or better, he can put a bullet in my head. You knew your old man was sick, right? The least you could have done was get him help.'

'We tried,' Stan said. 'He was in institutions most of his adult life. It didn't do any good. Then he ran off. When he finally called me, I hadn't seen him in eight years. Imagine that. Eight years. He calls me and tells me he needs to talk to me as a reporter. He made that clear. As a reporter. No matter what he told me, I couldn't reveal the source. He made me promise. I was confused as all hell. But I agreed. And then he told me his story. What he'd been doing. I could barely breathe. I wanted to die. I wanted to just dry up and die.'

Greg put his fingers to his mouth. Stan concentrated on the road. Myron stared out the window. He thought about the father of three young children, age forty-one; the female college student, age twenty; and the young newlyweds, ages twenty-eight and twenty-seven. He thought about Jeremy's scream over the phone. He thought about Emily waiting at the house, her mind sowing the seeds, sick and blackening.

They got off Route 78 and took 287 north. They exited onto winding streets with no straightaways. Bernardsville was about old money and rustic wealth, a town of converted mills and stone houses and waterwheels. There were fields of long brown grass swaying in death, everything a little too old and too neatly overgrown.

'It's on this road,' Stan said.

Myron looked out. His mouth was dry. He felt a tingle deep in his belly. The car traveled down another corkscrew of a street, the loose gravel crunching under the tires. There were deeply wooded lots commingling with your standard suburban front lawns. Plenty of center-hall colonials and those mid-seventies ranches that aged like milk left out on the counter. A yellow sign warned about children at play, but Myron saw none.

They pulled into a cake-dried driveway with weeds poking up through the cracks. Myron lowered his window. There was plenty of burnt-out grass, but the sweet summer smell of lillies still loomed and even cloyed. Crickets droned. Wildflowers blossomed. Not a hint of menace.

Up ahead Myron spotted what looked like a farmhouse. Black shutters stood out against the white clapboards. There were lights coming from inside, giving the house a glow that was big and soft and oddly welcoming. The front porch was the type that craved a swinging settee and a pitcher of lemonade.

When the car reached the front of the house, Stan shifted into park and turned off the ignition. The crickets eased up. Myron almost waited for someone to note that it was 'Quiet' and for someone else to add, 'Yeah, too quiet.'

Stan turned to them. 'I think I should go in first,' he said.

Neither man argued. Greg stared out the window at the house, probably conjuring up unspeakable horrors. Myron's left leg started jackhammering. It often did when he was tense. Stan reached for the door handle.

That was when the first bullet smashed through the front passenger-side window.

The glass exploded, and Myron saw Greg's head fly back at a rate it was never supposed to achieve. A thick gob of crimson smacked Myron in the cheek.

'Greg!'

No time. Instincts took over. Myron grabbed Greg, pushed him down, trying to keep his own head down too. Blood. Lots of it. From Greg. He was bleeding, bleeding heavily, but Myron couldn't tell from where. Another bullet rang out. Another window shattered, raining shards of glass down on Myron's head. He kept his hand on top of Greg, tried to cover him, protect him. Greg's own hand fumbled absently on his chest and face, calmly searching for the bullet hole. Blood kept flowing. From the neck. Greg's neck. Or collarbone. Whatever. He couldn't see through the blood. Myron tried to stop the flow with his bare hand, pushing the sticky liquid away, finding the wound with his finger, applying pressure with his palm. But the blood slipped through the cracks between his fingers. Greg looked up at him with big eyes.

Stan Gibbs put his hands over his head and ducked into a quasi-emergency-landing position. 'Stop!' he yelled, almost child-like. 'Dad!'

Another bullet. More glass shards. Myron reached into his pocket and pulled out his gun. Greg grabbed his hand and pulled it down. Myron looked at him.

'Can't kill him,' Greg said to Myron. There was blood in his mouth now. 'If he dies . . . Jeremy's only hope.'

Myron nodded, but he didn't put the gun away. He looked over at Stan. In the distance, they heard a helicopter. Then sirens. The feds were on their way. No surprise. There was no way they weren't going to follow. By air, at the very least.

Greg's breathing was short spurts. His eyes were going hazy-gray.

'We got to do something here, Stan,' Myron said.

'Just stay down,' Stan said. Then he opened the car door and shouted, 'Dad!'

No reply.

Stan got out of the car. He raised his hands and stood. 'Please,' he shouted. 'They'll be here soon. They'll kill you.'

Nothing. The air was so motionless that Myron thought he could still hear the echoes from the gun blasts.

'Dad?'

Myron lifted his head a little and risked a glance. A man stepped out from behind the side of the house. Edwin Gibbs wore full army fatigues with combat boots. He had an ammunition belt hanging off his shoulder. His rifle was pointed toward the ground. Myron could see it was Nathan Mostoni, though he looked twenty years younger. His head was high, chin up. His back was straight.

Greg made a gurgling sound. Myron ripped off his shirt and pushed it against the wound. But Greg's eyes were closing. 'Stay with me,' Myron urged. 'Come on, Greg. Stay here.'

Greg did not reply. His eyes fluttered and closed. Myron felt his heart slam into his throat. 'Greg?'

He felt for a pulse. It was there. Myron was no doctor, but it didn't feel strong. Oh damn. Oh come on.

Outside the car, Stan moved closer to his father. 'Please,' Stan said. 'Put down the rifle, Dad.'

The fed cars poured into the driveway. Brakes squealed. Feds jumped out of their vehicles, took position using the open doors as shields, aimed their weapons. Edwin Gibbs looked confused, panicked, Frankenstein's monster suddenly surrounded by angry villagers. Stan hurried toward him.

The air seemed to thicken, molasses-like. It was hard to move, hard to breathe. Myron could almost feel the officers tense up, fingers itchy, tips touching the cold metal of the trigger. He let go of Greg for a moment and shouted, 'You can't shoot him!'

A fed had a megaphone. 'Put down the rifle! Now!'

'Don't shoot!' Myron shouted.

For a moment nothing happened. Time did that in-and-out motion where everything rushes and freezes all at one time. Another fed car skidded up the driveway. A news van followed, screeching when it hit the brakes. Stan kept walking toward his father.

'You are surrounded,' the megaphone said. 'Drop the rifle and put your hands behind your head. Drop to your knees.'

Edwin Gibbs looked left, looked right. Then he smiled. Myron felt the dread rise up in his chest. Gibbs lifted his rifle.

Myron rolled out of the car. 'No!'

Stan Gibbs broke into a sprint. His father spotted him, his face calm. He aimed the rifle at his approaching son. Stan kept running. Time did stop this time, waiting for the blast of gunfire. But it didn't come. Stan had gained on him too fast. Edwin Gibbs closed his eyes and let his son tackle him. The two men fell to the ground. Stan stayed on top of his father, blanketing him, leaving no space open.

'Don't shoot him,' Stan yelled. His voice sounded hurt, again so childlike. 'Please don't shoot him.'

Edwin Gibbs lay on his back. He let go of the rifle. It dropped into the grass. Stan pushed it away, still on top of his father, still shielding him from harm. They stayed there until the officers took over. They gently removed Stan and then rolled Edwin Gibbs onto his stomach, cuffing his hands behind his back. The news camera caught it all.

Myron turned back to the car. Greg's eyes were still closed. He wasn't moving. Two of the officers ran toward the car, calling into their radios for an ambulance. Nothing Myron could do for Greg now. He looked back at the farmhouse, his heart still lodged in his throat. He ran toward the house and grabbed the knob. The door was locked. He used his shoulder. The door came down. Myron stepped into the foyer.

'Jeremy?' he called out.

But there was no reply.

36

They didn't find Jeremy Downing.

Myron checked every room, every closet, the basement, the garage. Nothing. The feds streamed in with him. They started knocking down walls. They used a heat sensor to check for underground caves or hidden places. Nothing. In the garage, they found a white van. In the back of it, they found one of Jeremy's red sneakers.

But that was it.

News vans, lots of them, gathered at the end of the driveway. What with the kidnapped boy, his famous father shot and in critical condition, a potential serial killer in custody, the connection to Stan Gibbs and the famed plagiarism charges – the story was getting the full, round-the-clock, give-it-a-banner-and-theme-music, death-of-Diana coverage. Stiffly coiffed correspondents flashed their best grim-news teeth and led with phrases like 'the vigil continues' or 'the search is reaching its xth hour' or 'behind me lurks the lair' or 'we'll be here until.'

A recent photograph of Jeremy, the one Emily had on the Web, ran continuously on all the stations. Brokaw, Jennings and Rather interrupted their programming. Viewers called in tips, but so far none amounted to anything.

And the hours passed.

Emily drove to the scene. It played on all the usual outlets, her head lowered, hurrying toward a waiting car like an arrested felon, the flashbulbs creating a grotesque strobe effect. Cameramen elbowed each other out of the way to capture a glimpse of the stricken mother collapsing in the back of the car. They even got a shot of her through the passenger seat crying. Great TV.

Nightfall brought out searchlights. Volunteers and law officials scoured the nearby grounds for signs of recent graves or digging. Nothing. They brought in dogs. Nothing. They spoke to neighbors, some of whom 'never trusted that family' but most gave the standard 'seemed like nice folk, real quiet neighbors' spiel.

Edwin Gibbs had been taken into custody. They tried to question him at the Bernardsville Police Station, but he wasn't talking. Clara Steinberg became his attorney. She stayed with him. So did Stan. They pleaded with Edwin, Myron guessed, but so far, he hadn't talked.

Back at the farmhouse, the wind picked up. Myron's bad knee ached, each step giving him a fresh jolt of pain. The pain was unpredictable, arriving whenever it damn well pleased, staying on like the most unwelcome houseguest. There was no side benefit to the knee pain, no weather forecasting or anything like that. Some days it just ached. Nothing he could do about it. He approached Emily and put his arm around her.

'He's still out there,' Emily said to the dark.

Myron said nothing.

'He's all alone. And it's night. And he's probably scared.'

'We'll find him, Em.'

'Myron?'

'Hmm.'

'Is this more payback for that night?'

Another search party returned, their shoulders slumped in resignation, if not defeat. Odd thing, these search parties. You wanted to find something, yet you didn't want to find something.

'No,' Myron said. 'I think you were right. I think our mistake was the best thing that could have happened. And maybe there's a price to pay to have something so good.'

She closed her eyes, but she did not cry. Myron stayed next to her. The wind howled, scattering the surrounding voices like dead leaves, whipping branches, and whispering in your ear like the most frightening lover.

37

Myron and Win looked through the one-way glass at Clara Steinberg's back and the faces of Stan and Edwin Gibbs. Kimberly Green stood with them. So did Eric Ford. Emily had gone to the hospital to sit vigil while Greg was in surgery. No one seemed to know if he'd make it.

'Why aren't you listening in?' Myron asked.

'Can't,' Ford replied. 'Attorney-client.'

'How long they been at it?'

'On and off since we took him into custody.'

Myron checked the clock behind his head. Nearly three in the morning. Evidence collection teams had leveled the house, but still no clue where Jeremy was. Fatigue lined everyone's face, except maybe Win's. Fatigue never registered on his face. Win must internalize it. Or maybe it had something to do with having little to no conscience.

'We don't have time for this,' Myron said.

'I know,' Eric Ford said. 'It's been a long night for all of us.'

'Do something.'

'Like what?' Ford snapped. 'What exactly would you like me to do?'

Win picked up that one. 'Perhaps you could speak to Ms Steinberg in private.'

That hooked Ford's attention. 'What?'

'Take her into another room,' Win said, 'and leave me alone with your suspect.'

Eric Ford looked at him. 'You shouldn't even be here. He' – a gesture toward Myron – 'represents the Downing family, as much as I don't like it. But you got no reason to be here.'

'Make a reason,' Win said.

Eric Ford waved his hand as if this wasn't worth his time.

Win kept the voice at a low, soothing level. 'You don't have to be a part of it,' he said. 'Simply talk to his attorney. Leave Gibbs alone in the room. That's all. Nothing unethical about that.'

Ford shook his head. 'You're crazy.'

'We need answers,' Win said.

'And you want to beat them out of him.'

'Beating leaves marks,' Win said. 'I never leave marks.'

'That's not how it works, pal. Ever heard of the U.S. Constitution?'

'It's a document,' Win said, 'not a trump card. You have a choice. The obscure rights of that subhuman' – Win gestured through the glass – 'or a young boy's right to live.'

Ford leaned his forehead against the glass.

'If the boy dies while we're standing here,' Win said, 'how will you feel then?'

Ford shut his eyes. In the holding room, Clara Steinberg rose from her chair. She turned, and for the first time, Myron saw her face. He knew that she had represented bad people before – very, very bad people – but whatever horrors she was now hearing had washed away her skin tone and etched in something that would probably never leave. She approached the one-way mirror and knocked. Ford hit the sound switch.

'We need to talk,' she said. 'Let me out.'

Eric Ford met Clara and Stan by the door. 'Let's head down this way,' he said.

'No,' Clara said.

'Pardon me?'

'We'll talk in here,' she said, 'where I can watch my client. Wouldn't want an accident, now, would we?'

There were no chairs so they all stood by the one-way window – Kimberly Green, Eric Ford, Clara Steinberg, Stan Gibbs, Myron and Win. Stan kept his head down and plucked at his lower lip with his fingers. Myron tried to meet his eyes. Stan never gave him the chance.

'Okay,' Clara said. 'First off, we need a D.A.'

'What for?' Eric Ford asked.

'Because we want a deal.'

Ford tried to snicker. 'Are you out of your mind?'

'No. My client is the only one who can tell you where Jeremy Downing is. He'll only do so under specific conditions.'

'What conditions?'

'That's why we need a D.A.'

'A D.A. will back whatever I agree to,' Eric Ford said.

'I'll still want it in writing.'

'And I want to hear what you're looking for here.'

'Okay,' Clara said, 'here's the deal. We help you find Jeremy Downing. In exchange, you guarantee not to seek the death penalty for Edwin Gibbs. You also agree to psychiatric tests. You then recommend he be placed in a proper mental health facility, not a prison.'

'You have to be kidding me.'

'There's more,' Clara said.

'More?'

'Mr Edwin Gibbs will also agree to donate bone marrow to Jeremy Downing if the need arises. I understand that Mr Bolitar is representing the family here. For the record, we should note that he is present as a witness to this agreement.'

No one said anything.

'So we clear?' Clara said.

'No,' Ford said, 'we're not.'

Clara adjusted her eyeglasses. 'This deal is nonnegotiable.' She turned to leave, her gaze snagging on Myron's. Myron just shook his head.

'I'm his attorney,' she said to him.

'And you'll let a boy die for him?' Myron said.

'Don't start,' Clara said, but her voice was soft.

Myron studied her face again, saw no give. He turned to Ford. 'Agree,' he said.

'Are you nuts?'

'The family cares about retribution. But they care more about finding their son. Agree to her terms.'

'You think I'm taking orders from you?'

Myron's voice was soft. 'Come on, Eric.'

Ford frowned. He rubbed his face with his hands and then dropped them back to his side. 'This agreement assumes, of course, that the boy is still alive.'

'No,' Clara Steinberg said.

'What?'

'Alive or dead does not change the state of Edwin Gibb's mental health.'

'So you don't know if he's alive or—'

'If we did, it would be an attorney-client communication and thus confidential.'

Myron looked at her in stark horror. She met his eyes and would not blink. Myron tried Stan, but his head was still lowered. Even Win's face, usually the model of neutrality, was on edge. Win wanted to hurt somebody. He wanted to hurt somebody badly.

'We can't agree to that,' Ford said.

'Then there's no deal,' Clara said.

'You have to be reasonable—'

'Do we have a deal or not?'

Eric Ford shook his head. 'No.'

'See you in court, then.'

Myron moved into her path.

'Step aside, Myron,' Clara said.

He just looked down at her. She raised her eyes.

'You think your mother wouldn't be doing the same thing?' Clara said.

'Leave my mother out of this.'

'Step aside,' she said again. Aunt Clara was sixty-six. For the first time since he'd known her, she looked older than her age.

Myron turned back to Eric Ford. 'Agree,' he said.

He shook his head. 'The boy is probably dead.'

'Probably,' Myron repeated. 'Not definitely.'

Win spoke up this time. 'Agree,' he said.

Ford looked at him.

'He won't get off easily,' Win said.

Stan's head finally rose at that one. 'What the hell is that supposed to mean?'

Win gave him flat eyes. 'Absolutely nothing.'

'I want this man kept away from my father.'

Win smiled at him.

'You don't get it, do you?' Stan said. 'None of you get it. My father is sick. He's not responsible. We're not making this up. Any competent psychiatrist in the world will agree. He needs help.'

'He should die,' Win said.

'He's a sick man.'

'Sick men die all the time,' Win said.

'That's not what I mean. He's like someone who has a heart condition. Or cancer. He needs help.'

'He kidnaps and probably kills people,' Win said.

'And it doesn't matter why he does it?'

'Of course it doesn't matter,' Win said. 'He does it. That's enough. He should not be put in a comfortable mental hospital. He should not be allowed to enjoy a wonderful film or read a great book or laugh again. He should not be able to see a beautiful woman or listen to Beethoven or know kindness or love – because his victims never will. What part of that don't you understand, Mr Gibbs?'

Stan was shaking. 'You agree,' he said to Ford. 'Or we don't help.'

'If the boy dies because of this negotiation,' Win said to Stan, 'you will die.'

Clara stepped into Win's face. 'You threatening my client?' she shouted.

Win smiled at her. 'I never threaten.'

'There are witnesses.'

'Worried about collecting your fee, Counselor?' Win asked.

'That's enough.' It was Eric Ford. He looked at Myron. Myron nodded. 'Okay,' Ford said slowly. 'We agree. Now, where is he?'

'I'll have to take you,' Stan said.

'Again?'

'I wouldn't be able to give you directions. I'm not even sure I can find it after all these years.'

'But we come along,' Kimberly Green said.

'Yes.'

There was an empty space, a sudden stillness that Myron didn't like.

'Is Jeremy alive or dead?' Myron asked.

'Truth?' Stan said. 'I don't know.'

38

Eric Ford drove with Kimberly Green riding shotgun and Myron and Stan in the backseat. Several cars' worth of agents followed them. So too did the press. Nothing they could do about that.

'My mother died in 1977,' Stan said. 'Cancer. My father was already unwell. The one thing in his life that mattered to him – the one good thing – was my mother. He loved her very much.'

The time on the car clock read nearly 4:03 A.M. Stan told them where to turn off Route 15. A sign read DINGSMAN BRIDGE. They were heading into Pennsylvania.

'Whatever sanity was still there, my mother's death stripped away. He watched her suffer. Doctors tried everything – used all their technological advances – but it only made her suffer more. That's when my father started with the strength of the mind. If only my mother hadn't relied on technology, he thought. If only she used her mind instead. If only she'd seen its limitless potential. Technology killed her, he said. It gave her false hope. It stopped her from using the one thing that could save her – the limitless human brain.'

No one had a comment.

'We had a summerhouse out here. It was beautiful. Fifteen acres of land, walking distance to a lake. My father used to take me hunting and fishing. But I haven't been out here in years. Haven't even thought about the place. He took my mother out here to die. Then he buried her in the woods. See, it's where her suffering finally ended.'

The obvious question hung in the air, unasked: *And who else's?*

Myron would later remember nothing about the drive. No buildings, no landmarks, no trees. Outside his window was total night, the black folding over black, eyes squeezed shut in the darkest of rooms. He sat back and waited.

Stan told them to stop at the foot of a wooded area. More crickets sounded. The other cars pulled up alongside them. Feds got out and started combing the area. Beams from powerful flashlights revealed uneven earth. Myron ignored them. He swallowed and ran. Stan ran with him.

Before morning broke, the federal officers would find graves. They'd find the father of three children, the female college student, and the young newlyweds.

But for now, Myron and Stan kept running. Branches whipped Myron's face. He tripped over a root, curled into a roll, stood back up, kept running. They spotted the small house, barely visible in the faint moonlight. There were no lights on inside, no hint of life. Myron did not bother trying the knob this time. He took it full on, crashing the door down. More darkness. He heard a cry, turned, fumbled for the light switch, flipped it up.

Jeremy was there.

He was chained to a wall – dirty and terrified and still very much alive.

Myron felt his knees buckle, but he fought them and stayed upright. He ran to the boy. The boy stretched out his arms. Myron embraced him and felt his heart fall and shatter. Jeremy was crying. Myron lifted his hand and stroked the boy's hair and shushed him. Like his father. Like his father had done to him countless times. A sudden, beautiful warmth streamed through his veins, tingling his fingers and toes, and for a moment, Myron thought that maybe he understood what his father felt. Myron had always cherished being on the son side of the hug, but now, for just the most fleeting of moments, he experienced something so much stronger – the intensity and overwhelming depth of being on the other side – that it shook every part of him.

'You're okay,' Myron said to him, cupping the boy's head. 'It's over now.'

But it wasn't.

An ambulance came. Jeremy was put inside. Myron called Dr Karen Singh. She didn't mind being woken at five in the morning. He told her everything.

'Wow,' Karen Singh said when he finished.

'Yes.'

'We'll get someone to harvest the marrow right away. I'll start prepping Jeremy in the afternoon.'

'You mean with chemo.'

'Yes,' she said. 'You done good, Myron. Either way, you should be proud.'

'Either way?'

'Come by my office tomorrow afternoon.'

Myron felt a thumping in his chest. 'What's up?'

'The paternity test,' she said. 'The results should be in by then.'

Jeremy was on his way to the hospital. Myron wandered back outside. The feds were digging. The news vans were there. Stan Gibbs watched the mounds of earth grow, his face now beyond emotion. No sound, not even the crickets now, except for shovel hitting dirt. Myron's knee was acting up. He felt bone-weary. He wanted to find Emily. He wanted to go to the hospital. He wanted to know the results of that test and then he wanted to know what he was going to do with them.

He climbed back up the hill toward the car. More media. Someone called out to him. He ignored them. There were more federal officers working in silence. Myron walked past them. He didn't have the heart to hear what they'd found. Not just yet.

When he reached the top of the landing – when he saw Kimberly Green and the lifeless expression on her face – his heart took one more plummet.

He took another step. 'Greg?' he said.

She shook her head, her eyes hazy and unfocused. 'They shouldn't have left him alone,' she said. 'They should have watched him. Even after a careful search. You can never search too carefully.'

'Search who?'

'Edwin Gibbs.'

Myron was sure he'd heard wrong. 'What about him?'

'They just found him,' she said, having trouble with the words. 'He committed suicide in his cell.'

39

Karen Singh summed it up for them: You can't get bone marrow from a dead man.

Emily did not collapse when she heard the news. She took the blow without blinking and immediately segued to the next step. She was on a calmer plane now, somewhere just outside panic.

'We have incredible access to the media right now,' Emily said. They were sitting in Karen Singh's hospital office. 'We'll make pleas. We'll set up bone marrow drives. The NBA will help. We'll get players to make appearances.'

Myron nodded, but the enthusiasm wasn't there. Dr Singh mimicked his motion.

'When will you have the paternity results?' Emily asked.

'I was just about to call for them,' Dr Singh said.

'I'll leave you two alone, then,' Emily said. 'I have a press conference downstairs.'

Myron looked at her. 'You don't want to wait for the results?'

'I already know the results.'

Emily left without a backward glance. Karen Singh looked at Myron. Myron folded his hands and put them in his lap.

'You ready?' she asked.

He nodded.

Karen Singh picked up the phone and dialed. Someone on the other end answered. Karen read off a reference number. She waited, tapping a pencil on the desk. Someone on the other end said something. Karen said, 'Thank you,' hung up, focused her eyes on Myron.

'You're the father.'

Myron found Emily in the hospital lobby, giving the press

conference. The hospital had set up a podium with their logo perfectly positioned behind it, sure to be picked up by any and all television cameras. Hospital logo. Like they were McDonald's or Toyota, trying to sleaze some free advertising. Emily's statement was direct and heartfelt. Her son was dying. He needed new bone marrow. Everyone who wanted to help should give blood and get registered. She plucked the strings of societal grieving, making sure it rang personal in the same way that Princess Diana's and John Kennedy Jr's deaths rang personal, wanting the public to mourn as if they actually knew him. The power of celebrity.

When she finished her statement, Emily hurried off without answering questions. Myron caught up to her in the closed-off area near the elevators. She glanced at him. He nodded, and she smiled.

'So now what are you going to do?' she asked him.

'We have to save him,' Myron said.

'Yes.'

Behind them the press were still yelling out questions. The sound trickled and then faded into the background. Someone ran by with an empty gurney.

'You said Thursday was the optimum day,' Myron said.

Hope lit her eyes. 'Yes.'

'Okay, then,' he said. 'We try it on Thursday.'

The bullet that had struck Greg had entered in the lower part of his neck and traversed toward his chest. It had stopped short of the heart. But it had done plenty of damage anyway. He survived surgery but remained unconscious in 'critical' and 'guarded' condition. Myron looked in on him. Greg had tubes in his nose and a frightening assortment of machinery Myron hoped never to understand. He looked like a corpse, waxen and gray-white and sucked dry. Myron sat with him for a few minutes. But not very long.

He returned to the offices of MB SportsReps the next day.

'Lamar Richardson is coming in this afternoon,' Esperanza said.

'I know.'

'You okay?'

'Dandy.'

'Life goes on, huh?'

'Guess so.'

Special Agent Kimberly Green came semi-bouncing by a few minutes later. 'It's all wrapping up,' she told him, and for the first time he saw her smile.

Myron sat back. 'I'm listening.'

'Edwin Gibbs, under his Dennis Lex/Davis Taylor identity, still had a locker at work. We found the wallets of two of his victims, Robert and Patricia Wilson, in there.'

'They were the honeymoon couple?'

'Yes.'

They both took a moment, out of respect for the dead, Myron guessed. He pictured a healthy young couple beginning their life, coming to the Big Apple to see some shows and do a little shopping, walking the bustling streets hand in hand, a little scared about the future but ready to give it a go. *El fin.*

Kimberly cleared her throat. 'Gibbs also rented a white Ford Windstar using the Davis Taylor credit card. It was one of those automatic reservations. You just make a call, walk straight to the rental, and drive off. No one sees you.'

'Where did he pick up the van?'

'Newark Airport.'

'I assume that's the van we found in Bernardsville,' Myron said.

'The very.'

'Tidy,' he said, using a Win word. 'What else?'

'Preliminary autopsies reveal that all the victims were killed with a thirty-eight. Two shots to the head. No other signs of trauma. We don't think he tortured them or any of that. His modus operandus seemed to involve the early scream and then he just killed them.'

'He ends the seed sowing for them,' Myron said, 'but not the families.'

'Right.'

'Because for his victims, the terror would be real. He wanted it all in the mind.' Myron shook his head. 'What did Jeremy tell you about his ordeal?'

'You didn't talk to him about it?'

Myron shifted in his chair. 'No.'

'Edwin Gibbs wore the same disguise he used at work – the blond wig and beard and glasses. He blindfolded Jeremy as soon as he had him in the van and drove straight to that cabin. Edwin told him to scream into the phone – even made him practice first to make sure he had it right. After the call, Edwin chained him up and left him alone. You know the rest.'

Myron nodded. He did.

'What about the plagiarism charge and the novel?'

She shrugged. 'It was like you and Stan said. Edwin read it, probably right after his wife was dying of cancer. It influenced him.'

Myron stared at her for a moment.

'What?' she said.

'You guys figured that part out when you first got the novel,' Myron said. 'That Stan hadn't plagiarized. That the book influenced the killer.'

She shook her head. 'No.'

'Come on. You knew that the kidnappings had taken place. You just wanted to put pressure on Stan so he'd talk. And maybe you wanted to embarrass him a little.'

'That's not true,' Kimberly Green said. 'I'm not saying some of our agents didn't take it personally, but we believed that he was the Sow the Seeds kidnapper. I already told you some of the reasons why. Now we know that a lot of the same evidence pointed to his father.'

'What same evidence?'

She shook her head. 'It's not important anymore. We knew Stan was more here than just a reporter. And we were right. We even thought he was getting stuff wrong on purpose – that he was using the book rather than what he'd really done just to throw us off.'

Her words didn't resonate the way the truth does, but Myron didn't argue the point. He scanned his Client Wall and tried to bring his focus around to Lamar Richardson's visit. 'So the case is closed.'

She smiled. 'Like legs in a nunnery.'

'You make that one up?'

'Yup.'

'Good thing you carry a gun,' Myron said. 'So are you going to get a big promotion?'

She rose. 'I think I get to be a super-secret-special agent now.'

Myron smiled. They shook hands. Kimberly left then. Myron sat alone for a while. He rubbed his eyes and thought about what she'd said and what she hadn't said and realized that something was still very wrong.

Lamar Richardson, shortstop extraordinaire, showed up on time and by himself. Positively shocking. The meeting went well. Myron gave his standard spiel, but the standard spiel was pretty good. Damn good, actually. All businesspeople need a spiel. Spiel is good. Esperanza spoke up too. She had started developing her own spiel. Well honed. The perfect complement to Myron's. Quite the partnership, this was becoming.

Win stopped by briefly as planned. If recruitment was a baseball game, Win was the big closer. People knew his name. They checked out his reputation – er, his business reputation, that is. When prospective clients learned that Windsor Horne Lockwood III himself would handle their finances, that Win and Myron further insisted that clients meet with Win at least five times a year, they started smiling. Score one for the small agency.

Lamar Richardson played it close to the vest. He nodded a lot. He asked questions but not too many. Two hours after arriving, he shook their hands and said he'd be in touch. Myron and Esperanza walked him to the elevator and bade him good-bye.

Esperanza turned to Myron. 'Well?'

'Got him.'

'How can you be so sure?'

'I'm all-seeing,' Myron said. 'All-knowing.'

They moved back into Myron's office and sat down. 'If Lamar chooses us over IMG and TruPro' – she stopped, smiled – 'we're baaaaack.'

'Pretty much.'

'And that means Big Cyndi will come back.'

'That's supposed to be a good thing, right?'

'You're starting to love her, you know.'

'Yeah, don't rub it in.'

Esperanza studied his face. She did that a lot. Myron didn't much believe in reading faces. Esperanza did. Especially his. 'What happened in that law office?' she asked. 'With Chase Layton?'

'I boxed his ears once and punched him seven times.'

Her eyes stayed on his face.

'You're supposed to say, "But you saved Jeremy's life," ' Myron added.

'No, that's Win's line.' She adjusted herself and faced him full. She wore an aquamarine business suit, cut low with no blouse, and it was a wonder Lamar had been able to concentrate on anything. Myron was used to her, but the effect was still there, still dazzling. He just saw the dazzle from a different angle.

'Speaking of Jeremy,' she said.

'Yes.'

'You still blocking?'

Myron thought about it, remembered the embrace in that cabin, stopped. 'More than ever,' he said.

'So what now?'

'The blood test came back. I'm the father.'

Something popped onto her face – regret maybe – but it didn't stay long. 'You should tell him the truth.'

'Right now I just want to save his life.'

She kept studying the face. 'Maybe soon,' she said.

'Maybe soon what?'

'You'll stop blocking,' Esperanza said.

'Yeah, maybe.'

'We'll chat then. In the meantime . . .'

'Don't be stupid,' he finished for her.

The health club was located in a chi-chi hotel in midtown. The walls were fully mirrored. The ceiling and the trim and the front desk were whole-milk white. Same with the clothes worn by the personal trainers. The weights and exercise machines were sleek and chrome and so beautiful you didn't want to touch them. Everything about the place gleamed; you were almost tempted to work out in sunglasses.

Myron found him on a bench press, struggling without a spotter. Myron waited, watching him wage war on gravity and the barbell. Chase Layton's face was pure red, his teeth gritted, veins in his forehead doing their pop-up video. It took some time, but the attorney achieved victory. He dropped the weight onto the stand. His arms fell to his sides like he'd missed a brain synapse.

'You shouldn't hold your breath,' Myron said.

Chase looked over at him. He didn't seem surprised or upset. He sat up, breathing heavily. He wiped his face with a towel.

'I won't take up much of your time,' Myron said.

Chase put the towel down and looked at him.

'I just wanted to say that if you want to press charges, Win and I won't get in your way.'

Chase did not reply.

'And I'm very sorry for what I did,' Myron said.

'I watched the news,' Chase said. 'You did it to save that boy's life.'

'Doesn't excuse it.'

'Maybe not.' He stood and added a plate to both sides of the bar. 'Frankly, Mr Bolitar, I'm not sure what to think.'

'If you want to press charges—'

'I don't.'

Myron was not sure what to say, so he settled for 'Thank you.'

Chase Layton nodded and sat back on the bench. Then he looked at Myron. 'Do you want to know what the worst part of it is?'

No, Myron thought. 'If you want to tell me.'

'The shame,' Chase said.

Myron started to open his mouth, but Chase waved him quiet.

'It's not the beating or the pain. It's the feeling of total helplessness. We were primitive. We were man to man. And there was nothing I could do but take it. You made me feel like' – he looked up, found the words, looked straight at Myron –'like I wasn't a real man.'

The words made Myron cringe.

'I went to these great schools and joined all the right clubs and made a fortune in my chosen profession. I fathered three kids and raised them and loved them the best I could. Then one day you punch me – and I realize that I'm not a real man.'

'You're wrong,' Myron said.

'You're going to say that violence is no measure of a man. On some level you're right. But on some level, the base level that

242

makes us men, we both know you're wrong. Don't pretend you don't know what I'm talking about. It'd just be a further insult.'

Myron swallowed down the clichés. Chase took deep breaths and reached for the bar.

'Need a spotter?' Myron said.

Chase Layton gripped it and jerked it off the stand. 'I don't need anybody,' he said.

Thursday came. Karen Singh introduced him to a fertility expert named Dr Barbara Dittrick. Dr Dittrick handed Myron a small cup and told him to masturbate into it. There were more surreal and embarrassing experiences in life, Myron guessed, but being led to a small room to masturbate into a cup while everyone waited for you in the next room had to be right up there with the best of them.

'Step in here, please,' Dr Dittrick said.

Myron frowned at the cup. 'I usually insist on flowers and a movie.'

'Well, at least you got the movie,' she said, pointing at the television. 'The TV has X-rated videos.' She left the room and closed the door behind her.

Myron checked the titles. *On Golden Blonde. Father Knows Breast* (starring Robert Hung). *Field of Wet Dreams* ('If you watch it, they will come'). He frowned and passed. So to speak. He stared at the swivel leather chair, one of those lean-back kind, where probably hundreds of other men had sat and . . . He covered it with paper towels and did his bit, though it took some time. His imagination was spinning in the wrong direction, generating an aura about as erotic as mole hair on an old man's buttock. When he was, uh, finished, he opened the door and handed the cup to Dr Dittrick and tried to smile. He felt like the world's biggest doofus. She wore rubber gloves, even though the, uh, specimen was in a cup. Like it might scald her. She brought it to a lab where they 'washed' (their expression, not his) the semen. The semen was declared 'serviceable but slow.' Like it was falling behind in algebra.

'Funny,' Emily said. 'I usually found Myron to be serviceable but quick.'

'Ha-ha,' Myron said.

A few hours later Emily was in a hospital bed. Barbara Dittrick smiled while inserting what looked suspiciously like a turkey baster into her and pressed the plunger. Myron took her hand. Emily smiled.

'Romantic,' she said.

Myron made a face.

'What?'

'Serviceable?' he said.

She laughed. 'But quick.'

Dr Dittrick finished her part. Emily stayed prone for another hour. Myron sat with her. They were doing this to save Jeremy's life. That was all. He didn't let the future enter the equation. He didn't consider the long-term effects or what this might one day mean. Irresponsible, sure. But first things first.

They had to save Jeremy. The hell with the rest.

Terese Collins called him from Atlanta that afternoon. 'Can I come up and visit?' she asked.

'The station will give you more time off?'

'Actually, my producer encouraged me.'

'Oh?'

'You, my studly friend, are part of a huge story,' Terese said.

'You used the words "studly" and "huge" in the same sentence.'

'That turn you on?'

'Well, it might a lesser man.'

'And you are that lesser man.'

'I thank you,' he said.

'You're also the only one in this story who won't talk to the press.'

'So you just want me for my mind,' Myron said. 'I feel so used.'

'Dream on, hot buns. I want your bod. It's my producer who wants your brain.'

'Your producer cute?'

'No.'

'Terese?'

'Yes.'

'I don't want to talk about what happened.'

'Good,' she said. 'Because I don't want to hear it.'

There was a brief silence.

'Yeah,' Myron said. 'I'd like it very much if you came up.'

*

Ten days later, Karen Singh called him at home.

'The pregnancy didn't take.'

Myron closed his eyes.

'We can try again next month,' she said.

'Thanks for calling, Karen.'

'Sure.'

There was empty space. 'Anything else?' Myron asked.

'There's been a lot of marrow drives,' she said.

'I know.'

'One donor looks like a match for an AML patient in Maryland. A young mother. She would have probably died if it weren't for these drives.'

'Good news,' Myron said.

'But no matches for Jeremy.'

'Yeah.'

'Myron?'

'What?'

'I don't think we have much time here.'

Terese returned to Atlanta later that day. Win invited Esperanza to his place for a night of mindless television. The three of them sat in their customary spots. Fritos and Indian takeout were on the night's menu. Myron had the remote. He paused when he saw a familiar image on CNN. A basketball superstar simply known as 'TC,' one of the NBA's most controversial players and a teammate of Greg's, was on *Larry King Live*. His hair was razor-carved to spell out *Jeremy*, and both gold earrings had Jeremy's name on them. He wore a ripped T-shirt that simply read HELP OR JEREMY DIES. Myron smiled. TC was something else, but he'd get the people out in droves.

More flipping. Stan Gibbs was on some talking-head show on MSNBC. Nothing new. The only thing the press loves as much as tearing somebody down is a story of redemption. Bruce Taylor had gotten the exclusive, as promised, and he'd set the tone. The public was mixed on what Stan had done, but for the most part, they sympathized with him. In the end, Stan had risked his own life to catch a killer, saved Jeremy Downing from certain death, and been wrongly accused by a too-eager-to-convict media. The fact that Stan had been confused about turning in his own father played for him, especially since the media was anxious to wipe away the awful mar of plagiarism they'd so quickly tattooed on him. Stan got his column back. Rumor had it his show was coming back too but in a better time slot. Myron wasn't sure what to think. Stan was no hero to him. But so few people were.

Stan, too, was pounding the bone-marrow-drive drum. 'This boy needs our help,' he said directly into the camera. 'Please come down. We'll be here all night.'

A blond talking head asked Stan about his own part in this drama, about tackling his father, about racing to the cabin. Stan played the modesty card. Wise. The man knew the media.

'Boring,' Esperanza said.

'Agreed,' Win said.

'Isn't there a *Partridge Family* marathon on TV Land?'

Myron suddenly stopped.

'Myron?' Win said.

He did not reply.

'Hello, world.' Esperanza snapped her fingers in Myron's face. 'There's a song that we're singing. Come on, get happy.'

Myron switched off the television. He looked at Win, then at Esperanza. 'Say one last good-bye to the boy.'

Esperanza and Win exchanged a glance.

'You were right, Win.'

'About what?'

'Human nature,' Myron said.

40

Myron called Kimberly Green at her office. She answered the line and said, 'Green.'

'I need a favor,' Myron said.

'Shit, I thought you were out of my life.'

'But never your fantasies. You want to help me or not?'

'Not.'

'I need two things.'

'Not. I said "not." '

'Eric Ford said that the supposedly plagiarized novel was sent directly to you.'

'So?'

'Who sent it?'

'You heard him, Myron. It was sent anonymously.'

'You have no idea.'

'None.'

'Where is it now?'

'The book?'

'Yes.'

'In an evidence locker.'

'Ever do anything with it?'

'Like what?'

Myron waited.

'Myron?'

'I knew you guys were holding something back,' he said.

'Listen to me a second—'

'The author of that novel. It was Edwin Gibbs. He wrote it under a pseudonym after his wife died. It makes perfect sense now. You were searching for him right from the get-go. You knew, dammit. You knew the whole time.'

'We suspected,' she said. 'We didn't know.'

'All that crap about thinking he was Stan's first victim—'

'It wasn't total crap. We knew it was one of them. We just didn't know which one. We couldn't find Edwin Gibbs until you told us about the Waterbury address. By the time we got there, he was already on his way to kidnap Jeremy Downing. Maybe if you had been more forthcoming—'

'You guys lied to me.'

'We didn't lie. We just didn't tell you everything.'

'Jesus, you ever listen to yourself?'

'We owed you nothing here, Myron. You weren't a federal agent on this. You were just a pain in the ass.'

'A pain in the ass who helped you solve the case.'

'And for that I thank you.'

Myron's thoughts entered the maze, turned left, turned right, circled back.

'Why doesn't the press know about Gibbs being the author?' Myron asked.

'They will. Ford wants all his ducks in a row first. Then he'll hold yet another big press conference and present it as something new.'

'He could do that today,' Myron said.

'He could.'

'But then the story dies down. Right now the rumors keep it going. Ford gets more time in the limelight.'

'He's a politician at heart,' she said. 'So what?'

Myron took another few turns, hit a few more walls, kept feeling for the way out. 'Forget it,' he said.

'Good. Can I go now?'

'First I need you to call the national bone marrow registry.'

'Why?'

'I need to find out about a donor.'

'This case is closed, Myron.'

'I know,' he said. 'But I think a new one might be opening.'

Stan Gibbs was at the anchor chair when Myron and Win arrived. His new cable show, *Glib with Gibbs*, was filming in Fort Lee, New Jersey, and the studio, like every television studio Myron had ever seen, looked like a room with the roof ripped off. Wires and lights hung in no discernible pattern. Studios, especially newsrooms, were always much smaller in person than on television. The desks, the chairs, the world map in the background. All smaller. The power of television. A room on a nineteen-inch screen somehow looks smaller in real life.

Stan wore a blue blazer, white shirt, red tie, jeans and sneakers. The jeans would stay under the desk and never get camera time. Classic anchorman-wear. Stan waved to them when they entered. Myron waved back. Win did not.

'We need to talk,' Myron said to him.

Stan nodded. He sent away the producers and motioned Myron and Win to the guest chairs. 'Sit.'

Stan stayed in the anchor chair. Win and Myron sat in guest chairs, which felt pretty strange, as though a home audience were watching. Win checked his reflection in a camera glass and smiled. He liked what he saw.

'Any word on a donor?' Stan asked.

'None.'

'Something will come through.'

'Yeah,' Myron said. 'Look, Stan, I need your help.'

Stan intertwined his fingers and rested both hands on the anchor desk. 'Whatever you need.'

'There's a lot of things that don't add up with Jeremy's kidnapping.'

'For example?'

'Why do you think your father took a child this time? He never did that before, right? Always adults. Why this time a child?'

Stan mulled it over, chose his words one at a time. 'I don't know. I'm not sure taking adults was a pattern or anything. His victims seemed pretty random.'

'But this wasn't random,' Myron said. 'His choosing Jeremy Downing couldn't have been just a coincidence.'

Stan thought about that one too. 'I agree with you there.'

'So he picked him because he was somehow connected with my investigation.'

'Seems logical.'

'But how would your father have known about Jeremy?'

'I don't know,' Stan said. 'He might have followed you.'

'I don't think so. You see, Greg Downing stayed up in

249

Waterbury after our visit. He kept his eye on Nathan Mostoni. We know he didn't travel out of town until the day before the kidnapping.'

Win looked into the camera again. He smiled and waved. Just in case it was on.

'It's strange,' Stan said.

'And there's more,' Myron said. 'Like the call where Jeremy screamed. With the others, your father told the family not to contact the cops. But he didn't this time. Why? And are you aware that he wore a disguise when he kidnapped Jeremy?'

'I heard that, yes.'

'Why? If he planned on killing him, why go to the trouble of donning a disguise?'

'He kidnapped Jeremy off the streets,' Stan said. 'Someone might have been able to identify him.'

'Yeah, okay, that makes sense. But then why blindfold Jeremy once he was in the van? He killed all the others. He would have killed Jeremy. So why worry about him seeing his face?'

'I'm not sure,' Stan said. 'He might have always done it that way, for all we know.'

'I guess,' Myron said. 'But something about it all just rings wrong, don't you think?'

Stan thought about it. 'It rings funny,' he said slowly. 'I'm not sure it rings wrong.'

'That's why I came to you. All these questions have been swirling in my head. And then I remembered Win's credo.'

Stan Gibbs looked over at Win. Win blinked his eyes and lowered them modestly. 'What credo is that?'

'Man is into self-preservation,' Myron said. 'He is, above all, selfish.' He paused a moment. 'You agree with that, Stan?'

'To some degree, of course. We're all selfish.'

Myron nodded. 'You even.'

'Yes, of course. And you too, I'm sure.'

'The media is making you out to be this noble guy,' Myron said. 'Torn between family and duty and ultimately doing the right thing. But maybe you're not.'

'Not what?'

'Noble.'

'I'm not,' Stan said. 'I did wrong. I never claimed to be a saint.'

Myron looked at Win. 'He's good.'

'Damn good,' Win agreed.

Stan Gibbs frowned. 'What are you talking about, Myron?'

'Follow me here, Stan. And remember Win's credo. Let's start at the beginning. When your father first contacted you. You talked to him and you decided to write the Sow the Seeds story. What was your motive at first? Were you trying to find an outlet for your fear and guilt? Was it simply to be a good reporter? Or – and here's where we're using the Win credo – did you write it because you knew it would make you a big star?'

Myron looked at him and waited.

'Am I supposed to answer that?'

'Please.'

Stan looked in the air and rubbed his fingertips with his thumb. 'All of the above, I guess. Yes, I was excited by the story. I thought it could very well be a big deal. If that's selfishness, okay, I'm guilty.'

Myron glanced at Win again. 'Good.'

'Damn good.'

'Let's keep following this track, Stan, okay? The story did indeed become a big deal. So did you. You became a celebrity—'

'We covered this already, Myron.'

'Right. You're absolutely right. Let's skip to the part where the feds sued you. They demanded to know your source. You refused. Now again there might be several reasons for this. The First Amendment, of course. That could be it. Protecting your father would be another. The combination of the two. But – and again Win's credo – what would be the selfish choice?'

'What do you mean?'

'Think selfishly and you really have only one option.'

'That being?'

'If you caved in to the feds – if you said, Okay, now that I'm in legal trouble, my source is my father – well, how would that have looked?'

'Bad,' Win said.

'Damn bad. I doubt you'd have been much of a hero if you sold out your father – not to mention the First Amendment – just to save your hide from vague legal threats.' Myron smiled. 'See what I mean about Win's credo?'

'So you think I acted selfishly by not telling the feds,' Stan said.

'It's possible.'

'It's also possible that the selfish thing was also the right thing.'

'Possible too,' Myron agreed.

'I never claimed to be a hero in all this.'

'Never denied it either.'

Stan smiled this time. 'Maybe I didn't deny it because I'm using Win's credo.'

'How's that?'

'Denying it would harm me,' Stan said. 'As would boasting about it.'

Myron didn't have a chance to look before he heard Win say, 'Damn good.'

'I still don't see the relevance of any of this,' Stan said.

'Stick with me, I think you will.'

Stan shrugged.

'Where were we?' Myron asked.

'The feds take him to court,' Win said.

'Right, thanks, the feds take you to court. You battle back. Then something happens you totally didn't foresee. The plagiarism charges. For the sake of discussion, we'll assume the Lex family sent the book to the feds. They wanted to get you off their back – what better way to do that than to ruin your reputation? So what did you do? How did you react to the charges of plagiarism?'

Stan kept quiet. Win said, 'He disappeared.'

'Correct answer,' Myron said.

Win smiled and nodded a thank-you into the camera.

'You took off,' Myron said to Stan. 'Now the question again is why. Several things come to mind. It could have been because you were trying to protect your father. Or it might have been that you were afraid of the Lex family.'

'Which would certainly fit Win's credo,' Stan said. 'Self-preservation.'

'Right. You were afraid they'd harm you.'

'Yes.'

Myron trod gently. 'But don't you see, Stan? We have to think selfishly too. You're presented with this serious plagiarism charge. What choices did you have? Two really. You could either run off – or you could tell the truth.'

Stan said, 'I still don't see your point.'

'Stay with me. If you told the truth, you would again look like a louse. Here you've been defending the First Amendment and your father and whoops, you get in trouble and you sell them out. No good. You'd still be ruined.'

'Damned if you do,' Win said. 'Damned if you don't.'

'Right,' Myron said. 'So the wise move – the selfish move – was to vanish for a while.'

'But I lost everything by vanishing.'

'No, Stan, you didn't.'

'How can you say that?'

Myron lifted his palms to the skies and grinned. 'Look around you.'

For the first time, something dark flicked across Stan's face. Myron saw it. So did Win.

'Let's continue, shall we?'

Stan said nothing.

'You go into hiding and start counting your problems. One, your father is a murderer. You're selfish, Stan, but you're not inhumane. You want him off the streets, yet you can't tell on him. Maybe because you love him. Or maybe there's Win's credo.'

'Not this time,' Stan said.

'Pardon?'

'Win's credo doesn't apply. I kept quiet because I loved my father and because I believe in protecting sources. And I can offer proof.'

'I'm listening,' Myron said.

'If I wanted to turn my father in – if that would have been in my best interest – I could have done it anonymously.' Stan leaned back and folded his arms.

'That's your proof?'

'Sure. I didn't do the selfish thing.'

Myron shook his head. 'You got to go deeper.'

'Deeper how?'

'Turning your father in anonymously wouldn't help you, Stan. Not really. Yes, you needed to put your father behind bars. But more than that, you needed to be redeemed.'

Silence.

253

'So what would answer both those needs? What would put your father away and put you back on top – maybe even more on top than before? First, you had to be patient. That meant staying hidden. Second, you couldn't be the one who turned him in. You had to set him up.'

'Set up my father?'

'Yes. You had to leave a trail for the feds to follow. Something subtle, something that would lead to your father, and something you could manipulate at any time. So you took a fake ID, Stan – the same way your father had. You even took a job where people would spot the disguise your father used and hey, maybe you could also tie in your dad's old nemesis the Lex family in the process.'

'What the hell are you talking about?'

'You know what bugged me? Your father had been so careful in the past. Now all of a sudden he's leaving incriminating evidence in a locker. He rents the kidnap van on a credit card and leaves a red sneaker in it. It didn't make any sense. Unless someone was setting him up.'

Stan's look of disbelief was almost genuine. 'You think I killed these people?'

'No,' Myron said. 'Your father did.'

'Then what—?'

'You're the one who used the Dennis Lex identity,' Myron said, 'not your father.'

Stan tried to look stunned, but it wasn't happening.

'You kidnapped Jeremy Downing. And you called me and pretended to be the Sow the Seeds killer.'

'And why did I do that?'

'To have this heroic ending. To have your father arrested. To have yourself redeemed.'

'How the hell does calling you—'

'To get me interested. You probably learned about my background. You knew I'd investigate. You needed a dupe and a witness. Someone outside the police. I was that dupe.'

'The dupe du jour,' Win added.

Myron shot him a look. Win shrugged.

'That's ridiculous.'

'No, Stan, it adds up. It answers all my earlier questions. How did the kidnapper happen to choose Jeremy? Because you followed me after I left your condo. You saw the feds pick me up. That's how you knew I'd spoken to them. You followed me to Emily's house. From there, any old newsman worth a damn could have figured out her son was the sick kid I told you about. His illness wasn't a secret. So Jeremy's being taken is no longer a coincidence, see?'

Stan folded his arms across his chest. 'I see nothing.'

'Other questions get answered too now. Like why did the kidnapper wear a disguise and make Jeremy wear a blindfold? Because you couldn't let Jeremy identify you. Why didn't the kidnapper kill Jeremy right away, like he had the others? Same reason you wore the disguise. You had no intention of killing him. Jeremy had to survive the ordeal unharmed. Otherwise you're no hero. Why didn't the kidnapper make his usual demand not to contact the authorities? Because you wanted the feds in. You needed them to witness your heroics. It wouldn't work without their involvement. I wondered how the media was always in the right spot – in Bernardsville, at the cabin. But you set that part up too. Anonymous leaks probably. So the cameras could witness and replay your heroics – your tackling your father, the dramatic rescue of Jeremy Downing. Good television. You knew the power of capturing those moments for all the world to see.'

Stan waited. 'You finished?'

'Not yet. You see, I think you went too far in spots. Leaving that sneaker in the van, for example. That was overkill. Too obvious. It made me wonder how neatly it all came together in the end. And then I start realizing that I was your main sucker, Stan. You played me like a Stradivarius. But even if I hadn't shown up, you just would have kidnapped someone else. Your main dupes were the feds. For crying out loud, that photograph of your father by the statue was the only picture in the whole condo. It even faced the window. You knew the feds were spying on you. You threw the truth about Dennis Lex right in their faces. Surely they'd go to the sanitarium and put it together. And if not, you could somehow get it out in the end, when they had you in custody. You were all set to cave in and tell on your father when I came through in the clutch. Me, the dupe du jour, saw the truth up at the sanitarium. You must have been so pleased.'

'This is crazy.'

'It answers all the questions.'

'That doesn't mean it's the truth.'

'The Davis Taylor address you used at work. It was the same address as your father's in Waterbury. So we would trace it back to him, to Nathan Mostoni. Who else would have done that?'

'My father!'

'Why? Why would your father change identities at all? And if your father needed a new identity, wouldn't he shed the old one? Or hell, at least change addresses? Only you could have pulled it off, Stan. You could have hooked up the extra phone line with no problem. Your father was pretty far gone. He was demented, at the very least. You kidnapped Jeremy. Then you probably told your father to meet you at the house in Bernardsville. He did what you said – for love or because of dementia, I don't know which. Did you know he'd arm himself like that? I doubt it. If Greg had died, you'd probably look worse. But I don't know for sure. Maybe the fact that he fired shots just made you look more heroic in the end. Think selfishly, Stan. That's the key.'

Stan shook his head.

' "Say one last good-bye to the boy," ' Myron said.

'What?'

'That's what the Sow the Seeds killer said to me on the phone. The boy. I made a mistake when he called me. I told him a boy needed help. After that, I only used the word "child." When I spoke to Susan Lex. When I spoke to you. I said a thirteen-year-old child needs a transplant.'

'So?'

'So when we talked in the car that night, you asked what I was really after, what my real interest in all this was. Remember?'

'Yes.'

'And I said I already told you.'

'Right.'

'And you said, "That boy who needs a bone marrow transplant?" You said, "That boy." How did you know he was a boy, Stan?'

Win turned toward Stan. Stan looked at Win's face.

'Is that your proof?' Stan countered. 'I mean, is this supposed to be a Perry Mason moment or something? Maybe you slipped up, Myron. Or maybe I just assumed it was a boy. Or I heard wrong. That's not evidence.'

'You're right. It's not. It just got me thinking, that's all.'

'Thoughts aren't proof.'

'Wow,' Win said. 'Thoughts aren't proof. I'll have to remember that one.'

'But there is proof,' Myron said. 'Definitive proof.'

'Impossible,' Stan said, but his voice warbled now. 'What?'

'I'll get to that in a moment. First let me back off on my indignation a little.'

'I don't understand.'

'At the end of the day, what you did was scummy, no question about it. But in its own way, it was almost ethical. Win and I often discuss the ends justifying the means. You could claim that's what happened here. You tried to turn your father in before he struck again. You did all you could to make sure nobody else was harmed. Jeremy was never in any real danger. You couldn't know that Greg would be shot. So in the end, you scared a boy, but so what? Next to the murder and destruction your father would have continued to wreak, it was nothing. So you did some good. The ends perhaps justified the means. Except for one thing.'

Stan didn't bite.

'Jeremy's bone marrow transplant. He needs that to live, Stan. You know that. You also know that you're the match, not your father. That was why you slipped him that cyanide pill. Because once we dragged your father to the hospital and realized that he wasn't a match, well, we would have investigated. We would have realized that Edwin Gibbs was not Davis Taylor né Dennis Lex. So you had to have him kill himself and then you pushed for a quick cremation. I don't mean to make it sound as harsh or cold as all that. You didn't murder your father. He took the pill all on his own. He was a sick man. He wanted to die. It's yet another case of the ends justifying the means.'

Myron took a moment and just looked into Stan's eyes. Stan did not look away. In a sense, this was more agenting work. Myron was negotiating here – the most important negotiation of his life. He had put his opponent in a corner. Now he needed to reach out. Not help him yet. He had to keep him in the corner. But he had to start reaching out. Just a little.

'You're not a monster,' Myron said. 'You just didn't count on the complication of being a bone marrow match. You want to do right by Jeremy. It's why you've gone so nuts trying to help the bone marrow drive. If they find another donor, it takes you off the hook. Because you're in this lie too deep now. You couldn't admit the truth – that you are the match. It would ruin you. I understand that.'

Stan's eyes were wide and wet, but he was listening.

'Before I told you that I had proof,' Myron said. 'We checked the bone marrow registry. Know what we found, Stan?'

Stan didn't reply.

'You're not registered,' Myron said. 'Here you are telling everybody to sign up and you yourself aren't in their computer. The three of us know why. It's because you'd be a match. And if you matched, there would be those questions again.'

Stan gave defiance one last shot. 'That's not proof.'

'Then how will you explain not registering?'

'I don't have to explain anything.'

'A blood test will prove it conclusively. The registry still has the blood that Davis Taylor gave during the marrow drive. We can do a DNA test with yours, see if it matches up.'

'And if I don't agree to a test?'

Win took that one. 'Oh, you'll give blood,' he said with just the slightest smile. 'One way or another.'

Something on Stan's face broke then. He lowered his head. The defiance was over. He was trapped in the corner now. No way to escape. He'd start looking for an ally. It always happened in negotiations. When you're lost, you look for an out. Myron had reached out before. It was time to do it again.

'You don't understand,' Stan said.

'Strangely enough, I do.' Myron moved a little closer to Stan. He made his voice soft yet unyielding. Total command mode. 'Here's what we're going to do, Stan. You and I are going to make a deal.'

Stan looked up, confused but also hopeful. 'What?'

'You are going to agree to donate bone marrow to save Jeremy's life. You'll do it anonymously. Win and I can set that up.

No one will ever know who the donor was. You do that, you save Jeremy, I forget the rest.'

'How can I believe you?'

'Two reasons,' Myron said. 'One, I'm interested in saving Jeremy's life, not ruining yours. Two' – he tilted both palms toward the ceiling – 'I'm no better. I bent rules here too. I let the ends justify the means. I assaulted a man. I kidnapped a woman.'

Win shook his head. 'There's a difference. His reasons were selfish. You, on the other hand, were trying to save a boy's life.'

Myron turned to his friend. 'Weren't you the one who said that motives are irrelevant? That the act is the act?'

'Sure,' Win said. 'But I meant that to apply to him, not you.'

Myron smiled and faced Stan again. 'I'm not your moral superior. We both did wrong. Maybe we can both live with what we've done. But if you let a boy die, Stan, you cross the line. You can't go home again.'

Stan closed his eyes. 'I would have found a way,' he said. 'I would have gotten another fake ID, given blood under a pseudonym. I was just hoping—'

'I know,' Myron said. 'I know all about it.'

Myron called Dr Karen Singh. 'I found a matching donor.'

'What?'

'I can't explain. But he has to stay anonymous.'

'I explained to you that all the bone marrow donors remain anonymous.'

'No. The bone marrow registry can't know about this either. We have to find a place that can harvest the marrow without knowing the patient's identity.'

'Can't be done.'

'Yeah, it can.'

'No doctor will agree—'

'We can't play these games, Karen. I have a donor. No one can know who he is. Make it work.'

He could hear her breathing.

'He'll have to be retested,' she said.

'No problem.'

'And pass a physical.'

'Done.'

'Then okay. Let's get this started.'

When Emily heard about the donor, she gave Myron a curious look and waited. He didn't explain. She never asked.

Myron visited the hospital the day before the marrow transplant was to begin. He peeked his head around the doorjamb and saw the boy sleeping. Jeremy was bald from the chemo. His skin had a ghostly glow, like something withering from a lack of sunshine. Myron watched his son sleeping. Then he turned and went home. He didn't come back.

He returned to work at MB SportsReps and lived his life. He visited his father and mother. He hung out with Win and Esperanza. He landed a few new clients and started rebuilding his business. Big Cyndi handed in her wrestling resignation and took over the front desk. His world was wobbly but back on the axis.

Eighty-four days later – Myron kept count – he got a call from Karen Singh. She asked him to visit her office. When he arrived, she wasted no time.

'It worked,' she said. 'Jeremy went home today.'

Myron started to cry. Karen Singh moved around her desk. She sat on the arm of his chair and rubbed his back.

Myron knocked on the half-open door.

'Enter,' Greg said.

Myron did so. Greg Downing was sitting up in a chair. He'd grown a beard during his long hospital stretch.

He smiled at Myron. 'Nice to see you.'

'Same here. I like the beard.'

'Gives me that Paul Bunyan touch, don't you think?'

'I was thinking more along the lines of Sebastian Cabot as Mr French,' Myron said.

Greg laughed. 'Going home on Friday.'

'Great.'

Silence.

'You haven't visited much,' Greg said.

'Wanted to give you time to heal. And grow that beard in fully.'

Greg tried another laugh, but he sort of choked on it. 'My basketball career is over, you know.'

'You'll get over it.'

'That easy?'

Myron smiled. 'Who said anything about easy?'

'Yeah.'

'But there are more important things in life than basketball,' Myron said. 'Though sometimes I forget that.'

Greg nodded again. Then he looked down and said, 'I heard about you finding the donor. I don't know how you did it—'

'It's not important.'

He looked up. 'Thank you.'

Myron was not sure what to say to that. So he kept quiet. And that was when Greg shocked him.

'You know, don't you?'

Myron's heart stopped.

'That was why you helped,' Greg said. His voice was pure flat-line. 'Emily told you the truth.'

The muscles around Myron's throat tightened. There was a whooshing sound in his head.

'Did you take a blood test?' Greg asked.

Myron managed a nod this time. Greg closed his eyes. Myron swallowed and said, 'How long . . . ?'

'I'm not sure anymore,' Greg said. 'I guess right away.'

He *knows*. The words fell on Myron, smacking down like raindrops, beading and rolling off, impenetrable. *He's always known . . .*

'For a while I fooled myself into believing it wasn't so,' Greg said. 'It's amazing what the mind can do sometimes. But when Jeremy was six, he had his appendix out. I saw his blood type on a chart. It pretty much confirmed what I'd known all along.'

Myron didn't know what to say. The realization pushed down on him, swept away the months of blocking like so many children's toys. The mind can indeed do amazing things. He looked at Greg and it was like seeing something in the proper light for the first time and it changed everything. He thought about fathers again. He thought about real sacrifice. He thought about heroes.

'Jeremy's a good boy,' Greg said.

'I know,' Myron said.

'You remember my father? Screaming on the sidelines like a lunatic?'

'Yes.'

'I ended up looking just like him. Spitting image of my old man. He was my blood. And he was the cruelest son of a bitch I ever knew,' Greg said. Then he added, 'Blood never meant much to me.'

A strange echo filled the room. The background noises faded away and there was just the two of them, staring at one another from across the most bizarre chasm.

Greg moved back to the bed. 'I'm tired, Myron.'

'Don't you think we should talk about this?'

'Yeah,' Greg said. He laid back and shut his eyes a little too tightly. 'Maybe later. But right now I'm really tired.'

At the end of the day, Esperanza stepped into Myron's office, sat down, and said, 'I don't know much about family values or what makes a happy family. I don't know the best way to raise a kid or what you have to do to make him happy and well adjusted, whatever the hell "well adjusted" means. I don't know if it's best to be an only child or have lots of siblings or be raised by two parents or a single parent or a gay couple or a lesbian couple or an overweight albino. But I know one thing.'

Myron looked at her and waited.

'No child could ever be harmed by having you in his life.'

Esperanza stood and went home.

Stan Gibbs was playing in the yard with his boys when Myron and Win pulled into the driveway. His wife – at least, Myron guessed it was his wife – sat in a lawn chair and watched. A little boy rode Stan like a horsey. The other boy lay on the ground giggling.

Win frowned. 'How very Norman Rockwell.'

Myron and Win stepped out of the car. Stan the horsey looked up. The smile stayed on when he saw them, but you could see it starting to lose its grip at the edges. Stan hoisted his son off his back and said something to him Myron couldn't hear. The boy gave an 'Aaaw, Dad.' Stan jumped to his feet and ruffled the boy's hair. Win frowned again. As Stan jogged toward them, his smile faded away like the end of a song.

'What are you doing here?'

Win said, 'Back together with the wife, are we?'

'We're giving it a go.'

'Touching,' Win said.

Stan turned toward Myron. 'What's going on here?'

'Tell the kids to go inside, Stan.'

'What?'

Another car pulled in the driveway. Rick Peck was driving. Kimberly Green was in the passenger seat. Stan's face lost color. He snapped a look at Myron.

'We had a deal,' he said.

'Remember how I told you that you had two choices when the novel was discovered?'

'I'm not in the mood—'

'I said you could run or you could tell the truth. Remember?'

Stan's façade tottered, and for the first time, Myron saw the rage.

'I left out a third choice. A choice you yourself pointed out to me the first time we met. You could have said that the Sow the Seeds kidnapper was a copycat. That he had read the book. It might have helped you out. Taken some of the heat off.'

'I couldn't do that.'

'Because it would have led to your father?'

'Yes.'

'But you didn't know your father had written the book. Isn't that right, Stan? You said you never knew about the book. I remember that from the first time we talked. I've been watching you say the same thing on TV. You claim you didn't even know your father wrote it.'

'All true,' Stan said, and the façade slipped back into place. 'But – I don't know – maybe subconsciously I suspected something somehow. I can't explain it.'

'Good,' Myron said.

'Damn good,' Win added.

'The problem was,' Myron said, 'you had to say you hadn't read it. Because if you had, well, Stan, you'd be a plagiarizer. All this work, all your big plans to regain your reputation – it would be for nothing. You'd be ruined.'

'We discussed this already.'

'No, Stan, we didn't. At least not this part of it.' Myron held up the evidence bag with the sheet of paper inside.

Stan set his jaw.

'Know what this is, Stan?'

He said nothing.

'I found it in Melina Garston's apartment. It says "With love, Dad." '

Stan swallowed. 'So?'

'Something about it bothered me from the beginning. First off, the word "Dad." '

'I don't understand—'

'Sure you do, Stan. Melina's sister-in-law called George Garston "Papa." When I spoke to him, he referred to himself as "Papa." So why would he sign a note like this "Dad"?'

'That doesn't mean anything.'

'Maybe, maybe not. The second thing that bothered me: Who writes a note like this – on the top inside of a folded card? People use the bottom half, right? But see, Stan, this wasn't a card. It was a sheet of paper folded in half. That's the key. Then there are those tears along the left edge. See them, Stan? Like someone had ripped it out of something.'

Win handed Myron the novel that had been sent to Kimberly Green. Myron opened it and laid the piece of paper inside it.

'Something like a book.'

It was a perfect match.

'Your father wrote this inscription,' Myron said. 'To you. Years ago. You'd known about the book all along.'

'You can't prove that.'

'Come on, Stan. A handwriting analyst will have no trouble with this. The Lexes weren't the ones who found the book. Melina Garston did. You asked her to lie for you in court. She did. But then she started growing suspicious. So she dug around your house and found this book. She's the one who mailed it to Kimberly Green.'

'You have no proof—'

'She sent it in anonymously because she still cared about you. She even tore out the inscription so no one, most especially you, would ever know where the book had come from. You had plenty of enemies. Like Susan Lex. And the feds. She probably hoped you'd think they did it. At least for a little while. But you knew

264

right away it was Melina. She didn't count on that. Or your reaction.'

Stan's hands tightened into fists. They started shaking.

'The victims' families wouldn't speak to you, Stan. And you needed that for your article. You ended up following the book more than reality. The feds thought it was to fool them. But that wasn't it. Maybe your father told you he was the killer, but nothing else. Maybe the real story wasn't as interesting, so you needed to embellish. Maybe you weren't that good of a writer and you really felt you needed those family quotes. I don't know. But you plagiarized. And the only one who could tie you to that book was Melina Garston. So you killed her.'

'You'll never prove it,' Stan said.

'The feds will dig hard now. The Lexes will help. Win and I will help. We'll find enough. If nothing else, the jury – and the world – will hear all you did in this. They'll hate you enough to convict.'

'You son of a bitch.' Stan cocked his fist and aimed it at Myron. With an almost casual movement, Win swept his leg. Stan fell down in a heap. Win pointed and laughed. Stan's sons watched it all.

Kimberly Green and Rick Peck got out of the car. Myron signaled them to wait, but Kimberly Green shook her head. They cuffed Stan hard and dragged him away. His sons still watched. Myron thought about Melina Garston and his silent vow. Then he and Win headed back to the car.

'You always intended to turn him in,' Win said.

'Yes. But first I had to make sure he went along with donating the bone marrow.'

'And once you knew Jeremy was okay—'

'Then I told Green, yes.'

Win started the car. 'The evidence is still marginal. A good attorney will be able to poke holes.'

'Not my problem,' Myron said.

'You'd be willing to let him walk?'

'Yes,' Myron said. 'But Melina's father has juice. And he won't.'

'I thought you advised him against taking the law into his own hands.'

Myron shrugged. 'No one ever listens to me.'

'That's true,' Win said.

Win drove.

'I just wonder,' Myron said.

'What?'

'Who was the serial killer here? Did his father really do it? Or was it all Stan?'

'Doubt we'll ever know,' Win said.

'Probably not.'

'It shan't matter,' Win said. 'They'll get him for Melina Garston.'

'I guess,' Myron said. Then he frowned and repeated, ' "Shan't"?'

Win shrugged. 'So is it finally over, my friend?'

Myron's leg did that nervous jig again. He stopped it and said, 'Jeremy.'

'Ah,' Win said. 'Are you going to tell him?'

Myron looked out the window and saw nothing. 'Win's credo about selfishness would say yes.'

'And Myron's credo?'

'I don't know that it's much different,' Myron said.

Jeremy was playing basketball at the Y. Myron stepped into the bleachers, the rickety kind that shake with each step, and sat. Jeremy was still pale. He was thinner than the last time Myron had seen him, but there'd been a growth spurt over the last few months. Myron realized how fast changes take place for the young and felt a deep, hard thud in his chest.

For a while, he just watched the flow of the scrimmage and tried to judge his son's play objectively. Jeremy had the tools, Myron could see that right away, but there was plenty of rust on them. That wouldn't be a problem though. Again with the young. Rust doesn't stay long on the young.

As Myron watched the practice, his eyes widened. He felt his insides shrivel. He thought again about what he was about to do, and a swelling tide rose inside of him, overwhelming him, pulling him under.

Jeremy smiled when he spotted Myron. The smile cleaved Myron's heart in two even pieces. He felt lost, adrift. He thought about what Win had said, about what a real father was, and he

266

thought about what Esperanza had said. He thought about Greg and Emily. He wondered if he should have spoken to his own father about this, if he should have told him that this wasn't a hypothetical, that the bomb had indeed landed, that he needed his help.

Jeremy continued to play, but Myron could see that the boy was distracted by his presence. Jeremy kept sneaking quick glances toward the stands. He played a little harder, picked up the pace a bit. Myron had been there, done that. The desire to impress. It had driven Myron, maybe as much as wanting to win. Shallow, but there you have it.

The coach had his players run a few more drills and then he lined them up on the baseline. They finished up with the aptly named 'suicides,' which was basically a series of gut-heaving sprints broken up by bending and touching different lines on the floor. Myron might be nostalgic for many things connected to basketball. Suicides were not one of them.

Ten minutes later, with most of the kids still trying to catch their breath, the coach gathered his troops, gave out schedules for the rest of the week, and dispersed the boys with a big handclap. Most of them headed toward the exit, slinging backpacks over their shoulders. Some went into the locker room. Jeremy walked over to Myron slowly.

'Hi,' Jeremy said.

'Hi.'

Sweat dripped off Jeremy's hair, his face coated and flushed from exertion. 'I'm going to shower,' he said. 'You want to wait?'

'Sure,' Myron said.

'Cool, I'll be right back.'

The gymnasium emptied out. Myron stood and picked up an errant basketball. His fingers found the grooves right away. He took a few shots, watching the bottom of the net dance as the ball swished through. He smiled and sat back down, still holding the ball. A janitor came in and swept the floor Zamboni-style. His keys jangled. Someone flipped off the overhead lights. Jeremy came back not long after that. His hair was still wet. He, too, had a backpack over his shoulder.

As Win would say, 'Showtime.'

Myron gripped the ball a little tighter. 'Sit down, Jeremy. We need to talk.'

The boy's face was serene and almost too beautiful. He slid the backpack off his shoulder and sat down. Myron had rehearsed this part. He had looked at it from all sides, all the pluses and minuses. He had made up his mind and changed it and made it up again. He had, as Win put it, properly tortured himself.

But in the end, he knew there was one universal truth: Lies fester. You try to put them away. You jam them in a box and bury them in the ground. But eventually they eat their way out of coffins. They dig their way out of graves. They may sleep for years. But they always wake up. When they do, they're rested, stronger, more insidious.

Lies kill.

'This is going to be hard to understand—' He stopped. Suddenly his rehearsed speech sounded so damn canned, filled with 'It's nobody's fault' and 'Adults make mistakes too' and 'It doesn't mean your parents love you any less.' It was patronizing and stupid and—

'Mr Bolitar?'

Myron looked up at the boy.

'My mom and dad told me,' Jeremy said. 'Two days ago.'

His chest shuddered. 'What?'

'I know you're my biological father.'

Myron was surprised and yet he wasn't. Some might say that Emily and Greg had made a preemptive strike, almost like a lawyer who reveals something bad about his own client because he knows the opposition will do it. Lessen the blow. But maybe Emily and Greg had learned the same lesson he had about lies and how they fester. And maybe, once again, they were trying to do what was best for their boy.

'How do you feel about it?' Myron asked.

'Weird, I guess,' Jeremy said. 'I mean, Mom and Dad keep expecting me to fall apart or something. But I don't see why it has to be such a big deal.'

'You don't?'

'Sure, okay, I see it, but' – he stopped, shrugged – 'it's not like the whole world's turned inside out or anything. You know what I mean?'

Myron nodded. 'Maybe it's because you've already had your world turned inside out.'

'You mean being sick and all?'

'Yes.'

'Yeah, maybe,' he said, thinking about it. 'Must be weird for you too.'

'Yeah,' Myron said.

'I've been thinking about it,' Jeremy said. 'You want to hear what I've come up with?'

Myron swallowed. He looked into the boy's eyes – serenity, yes, but not through innocence. 'Very much,' he said.

'You're not my dad,' he said simply. 'I mean, you might be my father. But you're not my dad. You know what I mean?'

Myron managed a nod.

'But' – Jeremy stopped, looked up, shrugged the shrug of a thirteen-year-old – 'but maybe you can still be around.'

'Around?' Myron repeated.

'Yeah,' Jeremy said. He smiled again and *pow*, Myron's chest took another blow. 'Around. You know.'

'Yeah,' Myron said, 'I know.'

'I think I'd like that.'

'Me too,' Myron said.

Jeremy nodded. 'Cool.'

'Yeah.'

The gym clock grunted and pushed forward. Jeremy looked at it. 'Mom's probably outside waiting for me. We usually stop at the supermarket on the way home. Want to come?'

Myron shook his head. 'Not today, thanks.'

'Cool.' Jeremy stood, watching Myron's face. 'You okay?'

'Yeah.'

Jeremy smiled. 'Don't worry. It's going to work out.'

Myron tried to smile back. 'How did you get to be so smart?'

'Good parenting,' he said. 'Combined with good genes.'

Myron laughed. 'You might want to consider a future in politics.'

'Yeah,' Jeremy said. 'Take it easy, Myron.'

'You too, Jeremy.'

He watched the boy walk out the door, again with the familiar gait. Jeremy didn't look back. There was the sound of the door closing, the echoes, and then Myron was alone. He turned toward the basket and stared at the hoop until it blurred. He saw the boy's first step, heard his first word, smelled the sweet clean of a young child's pajamas. He felt the smack of a ball against a glove, bent over to help with his homework, stayed up all night when he had a virus, all of it, like his own father had, a whirl of taunting, aching images, as irretrievable as the past. He saw himself hovering in the boy's darkened doorway, the silent sentinel to his adolescence, and he felt what remained of his heart burst into flames.

The images scattered when he blinked. His heart started beating again. He stared again at the basket and waited. This time nothing blurred. Nothing happened.

Acknowledgements

The author wishes to thank Sujit Sheth, M.D., Department of Pediatrics, Babies and Children's Hospital in New York, Anne Armstrong-Coben, M.D., Department of Pediatrics, Babies and Children's Hospital (and my love monkey), and Joachim Schulz, Executive Director, Fanconi Anemia Research Fund, all of whom offered up wonderful medical insights and then watched me take liberties with them; two fellow scribes, friends, and experts in their fields, Linda Fairstein and Laura Lippman; Larry Gerson, the inspiration; Nils Lofgren, for rocking me over the last hurdle; early reader and long-time but Maggie Griffin; Lisa Erbach Vance and Aaron Priest for another job well done; Jeffrey Bedford, FBI Special Agent (and not a bad freshman dorm counselor); as always, Dave Bolt; and mostly, Jacob Hoye, my editor for all the Myron Bolitar books – and now a father. That dedication is for you, too, Jake. Thanks, dude.

For those interested in becoming a bone marrow donor and perhaps saving a life, I urge you to contact the Anthony Nolan Trust at www.anthonynolan.org.uk or 0207 284 1234. For more information on Fanconi anemia, check out www.fanconi.org.

This book is a work of fiction. That means I make stuff up.